SACRIFICE AT MYSTERY HILL

Sacrifice at Mystery Hill

Because he was a ghost, Thomas Thornton, which had been his name in his eighteenth century reincarnation, was able to move right through the rocks, to slide through the small spaces between them with ease, even through the stone 'speaking tube' which led to the hollow space under the sacrificial altar. This was his favorite place to rest, snuggled up to the moss and decayed leaves that formed a soft bed. It smelled a little like death, too, musty and old and coppery, like blood, but it was a scent he had grown to love. It was also the place where *she* had died, so he felt closest to her there.

He had waited for her for centuries. Her death had been hard—and many souls who endured such a primitive and painful death were reluctant to return, but eventually they all did. After all, they had destinies to work out before they could go on to the next stage of existence, and so not coming back was not an option. The Coordinator, one of the Great Beings who tracked the journeys of all the souls, had told Thomas he would let him know when it was time. He, too, had his karma to work out before he could go on to the next level. His destiny was to overcome cowardice of that long ago primitive life when he could have saved her, but hadn't.

SACRIFICE AT MYSTERY HILL

Joan Conning Afman

A Wings ePress, Inc.

Paranormal Mystery Novel

Wings ePress, Inc.

Edited by: Jeanne Smith
Copy Edited by: Joan Powell
Senior Editor: Jeanne Smith
Executive Editor: Marilyn Kapp
Cover Artist: Trisha FitzGerald

Wings ePress Books
http://www.wings-press.com

Copyright © 2010 by Joan Conning Afman
ISBN 978-1-61309-867-7

Published In the United States Of America

Wings ePress Inc.
3000 N. Rock Road
Newton, KS 67114

Dedication

For Jim Walsh, with love, for all the right reasons, and with fond memories of T. D. Greenley of Farmingdale, an art professor who really did make a difference

Acknowledgments:

The author owes a debt of thanks to David Goudsward, who graciously allowed her to use material from his book "America's Stonehenge", which adds color and authentic background to "Sacrifice at Mystery Hill."

One

Because he was a ghost, Thomas Thornton, which had been his name in his eighteenth century reincarnation, was able to move right through the rocks, to slide through the small spaces between them with ease, even through the stone 'speaking tube' which led to the hollow space under the sacrificial altar. This was his favorite place to rest, snuggled up to the moss and decayed leaves that formed a soft bed. It smelled a little like death, too, musty and old and coppery, like blood, but it was a scent he had grown to love. It was also the place where *she* had died, so he felt closest to her there.

He had waited for her for centuries. Her death had been hard—and many souls who endured such a primitive and painful death were reluctant to return, but eventually they all did. After all, they had destinies to work out before they could go on to the next stage of existence, and so not coming back was not an option. The Coordinator, one of the Great Beings who tracked the journeys of all the souls, had told Thomas he would let him know when it was time. He, too, had his karma to work out before he could go on to the next

"

level. His destiny was to overcome cowardice of that long ago primitive life when he could have saved her, but hadn't.

~ * ~

It was the day of the summer solstice. The men of the tribe gathered at the four-foot -tall stone, carved in the shape of a leaning pyramid, to watch the sun rise precisely behind its pointed crest. In silence, they bowed to the god of summer, of crops to come, of the harvest, and walked in single file to where the sacrifice would be offered.

The chief, resplendent in his beaded ritual clothing, rich wolf cloak and feathered headdress, looked around the gathering. "If one man is willing to take her to wife and leave the tribe, she will be spared. Will anyone take her?" His curved sword glittered in the sun as he lifted it above the woman bound to the altar stone.

The chief was his father, whom he dared not offend, and a man and a woman driven from the tribe to survive on their own faced certain death. There was no way out for him, for her and for the child she carried within.

Frozen to the earth, his tongue numb and his heart dead, he had watched as the blade descended. Her scream of agony, blessedly brief, pierced the morning air. The chief carved her heart from her body and held it aloft on the tip of his sword. The tribe prostrated itself as the chief intoned the blessing upon them. Thomas, who was Achak in that incarnation, felt his soul bleed into the dirt.

~ * ~

He stretched, and his long arms and legs passed through the edges of the shield-shaped altar. He didn't understand why the so-called 'experts' who had swarmed over this particular collection of rocks for several centuries, trying to figure out who had built it—and for what purpose—had so much trouble believing that this stone had been used for human sacrifice. Wasn't it obvious, with its curved grooves around the edge, where the blood collected and ran down into the collection pit at the base of the stone? For wine, one of the archaeological experts had concluded, but his theory was quickly discarded when a similar rock was found in nearby Massachusetts that had a carving of a human form stretched out on the altar stone. This conclusion shouldn't have been so difficult to come by.

Thomas heard the sound of small boys in the distance. He sighed. They would use the sacred altar stone as a picnic table, of course, and their noisy chatter and activity would prevent any sleep he hoped to get, just to pass the time until she returned. Well, they were still a long way away. He would doze until then, and if they were particularly obnoxious, maybe have some fun with them.

~ * ~

Thomas blinked back to consciousness as the beer can clinked down on the stone above him. The boys were older than he'd envisioned—eleven, twelve maybe, but still much too young to be drinking beer.

"Hey," one of the boys called to the others, "think I could build a fire for the hotdogs here?" Thomas turned his head to look at him. Short for his age, he had a mop of too-long straw-colored hair and a round, freckled face. When the other boys didn't answer, he called again, "Mike! Glenn! How about I built the fire here?"

"Sure," the taller, skinny one named Glenn shouted back. "It'll take a while to get going, so we can do the sacrifice first."

For the first time Thomas noticed the blue denim backpack Mike had tossed on the ground.

The backpack wriggled. There was something alive in there.

Thomas clasped his hands on his chest as a heaviness descended on his heart. The boys had brought a helpless animal they intended to sacrifice—somebody's pet cat, or a beloved puppy? Although he had seen this happen countless times over the centuries, he never got used to it. Melancholy covered him like a cold blanket. Would mankind, starting with boy-kind, never tire of making the innocent suffer?

"Nah—Bunny can wait. I'm hungry now."

Thomas studied Mike, who seemed to be the leader of the group. He was a handsome kid, with a look of intelligence cast across his features. Auburn hair, river-water-colored eyes gray like the Spiket River which flowed past Mystery Hill and eventually dumped itself into the Merrimack.

Gray, mysterious, not giving up its secrets. Who had sailed up it, eons ago, and stayed around long enough to build this site? Nobody had ever come up with a definitive answer as to its beginnings.

Thomas allowed himself to feel a surge of disappointment in Mike. Such a boy should show traits of kindness, not cruelty.

Brendan's fire flared up sooner than he anticipated. While the boy fed it sticks and dried weeds, all three boys opened cans of beer and drank them, with exaggerated signs of enjoyment. Thomas remembered very well that beer was an acquired taste, and very seldom did anybody really like it at first.

Glenn looked around. "Where are the 'dogs'?"

"I've got 'em." Brendan tossed the stick with which he'd been tending the fire onto the ground, and walked back toward the altar stone where they'd all dumped their bags. He picked up one, fished around inside and brought out a package of franks, and a half dozen hot dog rolls wrapped in plastic. He turned and grinned at the others. "I didn't forget the mustard and relish either." He laid two jars on the altar.

The boys scrambled to find suitable sticks. Each jammed his hot dogs on the prongs and toasted two at once. When they were crisp and crackling, they stuck them in their buns, added the embellishments, snapped open new cans of beer, and settled down on the altar stone to eat.

The captive animal squealed and struggled inside the bag. The squeal told Thomas the victim was a rabbit.

"Shut up, Lindsey," Brendan snapped and aimed a kick at the bag.

The other two boys laughed, Mike the loudest. "You just wish it was your sister."

The rabbit whimpered, but didn't move again.

Anger surged through Thomas. Okay, these guys deserved a lesson. He knew he wasn't supposed to interact with humans, or do anything to interfere with their progress, or lack of it, but he had a soft heart as well as a steel-strong sense of justice, which he had developed over the centuries. And...well, sometimes he did pull a prank on deserving humans, just because he could.

He floated up through the rock and settled down, legs crossed Indian style, among the three boys. Mike looked around him and shivered. "You get a blast of cold air just now?"

Thomas knew the other two felt his presence also, but they blustered their way out of it. "Hey, Mikey, you think there's a ghost here?"

All three laughed, jostled and poked each other, nearly pushing Brendan off the rock.

Thomas picked up Glenn's second hot dog and raised it to his mouth. He always enjoyed these displays of his invisible presence, because, although humans thought ghosts could not interact with material objects, that simply was not true. It always disconcerted them to the max.

Maybe disconcerted was too mild a word.

Glenn watched his hotdog rise in the air. "Arghhh!" he yelled, making a grab for it.

Thomas moved it out of his way, easily avoiding his grasp. He took a bite of the frank. All three boys stared goggle-eyed at the hot dog, which suddenly lost a quarter of itself and disappeared into the air.

The boys scrambled off the rock, their dogs and beer cans spewing in many directions at once. Thomas took another bite, and another portion of Glenn's hot dog vanished.

The boys watched, frozen to the spot.

As the last bite of the dog and roll disappeared, the boys turned and ran, leaving their leftovers behind them. Thomas poured out the remaining beer and watched the amber liquid run down the grooves in the rock, where generations of innocent blood had run before. As the blood had, it dripped into the hole in the ground which had once held the receiving vessel. He smiled to himself as he heard the boys racing away through the woods, tree branches swishing in the wind, twigs snapping under their feet.

Thomas swirled himself around the bag which held the rabbit. He oozed himself inside it and widened the knot. The rabbit trembled, but as soon as Thomas made the opening wide enough, it squeezed out, and sat looking around at the rocks and trees.

"I know you're a domesticated bunny," Thomas told him, "but being loose in the woods is a lot better than the fate that was waiting for you. Come on. I'll show you a safe place." He guided the shaking rabbit to a tunnel under some of the rocks, where he would be safe for the time being.

The long summer afternoon waned. Thomas sighed, his longing for the one he had loved for centuries surging through him again. He had everything arranged. He would protect her this time, and no one would be able to stop him. When would she come back?

Two

Get ready.

The Coordinator, the powerful entity in the World Beyond, who—as his title indicated, was one of those who helped those souls who wished to reincarnate find suitable vehicles for their lives. He breathed his message into Thomas' spirit one hot day in the middle of August. *She* was back. If he, Thomas, wanted entry into this life, the Coordinator would arrange it. Thomas sent an immediate message back: yes, he was ready.

The Coordinator selected the most suitable situation, and Thomas went to work, preparing his new family for his life among them. He knew he had only two weeks or so to implant 'memories' in their minds, before his own consciousness of a previous life would begin to fade. Eventually, unless the past visited him in dreams, he would remember nothing of a former existence.

~ * ~

Sharon and Charlie Thorn lived in East Salem, on a pleasant street generically named Elm Drive. It wasn't that their name happened to be Thorn, so much like the Thornton he liked and had become used to—that was just a lucky coincidence, but the Thorn family itself was one he would have chosen to be born into, had he decided to be born for reincarnation.

He hadn't wanted to return until she was back. Now she was.

Humans didn't realize it, but there were several ways to reincarnate. One was being born, and you could select your family and setting. Most people opted to be born with old friends and relatives. Or, if you were of an adventuresome turn of mind and wanted to broaden your life experiences, you could opt for a lottery. This could throw you into life anywhere—a geisha in Japan, a member of the Taliban, a peasant in India, or a housewife in Oklahoma—but your karma would be greatly rewarded if the circumstances were new and difficult.

"More mashed potatoes, Thomas?" Sharon Thorn smiled at him and passed him the bowl.

He scooped out a healthy-sized second helping. "Thanks. It's sure good to be home again." He returned her smile, and looked at her with appreciation. She made a very acceptable mother, one any boy on the verge of leaving for college would be proud to have. Nothing remarkable—average height, a bit plump, brown hair and hazel eyes. Nothing unremarkable either—just an apple-pie mom.

Charlie, too, was a father who could hide in a crowd, and yet you wouldn't mind introducing him as your dad. On the thin side, he had dark hair graying and receding, and a bald spot encroaching, and deep blue eyes that saw more than he ever let on. Thomas thought the two of them would have made a perfect ad for the typical American parents.

"You always had a good appetite, Thomas." His father leaned forward on his elbows. "You'll probably gain weight in college unless you go out for a sport. Are you thinking of any particular one—basketball, maybe? You were always good at it."

Thomas smiled to himself. The pictures he had planted in his family's mind of his playing basketball in high school had really taken hold.

Then there was Mike.

"Tit-pinching! That's what he's good at!"

All eyes focused on Mike, who sat across the table from Thomas. Sharon gasped, and Charlie slapped his hand hard on the table. "Enough of that kind of talk, Mike."

Mike shrugged. "I don't know why he just didn't stay out in California. What's here to come back to?"

Thomas looked with annoyance at his younger brother. "College. Midstate. And I wasn't just in California. I wanted to see the country, so I worked my way around it. I had jobs in Kansas, North Dakota, Virginia and Texas, as well as California."

"It was two years well spent," his father put in. "You've matured, and you'll get a lot more out of college now."

"And I think a community college was a good choice," Sharon put in. "In two years, or even just after the first year, you can transfer to Keene, or somewhere else."

"I don't know why I picked Midstate," Thomas said. "Except I'm not sure of what I want to major in, so it seemed like the right place until I decide."

"You're twenty years old!" Mike giggled. "You'll be an old man compared to the rest of the guys."

Thomas regarded Mike. He was the only component of the family into which he had inserted himself whom he sometimes disliked. The kid could be a nasty brat, selfish and mean, and had perfected assorted methods of conning his parents and getting his own way. Well, now he had Thomas to cope with, and Mike was going to have to deal with someone he couldn't manipulate. Except that Thomas wouldn't be around much, as in two weeks he would leave for college.

This was the third way to reincarnate—full-fledged insertion into an already-formed situation. He'd spent several nights visiting them in dreams, replacing their memories of life with two sons with his own version of life with three sons. There were scenes of him being born, of being held by his older brother, Charlie Jr., of sandlot baseball games, Scouts, paper routes and camping trips with Dad and the three boys, and finally, Mike's arrival as the caboose-child. There were even photos created for the photo albums, the piano top and the computer, and video tapes. Thomas' favorite was their trip to Disney World; very creative, he told himself with a tinge of pride.

Thomas glared at Mike. "I'm leaving for Midstate in two weeks, but until then, I'm going to turn you inside out, little brother. You need to shape up in a hurry."

Mike stared back at Thomas, his gray eyes wide with disbelief. His mouth hung open, as evidently a smart-ass reply eluded him. Even Sharon and Charlie seemed stunned, as they sat in silence.

Sharon came back to life. "Oh, Thomas, he's just a kid. "You were just as obnoxious..." A puzzled look came over her face. She turned to her husband. "Wasn't Thomas just like that at Mike's age?"

Charlie regarded Thomas doubtfully and rubbed his chin. "You know, I don't remember..." His voice trailed off. "Those must have been the days when I worked sixty hours a week and wasn't home that much. But probably..."

Thomas filled Charlie's memory with pictures of himself helping Sharon with the dishes, running errands for Charlie, his paper route, mowing the elderly neighbor's lawn for no reward.

Charlie seemed to have trouble remembering his middle son at that age. Thomas knew he had only ten days or so to fill in the gaps in the family's memories. Little by little, he would lose his consciousness of himself as Thomas Thornton, and become for all earthly purposes Thomas Thorn. He wouldn't remember any other life.

~ * ~

"Time for the news," Charlie announced as he got up from his chair and patted his stomach. Dessert had been his father's favorite, strawberry shortcake, although the berries weren't as sweet and juicy as they were in early summer. He and Sharon retired to the living room and settled down in front of the television.

Thomas put the last plate in the dishwasher as Mike grabbed a Coke from the fridge and brushed past him.

"Goin' to Brendan's," he said as he headed for the kitchen door.

Thomas turned and grabbed a handful of Mike's tee-shirt. "Not so fast, Buddy."

Outraged, Mike took a swipe at his brother. "Hey, let go! You're not the boss of me."

Thomas pushed him back toward the Formica table and forced him into one of the four chairs. "I want to talk to you."

"I don't want to talk to you. Go to college and leave me alone. I liked it when you were gone."

Thomas ignored that and continued. "I saw what went on at Mystery Hill a few days ago. You and Glenn and Brendan."

Mike stared, incredulous. "What? You were spying on us?"

"Happened to be wandering by. You were going to sacrifice that helpless animal just for your own amusement."

Mike twisted away in his chair. "So what's it to you? It's a stupid rabbit. Plenty of them in the world."

Thomas heaved an inward sigh. He planted in Mike's brain the image of Mike frolicking on the lawn with a blond and white collie dog. The dog held a stick in his mouth and looked up at Mike with adoring brown eyes.

"How would you feel if it had been Trixie?"

A blaze of pain crossed Mike's face. "That's different. Dogs are family."

"So was Glenn's sister's rabbit. To her, anyway."

"Who gives a crap what that idiot Lindsey thinks?" Mike jumped up, ducked under Thomas' outstretched arm and made it to the door and out before he had time to react. Thomas heard his bike creak as Mike rode headlong out of the driveway and down the sidewalk.

Okay, plenty of time to deal with the kid in the next two weeks.

~ * ~

The Thorns had a good-sized flat back yard lined with maples, oaks, a magnolia tree that was glorious in the spring, and one good sized twisted pine. Several years ago, they'd installed an in-ground pool, and the year after that, Sharon's mother, Ivy, came to stay, parking a double-wide mobile home on the far side of it. A sturdy white fence encircled the entire yard, so it rather looked, when Ivy sat out on her concrete patio, that the pool belonged to her. And, often, she acted as though it did, too.

Thomas gazed out his bedroom window as he changed into his swim trunks. He grinned. Ivy sat out there, thin as a teenager in her magenta bathing suit, drinking what he assumed was one of her habitual evening margaritas. He loved Ivy. A refusing-to-grow-old lady in her seventies, she was a hippie leftover from the sixties, and much more likely to show up anywhere in a peasant blouse and gauzy skirt than the tailored suits her contemporaries wore. Her silver hair glittered in the fading sunlight, and she glanced up at the bedroom window, as if expecting to see Thomas there. He obliged and waved at her, grabbed a towel and headed down for a swim.

Ivy wandered over, draped herself over the edge of the pool and splashed her feet in the water. "How're you doing, Thomas? Only a couple more weeks left before you leave for college. We'll miss you. I know I will. It's been great having you home this summer."

"I'll miss you, too." He meant it—she was the liveliest person in the household, and he loved her free spirit. Nobody told Ivy what to do or think. She even had a boyfriend who lived in a yellow Victorian house down the street, and about once a week, much to her daughter's scandalized reaction, she spent the night with him.

"Want a margarita?" She set her own glass down on the tile. "I can run in and make you one. Apricot or raspberry?"

He laughed. Her margarita flavors were a family joke. These two were actually rather mundane, compared with what she often devised. "Apricot. And don't forget the salt. I'll swim laps 'til you get back. Take your time."

He plunged into the pool. He relished the slide of cool water over his body as he cut through it. That was one of the best things about being human—the sensations were so intense, especially after eons of feeling nothing pertaining to his body. When at last he came up for air, Ivy sat there, grinning at him, a second margarita by her side.

She raised hers to him in a mock toast. "Well, Thomas, here's to college, the best time of your life. What are you going to do for the next couple of weeks before you go?"

He squinted into the setting sun as he regarded her. Was there a hint of irony in her voice? What did she know that he didn't suspect?

The drink was frosty and sweet. She always used sea salt on the rim of her glass, even when she made fruit-flavored drinks.

He tried to ignore her question. "Great! You make the world's best margaritas."

"Answer my question, Thomas."

He met her gray eyes: river-water gray like Mike's. Eyes with secrets, eyes he couldn't read. He shrugged. "Ride herd on Mike. Someone has to tame that little guy."

"I couldn't agree more." She hesitated a moment, sipped at her drink, then threw him a small, lopsided smile. "Thomas, did you ever wonder why your brother, Charlie, is named after your father? Or why Mike is named after your grandfather, my late husband, and you wound up being Thomas, after no one in the family?"

Oops. She'd thrown him a curve. "I guess they just liked the name," he hedged. He scrambled to find a namesake and plant it in her memory. He conjured up an old friend of the family who'd died young. An auto accident—no, a sudden heart attack. He had been tall, brilliant, handsome, had been a mentor in business to his father; Ivy'd had a brief affair with him...

Ivy laughed out loud and held up her hand. "Oh, no you don't!"

Thomas drained his drink and plunged back into the pool. "I need to swim a few more laps—build up some muscle for the basketball team at Midstate."

She stood up and waited on the edge until he resurfaced. "Thomas."

The waning sunlight stroked her hair and ran down one side of her slim body. He read the hint of amusement in her eyes, but any signs of aging were hidden in the dusky shadows. For a second or two, he thought she probably looked much as she had fifty years ago. It was an eerie feeling, and he felt as if time were suspended as he stared up at her.

She smiled down at him, and her eyes twinkled. "Her name is Chloe."

Three

Ivy finished up her miniscule housekeeping duties, hung up the feather duster with a sigh of relief, poured herself a second cup of coffee and flicked on the TV as she plopped down in her favorite chair. In a few minutes, though, she tired of the morning news, and the endless bickering of the program hosts and their 'guests.' It was all the same thing—blaming the president, or the former president, cursing the rich for having money and the poor for having none, robberies, murders, and missing children. The older she grew, it seemed, the less she was able to tolerate man's inhumanity to man.

She pressed 'off' on the remote, and the screen went dark. She sat sipping the dark brew and thought of her grandson, Thomas. He had left for college before dawn this morning, driving his second hand Toyota, wanting to get there early and settle in at the dorm before signing up for his classes.

She knew she'd piqued his curiosity, and he wouldn't leave without wanting to talk to her. Late last evening there'd been a rap at her door.

"Why, hello, Thomas. Come to say goodbye to your old grandma?"

He laughed as she stood aside and he brushed past her. "You'll never be old, and I thought you preferred being called 'Ivy'."

She took a bottle of white wine out of the fridge and poured two glasses without asking him. He accepted the stemmed crystal glass, and inspected it before taking a sip.

"Nice, the way the colors swirl into the glass. Are these another of your antique store finds?"

She nodded. "I was lucky to find two of them. They were six dollars each, and a bargain, I'd say."

He nodded. "I agree." He took another sip, then set the glass down on a side table, leaned forward and pinned her with his eyes. "Ivy, what did you mean a couple weeks ago, out there by the pool, when you said, 'Her name is Chloe'?"

"You waited two weeks before you asked me that?" She sat back in her chair and swished the wine around in her glass. She gave him a conspiratorial smile. "Well, you know, Thomas, I've always been a little odd. I have 'experiences,' you might say. Prophetic dreams, for instance, and sometimes...well, sometimes I just know things."

Thomas nodded. "I remember once when I was a kid—we were all driving someplace, down to Portsmouth I think, on the Interstate, and all of a sudden you insisted that Dad pull off the road. I guess he thought you were going to be sick, 'cause he did it... And then that big semi roared by...out of control, and would have crushed us if we'd still been on the road."

She shook her head as if trying to clear her mind. "I sometimes feel I have one foot in another world, or as Stephen Hawking now says, 'many parallel worlds'." She paused, then locked her gray eyes with Thomas'. "I don't know if my, uhm, 'talents' are a blessing or a curse, but there are things I know, and I know you will meet a girl named Chloe, and she will play a big part in your life. I'm just giving you a heads up, that's all."

"How does it work?" he asked, obviously curious. "Do you see things in your head—or...?"

Ivy rubbed a hand across her eyes. "Sometimes it's just a very strong feeling that something will happen. Other times I absolutely know it will, but don't ask me how. A few times I've had a picture flash into my mind. Once in a while, I've sort of heard a voice...not an actual voice, but the words are there, just as if I had heard them."

"That's weird. Will you tell me about some of those experiences?"

She smiled. "Yes, but not tonight. I usually don't share them unless there's a reason to do so, or if someone else might profit from what I have to tell them."

"But why don't you tell them? Don't you think other people would find your 'experiences' fascinating? You could write a book, a novel and include them. I bet a lot of people have things happen to them they can't explain."

Ivy laughed. "Undoubtedly. But they also might lock me away in the loony bin." She raised the beautiful goblet, admiring it as much as the wine.

"Doubtful." Thomas grinned at her. "You're the most grounded person I've ever known—a little quirky, but right here, all the time." He drained his drink and set the glass down. "Why do you think these things happen to you, and not to most other people?"

Ivy shook her head. "I've wondered about that all my life. I think some people are just more open to the spirit world, or *other* worlds. When they have an unusual experience, something they can't explain, they don't ignore it or make up some more rational conclusion. They pay attention, and little by little these other worlds open up to them—because they're not shutting them out."

He leaned toward her. "Do you ever feel that these spirits might be evil? How do you know you can trust those, uhm... revelations?"

She pursed her lips. "Believe me, I've been told by more than one religious person—and I don't mean 'fanatics,' Thomas, because most of them have been good church-going Christians who are really concerned for my soul—that such experiences are all of the devil and will lead to the destruction of my soul. I don't agree with them. I think of it more as a gift that I just happen to be able to tune into."

"Why do you think that?"

She sighed. "Because every time I follow that hunch, or message, or whatever you want to call it, it turns out to be for my benefit. A few times, it's even saved my life, so how can I think it's evil?"

"Like what, Ivy? Just give me one example."

She considered. "Okay. I already told you one, but here's another. Many years ago, I was at a shopping mall. I was leaving the parking lot, and waiting for the red light on the main road to change. It turned green, and a voice in my head said, 'Don't go.' I sat on my brakes, and the cars behind me started beeping their horns, but I didn't move. Then—like a bat out of hell, as they say, came this yellow convertible about ninety miles an hour full of screaming and waving teenagers—right through the red light. If I'd ignored that voice and driven out into traffic, I'd have been hit, and maybe other people, too."

"Wow. That's impressive."

She giggled. "I rolled down my window, stuck my head out and gave the drivers in the cars behind me a 'so-there' look. They all had their mouths open, as if they couldn't believe what had happened."

Thomas stood and gazed down at her. "So, Ms. Fortune Teller, what happens next, after I meet this Chloe?"

She laughed and polished off her drink. "I don't know everything. I just feel she will be important in your life, and there's a reason you're going to meet her." She stood up. "Time to say goodbye, Thomas. I wish you a wonderful two years at Midstate. Beautiful campus."

He nodded. "I'll let you know, Ivy." He hugged her hard and left.

She watched him disappear into the darkness on the other side of the pool. She'd seen him mature in just the last two weeks. His face had filled out, he looked stronger and more solid, and even his thatch of sandy brown hair looked thicker.

Although she was tired and more than ready to sleep, she decided to look up that incident in the journal she kept about her strange experiences. Lately, if she didn't write everything down, it was gone from her head in a few hours. She didn't want that to happen. She truly believed the dreams she had and other strange coincidences were messages that helped her along life's often-rocky path.

She flipped through the yellow pages. The journal went back some fifty years, to when she had first started writing things down. It wasn't a diary in the usual sense of the word; she didn't write down the name of the boys she dated, or where they went, or what she thought about Sam and Joanne or anyone else. It wasn't that kind of record.

She opened to the first page.

October 15th, 1955

Judy gave me this journal for my birthday, and I've never used it. But I think I should write this down. It's so weird! I was feeling so down 'cause I got fired from the agency last week, and this week I started job-shopping again. I had on a very business-like gray dress that Mom made for me, and my big, fat art portfolio, and I thought I'd go to the department stores in Manchester and see if I could get a job in advertising or display. I went to McCall's and Stephenson's, but they had one-person departments, and told me they didn't need anyone. I thought I'd go over to the newspaper, see if there was something open there. I purposely decided not to go to Ellis Brothers, as they are the biggest department store around, and I had hardly any experience—just a few months at the art-supply store, and a month at the agency which let me go.

I was just crossing North Street, heading toward the newspaper offices, when I heard a voice in my head. It just said, "Go to Ellis Brothers." That was all. I heard it just as clearly as if someone had said it out loud. I turned right around in the middle of the street, and went up to the Personnel department. Scary lady—big and black-haired Miss Yagger told me the girl they had doing the art and clerical job in advertising was leaving for Germany to join her soldier-husband next week. She hired me on the spot.

This is the first time something strange like that has ever happened—except for thinking I heard someone call out my name—but I have a funny feeling it won't be the last.

Ivy laughed out loud. It certainly hadn't been the last. She'd lived a life filled with psychic adventures, most of which she'd never told anyone because she knew they'd never believe her. Once she had not followed the warning a voice had delivered, and a most unhappy period followed before she could correct the decision she'd made. These experiences seemed most to happen when she was discouraged, frustrated, or just plain unhappy. In every case, although sometimes it had taken a long time, her life had changed for the better.

She turned to the page with the Chloe incident, and closed the book with her finger marking the place. She could read it, of course, but she knew it by heart and preferred to remember it. It had been so strange—especially since the journal didn't mention Thomas being there at all.

It had been years ago, after she had retired to Florida, before she decided she needed to see her grandchildren grow up and parked her double-wide in her daughter's back yard. Sharon brought the boys to Florida with an express desire to go to Disney.

It hadn't been a lot of fun, except for Charlie, Jr. Mike balked at the first ride—the oh-so-tame teacup carousel. They all climbed into a green teacup and belted in, and Mike began to scream, "I want to ride in the yellow cup!" He kept it up all through the ride. After that, there was no getting him on any of the rides.

Ivy escorted Charlie on the Peter Pan flight, but that was all she got to do. Mike would have nothing to do with anything. Overtired and overexcited, he spent the entire day crying and throwing tantrums. Ivy could do nothing with him.

Where had Thomas been? Why couldn't she remember him?

"I don't want you! I want my mommy!"

After a while, Ivy gave up cajoling, bribing and pleading. "If you want to stay in the stroller and howl, Mikey, go ahead. I'm just going to sit here." She wriggled to get comfortable on the rocky ledge that lined the wide pedestrian path.

She wished she'd been able to go through the haunted mansion with Sharon and Charlie. She'd been through it on another trip, but there was much more to see, and she'd been looking forward to experiencing it again.

Mike fell asleep. The hood of the stroller sheltered him from the sun, but there was no shade for her. She sat broiling in the sun, and wished her daughter and grandson would soon come out the exit lane.

A large family group exited the Haunted Mansion. There were several adults and four or five children of varied ages. Ivy's attention fixed on a girl dressed in a Sleeping Beauty costume, the long, sky-blue dress and short yellow cape. Ivy couldn't tell her exact age—she might have been seven or eight, and tall for her age. The family walked briskly along, and when they passed Ivy, the girl turned her head, and with a familiarity that seemed to suggest she had known Ivy for a long time, smiled and said, "Hi."

Taken aback, and somewhat amused, Ivy managed a 'hi' in return. She didn't think, though, that this was one of those special times, a signal that meant something outside of the norm. Not until the next day.

Ivy opened the journal to where her finger held the page, and re-read the words she had written so long ago.

Thursday we went to Animal Kingdom. This went much better. Mike loved the animals and traipsing through the woodland paths. There was one section that was constructed to represent a ruined Indian palace. That's where the tigers were, and I stood alone at the railing, gazing at those fabulous beasts, while Sharon and the boys explored the ruins.

Suddenly I felt a presence beside me, and I looked down and saw with surprise that it was the girl who had spoken to me outside the Haunted Mansion. She'd left off her Sleeping Beauty costume, and wore jean shorts and a pink tee-shirt. Without looking at me, she said in a soft voice, "I came back to marry Thomas, and to take care of you when you're old and tired."

Before I could think of a reply—like 'who's Thomas?'— a woman whom I took to be her mother, came up and took the child by her arm. "Chloe Rose McAllister! How many times have I told you not to talk to strangers?" Impatiently, she tugged at her daughter's arm, and the child went away with her.

I looked after them, and knew that I had been granted a special moment. Okay, Chloe, we'll wait for you.

Ivy studied the words she had written. Chloe had said "Thomas," and Ivy had written that, but then crossed it out and substituted "Charlie." At the time, she thought she must have misheard what Chloe had said.

She'd never thought of this incongruity. Was it possible Thomas had not gone to Disney with them? What possible excuse could there have been for that? No, she decided, with a little smile to herself. It was more likely, just as she had been thinking, there was no Thomas then.

Ivy laughed out loud and closed the journal. If you lived long enough, life certainly got interesting.

Four

She saw him before he saw her.

Something about him caught her attention, although she couldn't have said what it was. He strode across the green lawn of the campus as if he owned the place, and yet, it wasn't arrogance in his posture as much as it was confidence that he knew who he was and where he belonged.

Sitting on one of the benches outside the Redfern art complex, Chloe McAllister paused in the sketch she was making, peered over the top of her drawing pad and followed him with her eyes. He wore a rust-colored sweater which complemented the October foliage of the trees on campus. Glints of sunlight played with his thick thatch of coppery-brown hair. He was tall, and walked with the grace of an athlete. She wondered if he played basketball. If so, they would be thrown together at the games, as she was in her second year of cheerleading.

A short, compact girl with curly blonde hair and sky-blue eyes appeared out of nowhere and plunked herself down on the bench beside Chloe.

"Chloe, I'm sorry I'm late. Professor Greenley went on and on about my term paper topic. I couldn't get away."

Chloe tore her eyes from Thomas, and smiled at her best friend. "It's okay, Gaia. I've just been admiring the new talent on campus." She flicked at finger at Thomas' retreating figure. Just before he turned a corner, one of the books under his arm fell to the ground, and he turned around to stoop down and pick it up.

Chloe squinted after him. "Do you know who that is? I've never seen him before."

Gaia threw her a curious look. "Oh, yeah. Thomas Thorn. I've been at a couple of things when he was there. He was at the Elk Horn last night. You should have come. He's hot, huh?"

"I told you I had a project to finish. Did you talk to him? Where's he from?"

"Hey, is this from Miss-Don't-Bother-Me-With-Boys-I've-Got-a-Career-to-Think About?" Gaia shrugged. "I think he's local, from around Salem. I talked to him a little while at the bar. I noticed him, too." She shot Chloe a playful grin. "Are we going to have a war over a guy? That'll be a new one for us."

Chloe laughed and closed up her drawing pad. "So before either of us has even had a date with this guy, we're competing for him? That's not so great for a friendship." She stood up and Gaia scrambled after her.

As they started off toward the dorm, Gaia took Chloe's arm. "Seriously though, there is something I'd like to talk to you about, that doesn't concern guys."

"Not another sorority bid, I hope. I've told you a zillion times I won't join anything that keeps other people out. It's just a principle of mine, that's all, and I can't get beyond it."

Tossing her blonde curls, Gaia snorted in disdain. "You've got too effin many principles, if you ask me. You have a black roommate, and you refuse to ask for a change and room with me, because it might hurt her feelings. Because she might take it the wrong way."

Miffed, Chloe turned to face her friend. "Look, if being an ethical person is too much for you, maybe you need a different best friend. Besides, Hannah's a nice person, a great roomie and we roomed together all last year. If you'd been in Johnson Hall last year, I'd be rooming with you. We can spend all the time we want together. Hannah has her own friends. If she ever suggests changing, I'll consider it."

Gaia threw up her hands. "Look, I didn't mean it that way. But—where do you get this stuff? You're not one of those religious persons who goes to church every Sunday and tries to convert everyone else. It just seems to be built into you, for some reason that I don't understand. It's not a moral sin to belong to a sorority or some other exclusive group."

"It's not a sin, but it's a decision I made a long time ago. I don't do 'exclusive,' sorry. Rejection hurts people more than beating them up, and I just won't be involved in that."

Stung by Gaia's words, Chloe relented a little. "What is it you want me to do now?"

Gaia strode on ahead of Chloe and kicked at the leaves with her sneakers. "Never mind. You're such a goody-goody you'd never go."

Chloe let out an exasperated sigh. "Wait up, Gaia! I'm not a goody-goody, you know that. I've smoked a little pot, had more to drink than I should on occasion, gone a little farther with some guys than I should have. My mom still thinks I'm a virgin, and I don't have the heart to disillusion her."

Gaia turned to face her. "Look, this is what college is for—experimentation in all kinds of things, and finding out who you are and what you want. Sometimes you act forty years old already. Chrissakes, let's have some fun while we're young!"

"Gaia, you're always searching—and for what, I can't figure out. If it isn't a new guy, it's some group…"

Gaia grabbed Chloe's shoulders. "Yes, I'm looking for something, and even I don't know what it is. I just know that something has always been missing in my life, and I need to find something to fill up that hole."

Glancing around the campus, Chloe acknowledged that there were elements of truth in what Gaia said, and she didn't want to lose Gaia's friendship. Except for cheerleading, she hadn't joined any clubs or groups, and she was quite satisfied with just a few good friends and day-to-day campus life. They had been best friends since they met in remedial algebra last year, and were joined at the hip, some people said, ever since Gaia had moved into Johnson Hall that fall. "What is it you want us to do?"

"Promise me you'll keep an open mind and not just automatically say 'no'."

"Okay, I promise." Chloe summoned up a smile for her friend.

Gaia's bright eyes looked cat-like and mysterious. She glanced around as if to make sure she wouldn't be overheard, and lowered her voice to almost a whisper. "What do you know about the ancient Druids?"

"Ancient sect. Stonehenge. Nature worshippers, that's about all. Are they offering a course in that? I'm up for that—but why all the secrecy?"

The blonde curls bounced as Gaia shook her head. "Nooooo… there's a group that meets off-campus, supposed to be top secret, but I heard about it at the Elk Horn and went to a meeting last night. They meet at midnight…"

"Gaia, you can't be serious. You don't want to fool around with that stuff."

Gaia set her lips. "You promised you'd listen."

Shifting her books to her other arm, Chloe sighed to herself and gave in. "Okay, okay. Tell me about it."

"They are trying to revive the ancient liturgies in the original language, and they practice the ancient rituals. Chloe, it's so cool! You wear a robe, and there's just something that happens, and you feel so a part of everything... a part of nature."

Chloe looked longingly toward the dorm. She wanted dinner, a hot shower and a long evening studying with compatible, silent Hannah in their room. Instead, she was listening to her best friend rattle on about a secret sect that wore white sheets and muttered things in a language no one on earth any longer spoke. "Uhm, Gaia, I don't know..."

Gaia actually stamped her foot. "You promised you'd listen!"

"Okay, I'm listening. I'm all ears." Chloe put a hand to her ear and cocked her head as if to hear better.

"The best part is, they're building their own Stonehenge, out in the woods beyond town. When it's finished, the meetings will take place there."

Chloe laughed. "How can they do that? Those rocks weigh tons, and even today the archeologists can't figure out how they got them there, when they aren't even from that region of England. The Stonehenge builders had to bring them hundreds of miles before they set them up."

"Yes, Miss Know-it-all, I realize that. They aren't building it to scale. Of course, they couldn't do that. These rocks are maybe two, two and a half feet high, but they are placing them in the exact same configuration as the original Stonehenge."

Chloe didn't say anything as she regarded her friend with a mixture of amusement and exasperation.

Finally, Gaia broke the silence. "So how about it? Will you join that group with me?

A breeze ruffled Chloe's hair, and she raised a hand to brush it away from her face. It looked as if Gaia wouldn't take no for an answer, but was their friendship really so fragile that it hinged on whether or not Chloe joined this ridiculous sect?

"I really don't think I'm interested in something like that," she began.

Gaia's face flushed deep pink with anger. "You are just no fun at all, Chloe McAllister! Fine! You just find someone else as self-righteous and boring as you are, and I will get a new best friend who wants to *live* life, not just talk about it."

"Gaia! Don't do this, please."

But Gaia was gone in a huff, and Chloe stood by herself in the middle of the quad. Students came and went all around her, chattering and laughing, but Chloe had never in her life felt so alone.

~ * ~

Her roommate, Hannah Stuart, wasn't in the dorm room. She busied herself with her books and papers. She had made an outline of the essay due on Thursday when Hannah returned from supper. She looked at Chloe in surprise. "Oh, hi there. You didn't go to dinner?"

"No. I fell asleep." Chloe sat up and rubbed her eyes. "What a strange dream." She laughed aloud. "My imagination must really be working overtime."

Hannah looked vaguely interested as she sat at her desk. Her dark eyes and black hair were startling against her caramel skin. She wore her hair short, and it was very curly.

She never tried to straighten it. Chloe thought Hannah was a beautiful girl and proud of whom she was. She didn't try to be something she wasn't.

"Well, what was the dream about?" Hannah picked up her sheaf of papers and leafed through them. "Am I glad I'm done with this! Try writing a paper in French when you're not even very good at English." She glanced back at Chloe. "Well?"

Chloe stifled a yawn. "Oh, really stupid. I can only remember bits and pieces. Something about a stone altar, and a pagan sacrifice, and one of Indian braves looked like..." her voice trailed off. "Like a guy I know."

Hannah shook her head. "Garbage in, garbage out. That's all it is." She opened her computer and began to type.

Chloe sat on her bed and gazed out the window at the darkening sky. She looked at her roommate's head bent over her laptop. Any other evening she could run down to Gaia's room, or Gaia would be popping into hers, all excited and full of ideas for things they could do, places they could go. It was true; Gaia was the one who provided all the fun. She turned and stared at Hannah's back. Well, she'd never know if she didn't ask, would she? "Hannah, would you want to go down to the Elk Horn with me, just for a little while?"

Hannah looked around, startled. "Oh, I don't think so. I have to finish this report, and I'm not really comfortable there anyway." She paused, then said what Chloe already knew. "We...you know, my friends and I tend to go to Jack's Place, on the other side of town."

"All right," Chloe said. "But I feel restless and I need to go out. I think I'll go by myself."

Hannah's eyebrows shot up. "What about Gaia?"

Chloe sighed in exasperation. "Oh, we had an argument. She went away angry, and I haven't heard from her since.

She might be at the Elk Horn, and looser after a couple of drinks."

When Hannah didn't answer, Chloe got up and threw on a heavy cable-knit sweater against the evening chill. Her ancient blue Chevy was really low on gas, but Chloe knew she could make it safely to the Elk Horn, which was only a mile or so away, and back with no trouble.

In just a few minutes, she pulled into the crowded parking lot.

As a cheerleader, she was well known among the students, and many of them called to her as she wormed her way through the crowd. Since the drinking age was twenty-one, it tended to be mostly older classmates and townies who frequented the bar. However, the age-old practice of borrowing someone else's license was still prevalent, and the bartenders tended to take a glance, and not ask questions as long as a license was flashed in front of them. She drank soda until an older student offered to buy her a beer. Or, she could join a table of students who had purchased a pitcher. Plastic glasses could be hidden in purses. It was easy to drink at the Elk Horn, whether you were twenty-one or not.

"Hey, Chloe, come and sit with us." Marcy Hughes, captain of the cheerleading squad waved to her. Two of the basketball players moved their chairs to make room for her, and Chloe joined their table. She took the plastic glass from her purse, and someone poured her beer from the pitcher. They had a basket of chips and salsa, and she helped herself to those.

As the chatter ebbed and flowed around her, she stole glances around the bar, trying to spot Gaia. When their eyes did meet, Gaia did not acknowledge Chloe, and looked away as if she didn't know her. Crushed, Chloe wondered what to do. She didn't want to walk over and confront her; a public bar was no place to carry on an argument.

Chloe joined in the banter at the table, but her heart wasn't in it. She stole glances at Gaia, and watched her flirt and laugh with the crowd around her. She never looked at Chloe.

What the hell? Maybe she's right and I'm a forty-year-old stick-in-the-mud. All work and no play. What would it hurt to go to one of those stupid meetings? I hate to lose my best friend over such a silly matter, but it seems to mean a lot to her. After two more drinks, she dug out her cell and texted Gaia. 'k. whre n wen?'.

She watched from the corner of her eyes as Gaia looked at her cell. After a moment, she turned full-face to Chloe, smiled and put her thumb and index finger together in an OK sign.

Relieved, Chloe nodded and smiled back.

After several more beers, Chloe knew she'd better stop drinking and get herself back to the dorm while she was still rational enough to drive. She didn't feel buzzed, and the plastic glasses were small, *but you know*, she told herself, *we forty-year olds are very practical people*. She laughed aloud. *And boring*, she reminded herself. *I am a boring person.*

She stood, and the room spun around her. Nobody seemed to be paying her any attention. *Now where did I leave that door?* Although it was not where she thought it was, she spied it on the opposite side of the bar and started toward it.

"Whoopsie!" she apologized as she stumbled and fell against a couple who were sitting on one chair, entwined around each other. They didn't even notice.

She made it to the door, pushed it open and staggered out into the open air. It hit her like a slap in the face. She stopped short as she saw the tall, copper-haired boy, the one she'd seen crossing campus at a distance, leaning against a lamppost. Their eyes met, and with a sensation that was almost physical, she felt something pass between them. She shivered all the way down to her toes. There was a feeling of familiarity, that he was someone she had known all her life. He straightened very slowly and looked at her. Not up and down, assessing her figure as a lot of guys did, but straight at her. Chloe couldn't move. They stood for what seemed to her an eternity, then he walked toward her and closed in the space between them. He looked down at her with eyes as gray as the river that flowed past the town.

"Tell me your name is Chloe."

She smiled. "Yes, it is, Thomas Thorn."

Five

The Elk Horn was nearly deserted. Thomas and his roommate, Jett Mason, having made a fast trip to town to pick up a few odds and ends, stopped in for a quick beer before heading back to the dorm. They both flashed borrowed IDs at Frank, the bartender, and after a disinterested glance, he filled two mugs, emblazoned with the Elk Horn logo, with draft beer and set them on the bar in front of them.

Thomas took a quick look around at the other patrons. He hoped Chloe might be there, but knew it was unlikely this time of day. He guessed right. She wasn't there, and a jolt of disappointment surged through him.

Jett waited until Frank wandered down to the other end of the bar, out of earshot. He lifted the mug and grinned at Thomas. "I have five of these already. One more makes my Christmas present to my dad. He went to college here, too, you know."

Thomas laughed. "He'll like that, for sure. Now tell me again about this so-called secret society you want me to join."

Jett glanced around to make sure he wouldn't be overheard. "Well, I know you like history, so I thought you might be interested. It's based on the Druids, and Stonehenge—you know, that strange rock formation in England..."

Thomas cut in. "That's archeology, not history, and it's a lot more than a rock formation. It was..."

Jett waved a hand to interrupt him. He took a hearty gulp of beer. "Yeah, I'm learning all about that through the group. Tonight is the last night we can bring in a prospective new member. So, do you want to come or not?"

Between homework and basketball practice, I haven't had a second to talk to Chloe. All I did was drive her home in her car. We talked for a few minutes, but we both had class assignments, but I did promise I would call. She'll think I'm not going to.

Thomas stumbled over his words. "Uh, there's this girl I met a couple of nights ago. I was hoping she'd want to go to a movie, or something."

"It's kind of late to ask her now. Why not go with me tonight and get with her on the weekend?"

Thomas stared into his beer and considered. He wasn't much for secret societies, but this might be interesting, simply from an historical or archeological perspective. If he didn't like it, he could always drop out. He didn't have to join.

He drained his drink and set the mug down with a clunk. He chuckled. "Okay, you're on. Tonight I become a Druid."

~ * ~

Thomas shivered as he and Jett approached the group of hooded figures, eerily outlined by the full moon above. He felt a tinge of apprehension as they joined the others, but shrugged it off, amused at himself. This was a bunch of college kids playing at being ancient Druids among a partial circle of two-foot high rocks. What could possibly be the least bit scary about this? If anything, it might turn out to be rather juvenile, and he'd never come back for session number two.

All the figures except one wore robes in somber shades of gray, brown or blue. The one who wore white stood silently by, watching the others don their garments. Here and there a giggle erupted, only to be shushed by someone else. When everyone had tied their rope belts, they turned and faced the figure in white. He raised a hand, as if in blessing, gestured slowly around the inner circle of stones, then moved his hand up and down in an obvious instruction to sit. Thomas and Jett found places in front of two of the larger rocks and lowered themselves to the ground.

Something about the way one of the smaller figures moved caught Thomas' attention. Although tall enough to be a boy, she moved with feminine grace, and as she walked toward the empty space beside him and sank down on the grass, he knew who it was.

He turned his head toward her, but realizing his hood hid his face in the darkness, he pushed the fabric back, just enough so she could recognize him. Their eyes met, and the feeling that he knew her, and had always known her, swept over him again. He reached out a hand to touch hers, but drew back when Jett nudged his knee.

Chloe also must have received a reprimand, as she turned her face away from him and lowered her head. He wondered who was with her. She looked vaguely like the girl he had seen at the Elk Horn, but in the dim light he couldn't be sure.

Elation filled him all of a sudden, and he shot Jett a grin and nudged him back. The figure in white walked into the center of the circle, and all the whispering and restless movements ceased at once.

"I am Dyfan. Welcome to our sacred circle. We come in peace."

His words echoed around the circle, as all repeated after him, "We come in peace."

Dyfan raised his arms in blessing, then folded them in front of him. He bowed his head. "Let us meditate on the three tenets of our faith: wisdom, creativity and love."

Thomas had a moment of panic. Meditate? He'd never meditated in his life. He stared at Dyfan. *What a phony!* Thomas didn't think the words, but they were there.

As if in answer, Dyfan began to instruct them. "Breathe deeply, clear your mind. Choose one of the words—'wisdom', 'creativity' or 'love', and allow it to take your mind to a new place. Picture the word in your mind. If you find yourself thinking of anything else—homework, football practice, a TV show, someone of the opposite sex, picture a windshield wiper brushing those thoughts away. Breathe deeply now..."

Thomas tried to keep thoughts of Chloe out of his mind, but there she was, sitting right next to him, and he could smell the light fragrance she wore...lilacs in the spring. Her presence was as tangible as his own. How was he supposed to ignore that? He breathed in and out, forcing himself into a slow rhythm as he let the word 'love' form in his mind. It came across in a masculine scrawl, dark blue on a lighter blue background. He gradually lost awareness of his body and his surroundings. He was aware only of a vague sound, like the waves of the ocean breaking on the sand. Over and over, the water washed up on the shore, and rinsed away the knowledge of Chloe's presence. He felt himself floating in mystical 'otherness.' He no longer knew where, or even who, he was.

~ * ~

A voice came out of the mist and entered his mind. "They will try to kill her again." He saw a ghostly shape float over the rocks so familiar to him, those of the Mystery Hill configuration in North Salem, his home town. He knew the ghost to be himself, but it was a Thomas of another place and time.

He heard himself say, "I will not let her die this time."

"You will need courage. Do you have that courage, Thomas?"

He saw Chloe, dressed in a white shift, bound with ropes to the rock which had been used as an ancient altar. A wreath of flowers encircled her head, and several white-robed persons danced around her, chanting and throwing flowers on her prone body as they moved. Chloe laid inert, her eyes wide and staring, her face frozen in fear.

"Do you have the courage, Thomas?"

"I have the courage."

"Watch the one who pretends to be her friend."

A white-robed figure came out from among the trees. Thomas knew those woods and those rocks by heart. He had spent centuries there, waiting for her. And, now, unless he saved her, she would die again, in the same place, in the same way. This time, if he had to, he would die for her.

The others parted and fell back as the priest approached the altar. He stood very still and gazed down at the victim. His hood hid his face, and Thomas could not identify his features.

"She is an acceptable sacrifice." Moonlight glittered on the blade of a wide, sharp knife as he raised it high in the air.

Thomas hurled himself at the priest, and felt himself pass through him, as unsubstantial as a gust of wind through the leaves of a tree.

He heard another sound: the lonely, plaintive sound of a flute.

His mind took over as he jolted himself back to reality. There was Jett sitting on one side of him, Chloe in a lotus position on the other. Murmurs ran around the circle, as the flute, which Thomas guessed came from a hidden CD player, brought them back to full consciousness. The meditation was over.

He glanced at his watch. An hour had gone by, and it felt like seconds.

Several people got up and stretched, and Thomas jumped to his feet, glad to be back from wherever the meditation had taken him. He turned, stretched a hand down to Chloe and drew her up beside him.

"I was going to call and ask you out tonight."

"I was otherwise occupied," she said with a toss of her head, which made her hood fall back. He caught the tease in her voice.

"So I see. I guess we both were."

He became aware of Jett and Chloe's friend, staring at them.

"I'm sorry. This is my roommate, Jett Mason."

Chloe turned to the pretty blond, whose expression registered shock as she stared at Thomas—and something else he couldn't read. Chloe introduced them.

Jett moved in to focus on Chloe's friend. "Gaia—it means 'earth,' doesn't it?"

"Yes, it does, but my name here is 'Carys.' It means 'little fair love.' She giggled, but her eyes never left Thomas' face.

This time he read her calculated message: *how interested are you in Chloe?*

Jett, vying for Chloe's attention, broke in. "Mine is 'Cadno,' which is Celtic for 'fox.' Dyfan will give you both your mystical names tonight."

Growing restless, Thomas shifted his gaze back to Chloe. "Is there more, or are we about finished here?"

Jett shook his head. "We're going to have an informal time now. Then Dyfan will give a message, which teaches us about the Druids and Stonehenge, so we can follow in their ways. And he will assign you Celtic names."

Thomas didn't know how much more he wanted to sit through. As he looked at Chloe, he knew she felt the same. "How about going out after?" he asked.

Whatever she was about to answer was preempted by Gaia. "All four of us? I'm up for that. But what's open at this hour? The Elk Horn sure isn't."

Jett jumped in. "IHOP is. We can go have breakfast."

Chloe smiled up at Thomas. "Uhm, pancakes. Yes, let's do that."

The group quieted down as Dyfan made his rounds about the circle, and urged everyone to be seated again.

Thomas resumed his seat on the ground, reached for Chloe's hand and held it tightly. He didn't care what Jett and Gaia thought. Something deep inside told him this was his girl, and he was going to hold onto her.

Six

"You get us a booth, and I'll be right there." Thomas gave Jett a wave and headed off to the men's room.

When he located his friends, in the last booth at the far end of the room, he was a little disconcerted to find Chloe wedged against the wall, Jett beside her. There was no option for Thomas except to take the seat across from Jett and next to Gaia. As he slid into the booth, she edged closer to him.

She gave his arm a squeeze. "Thought you'd never get here."

He shook off his feelings of annoyance as he picked up the menu. "A guy's gotta do what a guy's gotta do."

"So do girls," Gaia cooed, trying to catch his eye, and managed to close another inch between them.

Thomas ignored her and gave Chloe a long look. She glanced up from the menu and smiled at him. "I feel like pancakes, maybe one of the stuffed specials with fruit."

"Except strawberries," he said without thinking. "You're allergic to them, break out in nasty red bumps all over your pretty face." The moment it was out of his mouth, he realized that was something he couldn't possibly know. Where had that come from?

All three faces swerved toward him.

Jett laughed. "Are you already telling her what she can and can't do?"

"He's right." Chloe's face wore a puzzled look. "I am allergic to strawberries."

Gaia's voice held a hint of resentment as she said to no one in particular. "How does he know that? Oooohhh, oooohhh!" She made a mocking sound that was supposed to sound like a ghost.

The waitress, a middle-aged dyed blond who looked exhausted, came to take their order. Her name tag said her name was Donna. Thomas regarded her with sympathy. She probably had two or three children at home; maybe she worked a second job as well. He shook himself mentally. *Stop making assumptions about people you don't even know.*

Chloe ordered pancakes with peaches. Thomas and Jett opted for eggs and bacon. When Donna waited, pencil poised against her pad, Gaia sent a sweet smile across the table at Chloe. "You won't break out in red spots if I order the French toast with strawberries, will you?"

Thomas grimaced. He'd never liked French toast, bread soaked in eggs and then fried. Tasted like soggy cardboard to him. How could anyone eat that?

"Of course not. Go ahead."

Thomas, irritated, felt his nails bite into his palms. Gaia was getting on his nerves, and it wasn't taking much effort on her part, either. After Donna left, walking as though her feet hurt, he addressed Chloe. "What did you think about this evening?"

"It was interesting," she hedged.

Thomas felt Gaia stiffen beside him, and her voice rose.

"Interesting? Is that all you thought of it, Chloe? I find it fascinating—the way the Druids built Stonehenge without modern machinery or anything, how those blue stones came all the way from Wales, and the archeologists don't know how that was even possible..."

Donna arrived with a pot of coffee, four mugs and a pitcher of cream. Thomas took over the job of pouring a cup for everyone, and passed them around.

Chloe flushed at Gaia's reprimand. "Well, that part *is* fascinating. I like the history part, learning about something I have no knowledge about. But..."

"But what?" Gaia's voice was too loud, and several other diners turned around and stared at her. "Isn't it thrilling to feel yourself connected to something so—so ancient and mysterious? Something that feels so powerful?"

Even Jett seemed embarrassed. "Okay, okay, just keep your voice down, will you? We don't need the whole restaurant to hear us."

Thomas ignored the other two and addressed Chloe. "How do you like your new name? I think mine is sort of unimaginative. It doesn't take a lot of creativity to come up with 'red-headed' for me."

Chloe shivered. "Vala, the chosen one. It kind of gives me the creeps, if you want to know."

"Lochlan is a beautiful name," Gaia said, looking at Thomas. "I could name a son that."

"I liked his lecture," Jett cut in. "Like how Stonehenge was used for different purposes, first as a burial ground, later for religious ceremonies, and even as a healing center. And the pieces of bones and pottery suggest there might have even been human sacrifice."

"Yes!" Gaia was more than a little enthusiastic. "And during the meditation, you can actually feel yourself connect with the spiritual energy, whatever that is."

Silence greeted her outburst, and everyone stared at her. "Well, can't you? Didn't you?"

Just in time, Donna arrived with their plates. Thomas repressed the urge to jump up and help her as she set the unwieldy tray down on a three-legged stand. Although her face had few wrinkles, the bags under her eyes revealed the stress of her life.

"Thank you, Donna."

She smiled at him, an unexpectedly lovely smile that lit up her tired face.

Gaia dug into her strawberries with obvious relish. After a few swallows, she resumed her questions, her tone not quite so belligerent. "Didn't you feel the connection, any of you?"

Jett shrugged, as he picked up a piece of bacon and crunched on it. "It was restful. My mind wandered. I tried to get it off the football field, but it kept going back there, trying to make the winning touchdown."

Thomas laughed. "I'm a basketball guy myself, and I just got picked for the team."

Chloe leaned forward, and reached out a hand toward Thomas. "By the way, did you know that Jim Walsh, one of my art instructors, is also the basketball coach? That was a surprise to me when I started cheerleading last year."

Thomas raised his eyebrows over the rim of the coffee mug. "Really? I didn't know he taught art, too. That's an interesting combination..."

Chloe smiled at him. "He's not your typical art professor. He has a really interesting background. Majored in art, but then went into the Marines. Came back, took some training at the FBI to be one of those criminal profilers, but art won out, and here he is."

Gaia picked up her spoon and banged it on the table, like a gavel. "Can we please stick to the subject? I want to know what everyone felt during the meditation!"

Thomas saw Chloe jump, and her face paled a little.

"Chloe?" Gaia seemed determined to pry an answer, any answer, out of her friend."

Chloe put down her fork, half a peach clinging to it. "I—I felt something, not sure what it was. Is that what you call a 'connection with the past?'"

"What did it feel like?"

"Uhm...there seemed to be a—something, almost a presence, like I was tuning into a radio station. It was a little scary, and I guess I pushed it back. I didn't like it."

Gaia glared at her. "You can't be afraid of it. That's the road, the channel that connects you with the others, the ones who came before. You just let yourself go, tune into it and feel what happens."

Thomas decided to take her attention off Chloe. "If we all feel it, we connect, and become part of it. Is that it?"

Gaia heaved a huge sigh of relief. "Exactly! Somebody here gets it."

Jett changed the subject. "What did you think when Dyfan said some people actually believe extra-terrestrials had a hand in building Stonehenge?"

Thomas polished off the rest of his toast. "Could be. As someone once said, stranger things happen than this world dreams of."

"It is pretty hard to explain some of those things." Jett tried to refill his coffee, which emptied out the pot. There was only half a mug left. "Like the stone statues on Easter

Island, or the Nazca lines in Peru—they can only be understood from the air, and there were no airplanes when they were drawn in the earth."

This subject was obviously Gaia's meat and potatoes. "And like how they built the pyramids, all those huge stones fitting exactly together with no mortar."

"And those ancient buildings, built ten thousand years ago, undersea off the coast of Japan. Who lived there, and when?" Jett shrugged and drained his cup. "Well, we'll never know, I guess."

"And evil," Gaia added. "That's another subject. Why will some people commit such atrocious acts against other people? Does evil actually exist as an entity, or is it some kind of force that just gets into some people and takes over?"

Thomas thought of Mystery Hill. "None of you are native New Englanders, so you wouldn't know, but there's a place called 'America's Stonehenge' right near my home town. People who have researched it say really strange—and sometimes evil—things have gone on there over the years."

Gaia's head swiveled toward him as if it were wound on a spring. "Really? I didn't know that. What's it like?"

"Rocks," Thomas said. "Built into walls, tunnels, storage rooms—and yes, there is a stone they call the altar stone, which they think was used for human sacrifice."

Chloe gave a little shiver. "Can they prove that? Isn't it possible they just used animals?"

Donna interrupted the conversation by arriving with the bill. Thomas put it all on his credit card, and waved away his friends' objections, which weren't too insistent, he noted. He had saved a considerable amount of money during his two years roaming around the country, working at various jobs, and he could afford to treat now and then.

Thomas thought of how Mike and his friends intended to sacrifice the rabbit. "Some people think so. But there is another stone, the same shape as the altar stone, not far away in Massachusetts, which has a human figure carved into it stretched out, like a victim. That pretty much proved it."

Gaia was obviously fascinated. "Who built that site? The Indians? Had to be an early American tribe."

"Not necessarily." Thomas shrugged. "Some people say it might have been Norsemen, you know, coming in their Viking ships. Maybe even Phoenicians."

Jett snorted. "So far inland? I don't think so."

"There's a river," Thomas said, "the Spiket, which dumps into the Merrimack River, goes right up there."

"How far away is this place?" Gaia was more animated than Thomas had seen her all evening. "Can we go see it? Could we go right now?"

"No way! It's two o'clock and I'm ready for bed." Jett yawned. "Chloe, want to drive back with me?"

Chloe smiled and replied, "I came with Gaia. I think I'll go back with her. I'm ready to turn in, too."

"I thought we might do that together," Jett said, then held up his hands as Gaia looked daggers at him. "Just joking, guys." He attempted a laugh, but nobody else joined in, and Chloe looked embarrassed.

Turning back to Thomas, Gaia asked, "Seriously, Thomas, how far away is this place?"

"A couple of hours."

"How about making a trip up there soon, maybe this weekend? I want to see it."

Thomas shrugged. "Well… it's not a good time for me. I have an exam, a project due and basketball practice. But— you can go. Nobody's stopping you."

Gaia didn't answer, but he felt the surge of her anger.

He added, "But you'd better do it before the winter comes. It's no fun poking around there in the snow."

The four of them started to walk out of the restaurant. At the door, Thomas stopped. "Wait for me," he said to Chloe, and motioned for Jett and Gaia to go on ahead. "Meet us at the cars, okay?" Thomas headed back toward the table they had just left, slipped a twenty-dollar bill under the coffee pot, and hurried back to rejoin Chloe.

He took her hand and they walked outside, not in any hurry. The wind picked up and had an edge to it. Thomas scented the air, almost as a dog would do. "It feels like snow. It snows early in New Hampshire."

Chloe shivered, even though her thick, cable-knit sweater should have been enough for early fall weather. She turned her head to look up at him, and stopped walking, bringing him to a halt, too. "Did you feel anything during the meditation? I didn't want to upset Gaia more by telling her what it was really like for me."

"It seems to me she's pissed at everyone. I'm not going to worry about what she thinks, or Jett, either. What was it you felt? Do you want to tell me?"

They stood, gazing at each other, and Thomas sensed the same connection with her as he'd felt the first night outside the Elk Horn. "Tell me," he repeated in a softer voice.

She bit her lip, as if wondering if she should say the words aloud. Then it came out, in almost a whisper. "I felt evil. Something—or someone evil. And Dyfan scares me." She attempted a laugh. "That's silly, isn't it? Forget I even said that."

"Come on, you two." Gaia leaned against her car, her arms folded in front of her and a scowl on her face. Thomas wondered why she hadn't waited inside the car, where it would have been warmer.

As they walked toward Jett and Gaia, the trees, which had not yet lost all their leaves, rustled in the breeze above them. Thomas felt a sudden chill, which had nothing to do with the weather, as the words he'd heard in the meditation came back to him like an echo.

Watch the one who pretends to be her friend.

Seven

Chloe stared down at the library table.

Thomas looked across at her in disbelief. "I don't believe her! Gaia didn't say one word to you all the way home?"

"Not one word. When I tried to talk to her, she didn't answer. When we reached the dorm, she got out, slammed the door and left me sitting there, yelling after her."

"And you haven't heard from her since?" Thomas shook his head. "I got that she was annoyed at all of us for not being serious enough about the Stonehenge meeting, but this is ridiculous, don't you think?"

Chloe tucked an errant strand of honey-colored hair behind her ear. It immediately fell back around her face. "No phone messages, no text. When I went to her room to pick her up for first period class, she was already gone."

Thomas rubbed his chin. "You have first class together?"

"No. We walk across the quad together, then separate by the fountain. She goes to her class, and I go to mine."

"What's your first class?"

"Landscape painting."

He looked at her with curiosity. "Are you planning to major in art, or is this just an interest of yours?"

She shook her head. "I don't know yet. I love art, and I'm good at it, too, but I feel a strange little tug toward nursing, too." She managed a half-smile as she continued. "Professor Walsh saw I was upset and tried to cheer me up. He can be very funny, but today it didn't do any good."

Thomas nodded, sensing her sadness.

"This just hurts so much. Gaia and I have been such good friends ever since we met over a year ago. She was so bubbly I just couldn't help but like her. But, she's changed..." She paused, and a tear escaped from her eye. She dug a tissue from her pocket and swiped at it. "We used to have so much fun."

Thomas considered. "Did things start to change when she got involved in the Druid thing?"

"I didn't know she was involved in that until the day she invited—well, insisted I join, too."

"And when was that?"

"The day before I met you outside the Elk Horn. I went down there that night to tell her I'd go to the meeting with her."

Thomas gave an inward groan. He had hoped to avoid this particular conversation, but the way Gaia was treating Chloe made it impossible. "Listen," he said, as he reached out his hand to touch hers. "When we met that night..."

She attempted a faint laugh. "I was a bit wasted, I know."

He gave her hand a squeeze. "It's not about that. Gaia had called me and persuaded me to meet her there. I didn't want to. I'd been with her in a group a couple of times, but wasn't that into her. I was stalling for time when you showed up."

She let out a long breath. "Oh, then her recent attitude toward me makes a lot more sense. She did tell me she'd met someone she liked a lot, but I didn't know it was you. No wonder she thinks I'm being a rotten friend."

Thomas stood and began to gather up his books. "Let's get out of here. I need some fresh air, and I have an idea." He waited, watching her face for any sign of reluctance, now that she knew he'd been seeing Gaia before he met her.

She was quiet as they left the library and walked down the wide steps. In a humorous imitation of famous libraries which had lions on pedestals at the sides of their stairs, Midstate had commissioned piles of granite books, about four feet high on each side. In addition to the sculptures, there were carved books, looking as though they'd fallen from the top of the pile, scattered around the pedestal bases, which students often used as seats.

Thomas stopped and sat on the top three piled volumes, which had Intro to Archeology carved into the granite, and pulled Chloe down beside him. "What are you thinking now?"

She didn't look at him, but picked at a thread in her sweater. When she did glance up and met his eyes, he was shocked to see tears in them. "Chloe..."

"I feel like I'm being forced to choose between you and my best friend," she whispered, "and I don't want to. I know she likes you, and that makes me feel disloyal."

"And it isn't fair that you have to do that, but I'm telling you I was never interested in her. She has no claims on me." He tried to put his arm around her, but she shrugged away. "Gaia isn't being fair, either, do you think? I never made any commitment to her. She asked me out, not the other way around."

She swiped at her eyes. Several girls passed them and threw her curious looks, then whispered to each other as they climbed the steps. One of them looked back at her and Thomas, and sent him an encouraging thumbs-up sign.

"Do you want to hear my idea?" Thomas tried to calm his apprehension that she would just get up and leave him there alone.

"What is it?" Her voice was toneless, as if she didn't care.

He cleared his throat. "Well, it's such a beautiful day, too nice to spend inside a musty library, and it's Friday and classes are over for the week. Why don't you get your camera, and we'll take a ride out to Mystery Hill, near where I live. You can take some pix for your landscape class, and I'll call my mom and invite us for dinner."

Chloe's face still registered nothing he could read. "Come on, Chloe," he urged. "If we get away from here, we can think better. I don't owe Gaia anything, and I'd like you to meet my family."

"You told Gaia you were too busy to go this weekend."

He shrugged. "It's not the weekend, it's Friday. It's only an hour's drive, and we'll be back tonight. And, I meant it—I am too busy to go this weekend."

"I owe her something," Chloe said. "It's called 'loyalty.' She scooped up her books and stood. "I don't know what to do, Thomas, but I have to talk to Gaia before I make any decisions about you and me." She walked off briskly in the direction of her dorm.

He watched her go, her lithe, athletic figure striding over the quad, which was framed in the vivid yellows, oranges and crimsons of the autumn trees. A large red leaf drifted down from a branch and caught in her hair. She stopped, as if she had run into a wall, reached up for the leaf and stared at it. She made a slow turn and looked back at Thomas.

His stomach roiled again as she walked back toward him, much more slowly than she had left. She held the leaf out to him.

He took it, and regarded her through narrowed eyes. "Does this have a secret message printed on it?"

She squinted at the leaf and pretended to read it. "It *says 'go with Thomas to Mystery Hill.'*"

~ * ~

"So what changed your mind?"

He tried to catch her eye, but she stared out the car window, not speaking. She'd made a hasty trip back to her dorm room, grabbed her camera, a sketch pad and a box of colored pencils, which she tossed into the back seat of his car.

"Hannah said Gaia stopped into my room twice this afternoon."

"And what does that have to do with why you changed your mind?"

She laughed without mirth. "Obviously it didn't, when we were at the library. It just hit me that Gaia hasn't shown that much loyalty to *me*. She lied to me about you, said she'd been out with you a couple of times, and she's been treating me like dirt. I decided I had the right to take some time to make up my mind if I have to choose between you two, and I hope I don't."

Thomas sighed. "I don't see why you have to make that choice, either. If you think it will help, I'll talk to Gaia myself, and try to straighten things out." He made a face. "Not that, that will be much fun. Did Hannah say Gaia left a message for you or anything? For Pete's sake, why didn't she call or text?"

"I turned my phone off in the library. Hannah said she seemed 'agitated,' whatever that means."

Thomas pretended to watch the road. He passed one of the yellow, diamond-shaped deer-crossing signs, and slowed his speed. You never could tell when one of those quick, graceful creatures would decide to dart in front of the car. He'd come close to hitting one a number of times.

"Did you call your mother?" By the tone of her voice, Thomas guessed Chloe wanted to change the subject.

"I did, and the family can't wait to meet you. My mother is preparing pheasant under glass, and baked Alaska for dessert."

He laughed at her incredulous expression. "Just kidding. She'll probably make meatloaf. If anyone cooked pheasant, it would be my grandmother, Ivy, and she'd probably have shot it, too."

Chloe brightened. "You call your grandmother 'Ivy?' Tell me about her."

Thomas edged with caution around a flatbed truck, and hoped a deer wouldn't choose that moment to try to cross the road. When he passed the truck loaded with Christmas trees, he relaxed against the back of the seat. "She's a piece of work," he said. "She's in her seventies, but she never got out of the sixties—the nineteen sixties, that is. She wears black jeans and tie-dyes her own tee-shirts. She makes jewelry from things she picks up on her daily walks."

He had Chloe's full attention at last. "What kind of things?"

"Oh, stones, shells, pieces of glass or metal, even twigs or nuts sometimes. It's amazing what she does when she works her magic on them. She comes up with some beautiful stuff. She gives them as gifts, and everyone is just blown away with what she can do with, literally, junk. She's one of a kind—you'll love her."

"I will. I just know I will." Chloe smiled at him at last—a full-blown happy grin. "What else should I know about your family before I meet them?"

"My older brother, Charlie, as I've already told you, is in Iraq. He's a real straight-arrow type, enlisted right after high school. But I'm sure he'll go to college when he comes home."

"Which is when?"

"We don't know. They keep recalling the same bunch of guys for another tour of duty."

"Anyone else?"

"My younger brother, Mike. He's a royal pain in the ass. Don't take anything he says personally. I tried to shape him up this summer, but it didn't do much good. My parents are much too easy on him."

"And your parents?"

"Salt of the earth." He turned to smile at her, and just in time saw the deer leap from the shrubbery. He turned the wheel hard, and winced as he heard the tires squeal when the car skidded on the road.

Chloe gasped and gripped her seat belt. "Oh, my God! You just missed him."

"Her," he said grimly. "No antlers. It's one of the hazards when you live in New Hampshire. Sometimes I think we have more deer than people."

She stretched to gaze after the deer. "They're so beautiful. What would you have done if you'd hit it?"

He couldn't resist saying it, and he made his voice dead-serious. "Why, put it in the trunk and take it home, of course. We'd have venison for dinner."

~ * ~

"Here we are." Thomas turned the car onto a long access road. The not-overly large sign at the beginning of the entrance proclaimed it to be "America's Stonehenge: Mystery Hill."

He paused the car at a larger, metal sign so Chloe could read the abbreviated explanation of the site. She scanned the words, which were printed white on black. "Huh, two thousand years old, and they think it could even be the remnants of a pre-Viking or even a Phoenician civilization. Wow! I can't wait to see it."

He took her hand as they got out of the car and started the short walk up the hill to a rustic cabin which served as the admission building and gift shop. She didn't pull away, which he took as an encouraging sign.

She gestured with her other hand at the stone wall that bordered a wooded area with a scattering of picnic tables to the right of the road. "Is that ancient, too?"

"I doubt it. There's an interesting rock in there, though. Want to see it?"

"Sure." They changed directions and headed for the stone wall. There wasn't a break in the rocks, so Thomas climbed over it, and turned back to help Chloe. She didn't seem to need his help, however, as, laughing, she scrambled over it by herself. He pointed to a huge gray rock which loomed up fifty feet or so from where they stood.

"Awesome!" Chloe aimed her camera and moved around the stone, taking shots from various angles.

Thomas watched her, enjoying every moment. Her movements were free and graceful, and the worry seemed to have dropped from her shoulders. Her expression mirrored her pleasure as she took pictures. When she had taken half a dozen, she leaned up against the rock and flattened herself against its rough surface, and stretched her arms out to the sides.

"Oh, Thomas, this is wonderful. It's so beautiful here, and so peaceful. I can't wait to see the rest of it."

Something dark, like an unwelcome memory from the past stirred in his mind... something activated by the way she lay flat against the rock. Feeling disturbed, he started toward her. She flashed him a smile, and moving away from the stone, she began to twirl in circles, her sneakers sending the many-colored leaves in all directions. Her long, honey-colored hair streamed out behind her. He stopped in his tracks to watch her, and the darkness in his mind faded away.

Inside, the sixtyish, gray-haired woman, whose name tag said *Annie,* took their ticket in a word-sparse, businesslike way. She gave him a slight nod. Thomas recognized her from his previous visits. With a cynical twist of humor, he thought she'd probably been there as long as the site itself.

Chloe moved about the shop, examining the souvenirs and other items for sale. "Look!" She exclaimed, as she stopped in front of a large, framed photograph on one wall.

Thomas, familiar with the picture, smiled as he joined her. "What do you think of that?"

The pattern of small and large rocks rose higher than a mere wall. In the center of the construction was an opening, which looked as though it led into a cavern. The opening was black against the assorted grays of the stones, and in front of the opening floated a misty, vaguely human-like shape. Chloe ran a finger over the photo and read the caption aloud: The ghost of Mystery Hill. She turned back to Thomas, amazement on her face.

"They took a picture of a ghost?"

Thomas grinned at her. "Even better than the Druids, isn't it? That bunch is just pretending with their miniature half-assed Stonehenge. Here we have the real thing."

Before she could reply, his cell phone rang. He groped for it in his pocket, flicked it open and read the numbers on the screen. "Hi, Mom—we're on our way. We'll only be another hour or so..."

He broke off, as his mother interrupted him. "Huh?"

Chloe turned away from the photo and laid a hand on his arm. "What is it?"

He clicked the phone closed, as he felt the color drain from his face. "It's Ivy. She's had a fall, and they've taken her to the hospital. We have to go home right away."

Chloe nodded. "Let's go. This can wait. Ivy can't."

Eight

"Strange things are said to have happened at Mystery Hill." Ivy took care not to put pressure on her arm in its cast. Even with her broken limb, she'd managed to make a pitcher of watermelon margaritas for Thomas and Chloe. "I'm sorry you didn't get to see the rest of it because of clumsy old me."

Thomas sat back and smiled as he watched Chloe fall under Ivy's spell. She had made herself helpful, and acted very solicitous toward Ivy, and even seemed to enjoy doing things for her. His whole family had embraced her as one of their own, and Mike was already head over heels in love with her. He had been the perfect little gentleman, and not one cuss word or fresh remark had passed his lips since he set eyes on her. Remembering how Mike had talked and acted before Thomas left for Midstate, he didn't know whether to be amused or feel in awe of the effect Chloe had on his younger brother.

Sitting out on Ivy's patio on the October-blue afternoon, Thomas relaxed. He hadn't realized how the situation among

Chloe, Gaia and himself had affected him. The tension drained away, little by little. Now he was home, and Chloe was with him, and it felt like they belonged there together.

Chloe leaned forward toward Ivy. "Like what? I saw the photograph of the ghost—that just blew my mind."

Ivy raised her frosted glass to take a sip, paused and gazed over the rim at the covered pool, closed for the season. "There's a story about a hunter—it must have been in the sixteen or seventeen hundreds, when New England was being settled, but was still a wild place. Anyway, he camped out in the mountains, and just as he was falling asleep, he heard strange sounds, which jolted him back to consciousness. He thought it must be a hungry owl or a lonely wolf, and he tried to go back to sleep, but..."

Thomas grinned. Ivy was a born story-teller, and she intended to get as much mileage out of this tale as possible.

Chloe set her glass down on the glass-topped table. "But...what?"

"According to native lore, he either saw with his own eyes, or he had a vision, of a line of strange-looking men walking in silence down a rock-lined trail. Apparently there was a shining silver—thing—carried along in the air ahead of them by some unseen force of some kind. When they reached a place where there was a cleft in the rocks, the silver shape simply disappeared into it. And the hunter heard a strange, loud laugh that echoed through the night. That really frightened him, and he built up his fire and didn't sleep any more."

Chloe shivered. "I wouldn't be able to sleep either."

Ivy drained the dregs of her drink and pushed the glass toward Thomas, indicating that she wished another. Chloe jumped up and grabbed the pitcher before Thomas could move. Carefully, she refilled Ivy's glass.

"Another hunter, in more or less the same time period, reported that he was shocked awake by unearthly screams in the middle of the night. It was hard to hear over the roar of the mountain stream where he had pitched camp, but it sounded to him like someone in extreme agony—and all night long he heard strange sounds."

"What kind of sounds?"

"Screams, chanting, laughter."

"He never went to investigate?"

Thomas' mind conjured up a picture of Chloe splayed against the rock at Mystery Hill, her arms outstretched. Uncomfortable with the image, he cut Ivy short. "This is just folklore, Chloe. Nobody knows for sure whether anyone saw or heard anything."

"You're right, Thomas." Ivy stood up and gestured to Chloe. "Let's talk about more pleasant things. Would you like to see some of my found-object jewelry?"

"I would love to." She jumped to her feet, turned and put a hand on Thomas' arm. "Do you mind if I go inside with her?"

"Not at all. I want a few words with Mike, anyway."

~ * ~

Ivy watched Chloe pick at the jewelry, which she laid out on a black cloth on the kitchen table. The scene at Disney World when she'd first seen Chloe came back to her full force. Chloe looked much the same, older naturally, but she still owned the same poise she'd had as a child. Her face was thinner, her hair a darker honey shade, and of course, she was taller, but Ivy would have known her anywhere. She wondered if Chloe remembered her, remembered that incident at all. Did she dare to ask? How could she bring up the subject?"

Well, Ivy, old girl, you'll never know if you don't ask.

She took a deep breath. "Chloe, do you remember ever seeing me before?"

Chloe looked up. "What? Where? What do you mean?"

"Disney. Magic Kingdom. Did you go there as a child?"

"Yes, a couple of times. Once when I was about three, but I don't remember that. And once when I was eight or nine." She started to laugh. "My mother bought me a Sleeping Beauty costume, long blue dress and yellow cape, and I wore it two of the three days we were there. I thought I was a princess. We have a slew of pictures of me in that dress."

Ivy nodded. "I saw you at Disney wearing that dress."

"Oh, Ivy, you couldn't possibly remember seeing me that long ago. There must have been dozens of girls wearing the same dress."

Ivy didn't answer, and Chloe narrowed her eyes. "Why are you so sure it was me?"

"When your family came down the exit from the Haunted Castle, you turned your head, smiled at me and said 'hi,' just as if you were an old friend. Do you remember doing that?"

She shook her head, looking amused. "Not really. I don't mean to hurt your feelings, Ivy, but I was a little girl, and I don't remember everything about that trip, just that I had such a fun time."

Ivy nodded. "The next day your family went to Animal Kingdom."

"Y-e-e-e-s-s-s." Chloe drew out the word. A concerned look crossed her face. "What are you getting at?"

"Do you remember the Indian temple ruins and the tigers?"

"Ivy, you're freaking me out. What are you getting at?"

Ivy didn't answer and began to pick up the jewelry and pack it into assorted boxes and velvet draw-string bags. If she told Chloe what she had said when they were admiring the tigers, she might not believe her. However, if she showed her the diary...

"Ivy?"

She made up her mind. *I hope she doesn't think I'm crazy.* She went into the living-dining area and took the old leather journal from a drawer in the desk. She flipped through the pages until she found the account detailing the Disney trip. She laid it on the table and pointed a finger at the date: April 26, 1999. "Start here."

She watched while Chloe read, her expression serious, her brow furrowed. When she reached the end, her face looked several shades paler. "This is so weird. But—why do you have 'Charlie' crossed out and 'Thomas' written above it?"

Ivy sighed. "That's the question all right, Chloe. I didn't write 'Thomas' because I don't remember Thomas being there. Sharon came to visit me in Florida with Charlie, Jr. and Mike, and the four of us went to Disney. No Thomas."

Chloe stared at her, wide-eyed. "How could that be?"

Just then Mike burst through the kitchen door, followed by an apologetic Thomas. "Sorry, girls, I couldn't keep him out of here any longer."

Mike gazed at Chloe, his eyes shining. "Hey, Chloe, will you play a video game with me?"

"I'd love to, Sir Michael. What are we going to play?"

"*World of Warcraft.*"

"You're on. I can beat you at that, easy."

It seemed to Ivy that Chloe looked relieved as she closed the diary and handed it back to her. She gave Ivy a quick hug, thanked her for the margaritas, and promised she'd see her before they left. She refused to meet her eyes, however, and left with Mike, chasing him across the lawn as if she were a kid herself.

"Oh, oh." Thomas gave Ivy a long, steady look. "What did you say to her?"

~ * ~

On the ride back to campus. Thomas tried to allow Chloe the privacy of her thoughts, but curiosity pricked at him like a gnat under his collar. She stared out the front window, not saying a word for miles. Finally, unable to endure her silence any longer, he reached for her hand and gave it a squeeze. "Hey, was my family that bad?"

She turned to him, a look of surprise on her face. "Of course not. I loved your family and felt so accepted by all of them. Mike is adorable, and Ivy—well, I just felt as if I've always known her."

He rolled his eyes. "I'm glad there's one person in the universe who thinks Mike is adorable. Do you feel we're moving too fast then?"

Chloe shook her head. "No, I'm comfortable with where we are. But..." she broke off and went back to staring out the window. "I need to ask you something."

"Ask me anything, Chloe."

She hesitated so long he thought she'd changed her mind. When the question came, which he had expected to be one of those girl-type questions: where are we going with this relationship—he was amazed that it was something so mundane.

Her amber eyes raked his face. "Do you remember going to Disney World as a kid?"

"Of course. It was the trip of my childhood. Mike was only three or so, and he threw tantrum after tantrum, drove Ivy crazy. She paid for everything and complained that she wasn't having any fun. That's Ivy! But Charlie and I went on every ride we could. We had an absolute blast. I'll never forget it."

"Are there any pictures from that trip?"

Thomas threw her a quick glance. "Of course there are. Why in the world are you asking about my Disney trip?"

Chloe folded her hands in her lap, then unfolded them to pick at a fingernail. "My family went there several times. I just wondered if any of our visits overlapped, that's all."

He laughed. "Well, that would be quite a coincidence, wouldn't it?"

He expected her to laugh along with him, but she stared straight ahead again, as if the gray asphalt highway were the most interesting thing in the world. He barely caught her murmured response. "Yes, that certainly would be a weird coincidence."

Nine

Hannah looked up from her computer and turned as Chloe closed the door to the dorm room after her, and threw her camera and sketch pad onto the bed.

"Good thing you're back. Gaia's been up here every few hours looking for you. She seemed sort of upset. She said you weren't answering your phone and she didn't know where you were."

"I turned it off while I was at Thomas' house. I didn't want to be rude when I was meeting his family. Then I sort of forgot to turn it back on."

Hannah's eyebrows shot upward. "Hmmm, I bet. I didn't know you were going to spend the weekend with them. I just thought you wanted to take some pictures of the strange rocky formations there."

"We didn't intend to stay. We just got to Mystery Hill when Thomas got a call that his grandmother, Ivy, had fallen, and we turned around and went to his place." She pulled off her sweater and dropped it on the bed. "I just loved his family, and it felt so much like home that we stayed for the weekend."

Hannah looked at what Chloe was wearing and grinned. "So his mom lent you some of her clothes? I don't remember your having any black jeans, or any tie-dyed tee-shirts either. His mom must be one of those perpetual hippie types."

Chloe laughed and sank back on her bed. "Not his mom, his grandmother, Ivy. His mom is the traditional apple-pie mom, but Ivy is a trip and a half. These are her clothes."

The door flew open, and Gaia, not bothering to knock, burst in. She planted her feet in front of Chloe's bed, and put her hands on her hips as she looked Chloe up and down, taking in her clothing.

"Well, I see you've decided to come back. Where were you, at a hippie reunion?"

Chloe sniffed. "By the way, it's nice to see you, too." She felt annoyed, but wasn't about to start playing games with Gaia. She filled her in briefly on what she and Thomas had done and about Ivy's accident.

To her surprise, Gaia laughed. "Well, I figured as much, but I got worried when I couldn't reach you on your cell. Want to go to lunch and tell me about it?"

"Sure. Just let me get out of these clothes."

Gaia took her place on the edge of the bed as Chloe fished around in her closet for a pair of her own jeans and a lightweight sweater. She couldn't believe what came out of Gaia's mouth next.

"Want to go to lunch with us, Hannah?"

"Huh?" Hannah swirled around in her chair, obviously astonished at the invitation.

Chloe pulled a brown sweater over her head and tied a blue and brown print scarf around her waist. "Yeah, come with us, Hannah. It's just lunch and you have to eat." *What the heck is up with Gaia? She's never asked Hannah to go anywhere with us.*

"Uh, no thanks, Gaia. I brought some fruit back from breakfast, and I have to finish this report. You two go, but thanks for asking."

Gaia chatted about nothing in particular on the short walk to the dining hall. She seemed like her old self, bouncing along beside Chloe, her blond curls tousled by the breeze.

Still wary, after Gaia's treatment of her the previous week, Chloe didn't volunteer any information about the past few days. "What did you do all weekend, Gaia?"

"Oh, hung around with Jett mostly. He's a cool guy, really. I'm glad I'm getting to know him better. We have a lot in common."

Chloe pushed the crust from her first piece of pizza to the edge of the plate and picked up the second piece. "Yeah? Like what?"

"Oh, we like the same movies, sci fi things like *Avatar*, and we both love Stephen King's novels, and of course we share an avid interest in our local Stonehenge group."

Chloe stiffened, anticipating another tense discussion about the group, but Gaia looked at her with innocent blue eyes and added, "and we both think chocolate is God's greatest gift to man, ever."

Chloe burst out laughing. Maybe the easy-going, fun-loving old Gaia was back after all. She sat back in her chair and relaxed.

"You'd get along great with Thomas then. He loves, and I do mean loves, Snickers bars." The minute the words left her mouth, she regretted saying it. No way did she want to bring up the subject of Thomas, with Gaia.

As if on cue, Gaia shoved her plate aside, put her elbows on the table, rested her chin in her hands and leaned forward. "Now, tell me all about Thomas and his family, and what's going on with you two. And fill me in on this Mystery Hill place. I want to know everything."

Chloe stiffened, and felt something shift inside as Gaia's eyes locked on hers.

~ * ~

"Uh, gotta go. Bye for now."

The door to the dorm room stood open, and Thomas walked in just as Jett cut his conversation short, clicked off his phone and shoved it back in his pocket. "Well, you decided to come back. Gaia and I wondered what the hell happened to you two."

"Spent the weekend at my place. We didn't intend to, but that's the way it played out." He shrugged out of his jacket and threw it over the back of his chair.

"How'd it go?"

"Great. My family loved her." Thomas noticed one of the Elk Horn beer mugs sitting on the corner of Jett's desk. He gestured toward it. "I see you spent the weekend at the Elk Horn. Finished up the set for your dad yet?

"Yeah. Gaia and I had a Circle meeting Saturday night, and I was able to snatch this last one."

Thomas flicked on his computer, watched the screen light up, and asked in an off-hand manner. "Circle meeting? What's that?"

"Druids' executive council. We call it the Circle, meaning the inner circle."

Thomas watched his email messages surface. Nothing from Chloe yet—well, how could there be? He'd hardly left her at the dorm. Nevertheless, he felt a sting of disappointment. He missed her already. He began to type a message to her, when what Jett said about the Druids' inner circle suddenly registered in his mind. He swung around in his chair. "Inner circle?"

"Helping Dyfan plan future meetings and events."

Thomas narrowed his eyes as he looked at Jett. "Events? What kind of events?"

Jett sat back and flashed a smile at Thomas. "We're not planning a human sacrifice," he joked, "so stop looking so worried. But we are planning a celebration for the Winter Solstice. We'll have some kind of celebration, then a big party. That's several months away, of course, but you and Chloe will get a big bang out of it."

"Oh, I'm not sure we'll be going to another meeting." Thomas turned back to his laptop. "We didn't dig the last one all that much. And I don't trust that character, Dyfan. Maybe you should cool it a little, too, Jett."

It wasn't just the silence that got Thomas' attention again. The air in the room seemed to chill and grow heavy. Thomas slowly revolved in his chair until he faced his roommate again. Jett's dark eyes seemed to burn in his face with an intensity Thomas had never seen. When he spoke, his voice was cold, but it also held something else—a new authority, or the hint of a threat.

"Gaia and I want you and Chloe involved in this with us."

Thomas stared at his friend. When he answered, his voice came out weaker than he intended. "You can't force us to join that group. We'll make up our own minds."

Jett continued to hold Thomas' eyes with his. He found that he could not look away, and there was something in Jett's steady gaze that began to break down his resistance. Thomas felt a strange throbbing in his head. He had an almost visual image of his resolve cracking; it was a hard, gray thing like a chunk of ice that developed black fissures, and became thinner and thinner until...

Just before the gray thing fractured, Thomas, with a great surge of will, tore his eyes from Jett's. They stung, and he rubbed a hand across them. He jumped to his feet, and ignoring Jett's instructions to 'sit down, Thomas,' grabbed his jacket from the bed and dashed from the room.

The cold air outside washed over him, and his head began to clear. What the hell had happened in there? He strode around the campus, not paying any attention to where he was going, head down and hands in his pockets, thinking. The more he thought about it, the less sure he was about what he had experienced. Had Jett tried to hypnotize him? Or had he imagined the whole thing? The more he thought about it, the more confused he became.

The temperature seemed to drop suddenly. He turned his collar up around his neck and rubbed his hands together to warm them. He circled the dorms, walked past the dining hall. He hadn't had lunch, but he wasn't hungry. He passed the science labs, the library with its granite stack of textbooks, and walked along the path lined with blue spruce trees that led to the Redfern art complex.

Chloe was there, sitting on a bench in the sculpture garden. She looked up as he approached, and he saw how pale her face was, as she sat there, shivering in a thin brown pullover sweater.

He sat beside her and, without a word, put his arm around her and drew her close to him.

"Oh, Thomas," she whispered, her voice shaking. "What are we going to do?"

He had no answer for her, except to hold her and bury his face in her lilac-scented hair, as the first light snow of the season began to fall.

Ten

The next full moon came along in mid-November.

"I guess we might as well go," Chloe said. "Gaia really wants us to, and I don't want to cause any more friction between us. There's no harm in it, is there? I really should support my best friend."

Thomas wanted to remind her of the evil presence she said she'd felt last time, but it didn't seem important any more. He reasoned that she might even have imagined it. As for him, Jett seemed to take it for granted that he would go, and Thomas didn't much care, one way or the other. It was just a bunch of kids playing grown-up as far as he was concerned.

"We'll go once more. Then it will be Thanksgiving, and you'll come home with me, won't you? After that..."

She hugged his arm to her. "We won't think about what comes after the next meeting, and yes, I would love to spend Thanksgiving with your family."

"Your mother won't mind?" He knew her parents were divorced and her father had since died, but she'd never said much about her family life.

"My mother has a new boyfriend, and they're going on a Caribbean cruise for Thanksgiving. Can you believe that?" For the first time Thomas heard a note of bitterness in her voice. She continued. "To me Thanksgiving is home, a fire in the fireplace, a turkey on the table, family and friends…"

He couldn't believe she started to cry. She mopped at her eyes with a tissue, and went on. "And I've never had that. The only time I remember Mom cooking a turkey, she and my dad had a big fight, and she took it out of the oven half-cooked and threw it out on the lawn. Those big black turkey vultures had a fine feast. We had egg salad sandwiches and soup for dinner. All the other years we ate out."

He took a deep breath and let it out slowly, giving her time to dry her tears. "You'll have a family this year, and turkey and cranberry sauce, and everything that goes with it, I promise."

She smiled up at him. "I just can't wait. I adore your family."

"A week to go," he said. "In the meantime, we'll give the Druids one more chance to impress us."

~ * ~

Thomas felt annoyed that Gaia had insisted on driving, but he gave in. *Just this once. After this, if there is an after this, Chloe and I will go in my car.* At half-past eleven, Gaia and Chloe pulled up in front of the dorm where Thomas and Jett lived. They were already waiting outside, and they scrambled into the back seat.

"Hope you're all bundled up. It's cold in the woods." Gaia tossed a look back at them, and pulled out into the road.

Thomas leaned forward toward her. "What's on the agenda tonight?"

Gaia met his eyes in the rear view mirror. "The stone circle is completed. We're going to have a bonding rite, which will include the principles of membership and vows of secrecy."

Chloe didn't say a word, and sat staring straight ahead.

Thomas tried to insert a joking note in his voice. "That won't include any blood-letting or cutting, will it?"

"Don't you want to be my blood brother, Thomas?" Gaia's lilting tone held a note of sarcasm.

"Not particularly." Thomas stared at the back of Chloe's head and wished she'd join in the conversation. Her light brown knit cap matched the color of her hair, which she had gathered into a knot at the back of her neck. The cap fit her head tightly and covered her ears. Her jacket was brown, too. The only thing that broke the monotony was a long, lavender scarf which she wound around her neck. One end trailed over her shoulder.

Playfully, Thomas tweaked one end of the scarf. "What do you think about that, Chloe? Do you want to be Gaia's blood sister?"

She turned in her seat just enough to catch his eye. "Do I have any choice?"

"No!" Gaia and Jett said together, and they both laughed.

The wheels of the car squealed as Gaia applied the brakes too hard in order to stop for a red light.

"Hey, lighten up, you two!" Jett knocked Thomas' arm with his fist. "This isn't a funeral we're going to."

~ * ~

Dyfan waited for his congregation with his arms folded in front of him, the full sleeves of his white robe draped in folds as if he were a statue. Thomas heard Chloe catch her breath as they walked into the circle. On the silvery-white altar stone in the center stood an unglazed terra cotta jar.

Candles flickering in red glass jars ringed the stone. Smaller stones had been brought in to complete the circle. Thomas had to admit that the effect of it all, sitting on a blanket of fresh snow, surrounded by the dark trunks of trees, was eerily beautiful. It did look like a sacred place.

In silence, they put on their robes. As before, Dyfan chose the colors, which were limited to white, two shades of blue, brown and gray, and black. His assistant, wearing black, handed out the robes, which were folded like shirts from the cleaners. Thomas wondered where they had come from, and who had paid for them, but since no one else asked, he didn't either. Thomas received a gray robe, and Chloe was given a pale blue garment. Jett and Gaia both received black ones, which didn't seem to bother them at all. Each hooded robe slipped easily over their heavy sweaters and jackets, and each came with a knotted rope belt to be tied loosely around the waist.

Dyfan unfolded his arms and made a circular gesture with his index finger, signaling to the others to choose a rock which would be their place in the circle.

"Come on," Thomas whispered, as he guided Chloe toward the far side of the altar stone, where they had sat at the previous meeting.

Thomas glanced around at the serious faces and stifled a chuckle. For the life of him, he could not take this gathering seriously. This was a bunch of college kids playing dress-up, for God's sake! He didn't remember ever seeing Dyfan, or whatever his real name was, around campus. He made a mental note to look for him, although whether he could recognize him in daylight was another question. He looked down at Chloe. Her eyes were fastened on the altar with the brown jar.

Dyfan called their Druid names, and Thomas had to give him credit. He'd memorized them all and didn't make any mistakes.

"Cadno."

Jett answered "present" in a low voice, as he stared at the ground.

"Carys."

Gaia replied, her voice nearly inaudible.

Dyfan went around the circle. "Tauren. Drakthul. Arthas. Seyine. Kargath." All the answers were muted, as if they were all standing in a church.

"Lochlan." Thomas muttered a reply to his assigned name.

"Vala."

Chloe hesitated just a second or two before responding. Even then, standing right beside her, Thomas barely heard her reply.

When Dyfan completed the calling of all the names in the circle, he walked with deliberate steps toward the center stone. He picked up the jar and held it high in the air with both hands, as Thomas had seen the priest do with the communion chalice.

"We are here to dedicate our sacred meeting place, and to pledge our loyalty to each other with blood."

Thomas heard Chloe's quick intake of breath, and wished he could put his arm around her.

Dyfan dipped his hand into the jar and brought it out again. He held up two fingers, which gleamed with something wet and red. He smiled. "Just food coloring and pancake syrup. We'll just pretend this time."

Thomas felt Chloe relax. But what did Dyfan mean, this time?

"The blood of an acceptable sacrifice." He looked around the circle, making sure every eye fastened on him. "When I approach you, hold out your hand, palm up, and you will receive the blessing of love."

Thomas couldn't stop a sarcastic thought. *Is he going to draw hearts on our palms?*

Thomas watched the first girl, whose name was Seyine, tremble as Dyfan approached her. She held out her hand, and Dyfan dipped his into the jar, and traced a circle onto her white palm. Several drops fell on the snow. "I bless you, daughter, in the name of the nature gods we serve."

One robed figure after another held out his or her hand, and Dyfan somberly marked each one with a bloody circle. When he reached Thomas, their eyes met, and despite his feelings of detachment, something in the other's expression reached a distant place within. He didn't want the scarlet circle, but as Dyfan gazed at him, he felt his hand stretch itself out almost of its own accord. Dyfan moved on to Chloe. Thomas dropped his hand to his side, and watched several red blotches appear on the snow at his feet. Doubt crossed his mind. It sure looked like blood to him.

Everything in him wanted to grab Chloe's hand and run, but his feet wouldn't move.

With a great effort, he turned his head to look at her. White-faced, she stared at her outstretched hand as if in a trance.

Dyfan motioned to the group to sit, and they sank down in front of their respective rocks. Their robes appeared to protect them from the cold, as Thomas felt nothing—not the cushion of the snow, nor the wet cold he expected.

Dyfan clasped his hands together in prayer. "We believe in three things," he began, "wisdom, creativity and love. In this present incarnation on this world, we seek to practice all three, in order to improve ourselves and help others…" His voice droned on, and before long Thomas' thoughts drifted.

~ * ~

"Kanti, Kanti…" He lay beside her, hidden from prying eyes by the walls of stone that surrounded them. His hand stroked her hair, dark as raven feathers, soft as a cloud, if only he could touch a cloud.

She murmured his name, Achak, and pressed her face to his shoulder. "I love you," she murmured in the strange language they shared.

"Your name means 'spirit,' and now our spirits are joined forever."

She didn't answer, and he knew from her deep, even breathing that she had fallen asleep. He pulled the deerskin blanket up over her naked body, letting his fingers trace its graceful outline as he covered her.

He studied her face for a long time before he folded his hands beneath his head and lay back himself. Her skin was paler than most of the women of the Tribe.

"Like she has white blood!" her father had spit. "She is tainted. I cannot approve of her to be your woman."

Her hair, though, couldn't have been blacker, and her eyes were like coals when the fire had died, except for the mischievous sparkle that dwelled there. She was small, but had the curves of a woman, and fit his body as if they had been designed for each other. And what was that feeling, that invisible connection he felt with her? If that didn't prove she was meant to be his woman, what did it mean?"

"I don't want another woman. I want Kanti." He backed away from his father's wrath.

"You will not defy your father, your chief. You are to inherit the leadership of the Tribe, and you must have a wife I have approved. You will lose everything if you join with this woman. I will not allow it."

Crestfallen, Achak mulled over the situation. He wanted Kanti. If he got her with child, his father would have to agree to their joining, wouldn't he? Achak was his only son. The chief spoke so often of having a grandson, or a fleet of male heirs, which he had not been privileged to sire. He had made enough remarks about his son's 'soft heart', his disappointment that Achak was not tall and powerfully built as he was, that he took more after his pretty, delicate mother. He had married the woman of his heart, and look what it had gotten him: one son, and that one inadequate in his eyes.

Achak sighed. The hunting had not been good this year, and soon the tribe would move on in search of more game. But before they did, they would celebrate the Summer Solstice. There would be a special sacrifice to the Great Spirit, prayers and entreaties for good corn crops, a great feast and a celebration.

Lulled by the quiet and the comfort of Kanti's nearness, he too fell asleep.

He woke with a jolt when he heard the shouts of the Tribe returning from their hunt. He woke Kanti. "Hurry! Get dressed. They are back and we have to get out of here."

It was too late. A dark form filled the entrance of the cave.

"Askook!" The snake.

Askook's face took on a triumphant look as he leered at Kanti's naked body. She shook her hair over her face and cupped her hands over her breasts, but Ashak knew the snake had seen her.

He pointed at Achak. "And this is why you could not go on the hunt? This is what caused that limp you've had the last few days? Your father will be most enlightened to hear about this."

"Askook—no!" But the snake had slithered away.

~ * ~

"Thomas, where are you?" He became aware of Chloe's laughter, and her feet, shaking snow from their robes. He got up slowly, his head still swimming with pictures. He shook his head, trying to ground himself, and the images slowly faded away.

The ceremony was over. He couldn't remember anything Dyfan had said after his opening statement.

Gaia stood in front of him, her blue eyes blazing with excitement. "Which goal are you going to work on, Thomas? I guess Chloe will want to work on her creativity, but me— I'm going with love. How about you?"

Thomas attempted a light-hearted laugh. "I guess that leaves wisdom for me."

Maybe this group is not such a waste of time after all. The opposite of love is hate, and if Gaia cannot manage love, or have the love she wants, she may well turn to hatred. Wisdom includes knowledge, and—I don't know why or how, but I have a feeling that I need to know how to protect Chloe.

Eleven

"It's not supposed to rain on Thanksgiving," Thomas observed. He cast an eye at the gray sky, heavy with clouds, threatening more rain than they'd already had, which had melted away all the snow.

"It's a good thing for me it did rain." Chloe prowled around the rocks at Mystery Hill, aiming her camera at places Thomas didn't find at all interesting.

"Is this the altar stone?" She stopped to gaze down at the large, flat stone, shaped like an irregular rectangle, the top narrower than the bottom.

"Yes. It's called 'the sacrificial table'."

"It gives me the creeps." She shivered and turned away. "Did they really sacrifice human beings there?"

"Uhm hmmm. That's what the books written about this place say, anyway. Can't prove it by me, though."

Yes, you can. You've seen it with your own eyes, Thomas. Where had that crazy thought come from? He pushed it away.

He leaned against one of the stone walls and watched her, thinking how much he loved her, and feeling his desire for her rise. Even at his young age, barely twenty years old, he was sure he wanted her with him for the rest of their lives. His family already seemed to take her for granted, especially Ivy. They hadn't even made love fully yet, a lot of touching and kissing, but not the love act itself. Of course, with Jett and Gaia always around...

"What kind of pictures are you trying to get?"

She glanced toward him and brushed back her damp hair. That was one of the things he loved about her. Unlike most girls who were beautiful, she didn't seem to care if she got messy, got wet, got caught in the rain. She was so natural.

"Mr. Walsh wants us to make a painting of something people don't usually notice," she said. "Just spaces, forms, negative shapes, values."

He didn't understand art language. "Like what?"

She laughed, then pointed upward. "See how those bare branches make spaces where the sky shows through? Those are negative spaces, and in a composition they're just as important as the tree limbs themselves."

He looked, saw what she meant, and nodded. "What else?"

She whirled around and pointed at the rocks. "Values. That's the various shades of a color, whether it's light, medium or dark. The rocks even have tinges of other colors—blue, lavender, green, brown. See them?"

All at once he did. "I do, now that you've pointed them out. Rocks were always just gray before."

Her laugh rang out again. "Things like the colors of a gasoline spill on the asphalt, the shadows of trees on the sidewalk—things people never notice."

He followed her as she disappeared around a wall of stones. The day had grown warmer, very mild for the end of November in New Hampshire, and he took off his heavy jacket. The sun looked as though it were trying to break through the clouds.

Chloe stooped and peered into a tunnel, then went in. Thomas watched as she stood in the center of the tunnel which formed a room, probably used for storage centuries ago. She shrugged out of her jacket and let it drop on the floor, which was dry and covered with pine needles.

"Chloe..." He could hardly breathe.

"Thomas."

He walked into her arms. He bent his head to kiss her neck. "You're all the shape, form, value and er...positive spaces I could ask for right now. You're the one great work of art I can actually appreciate."

~ * ~

Thomas was shocked at how much Ivy had failed in just a few weeks.

She caught his look. "It only takes one bad fall at this age to start you sliding downhill, sort of like you used to do on your sled."

He read the amusement in her eyes as he visualized himself coasting down the long hill at the end of their street. His Flexible Flyer had been a shiny blond wood sled with red lettering—or had it been blue? He gave up. "That was a long time ago."

"Yes, indeed." She smiled at him, leaned back in her rocker and closed her eyes.

The rain of the previous day had developed into a traditional snowfall. It started lightly, then grew in strength as it piled up around the house, formed drifts in the yard and coated the bare tree limbs. Thomas sat forward as a cardinal lit on a branch outside the window, making a bright red splotch in the white world outside. It cocked its head and regarded him from one beady eye.

"Hmmm. I think I'll come back as a bird next time. They seem to have such carefree lives, just flitting from tree to tree."

"Sorry, Thomas, but you can't do that." Ivy didn't even open her eyes as she spoke. "You have to build on the life you had before. If there were things you should have done, if there were people you hurt..." Her voice trailed off and her head lolled to one side as she drifted off to sleep. He barely heard her next sentence. "You have to fix all that in your next life."

The cardinal changed its position on the branch and looked at him from its other eye.

"Sorry," Thomas apologized to the bird, as he stood and stretched. "Ivy says I can't come out there with you. I have to stay here and do whatever it is I came to do. And right now that probably means basting the turkey.

He grinned at the cardinal and headed for the kitchen to see what he could do to help his mother and Chloe with Thanksgiving dinner.

Twelve

Gaia shivered in the cold sunshine, but she wouldn't have changed a thing for anything in the world. "This is the way Thanksgiving should be celebrated."

Jack Wayland speared a chunk of turkey directly from the platter on the altar stone, and bit off a piece. "Out here, in nature, the way the Pilgrims did it."

"This is actually better than my aunt's cooking, which isn't so hot even when she isn't drinking." Gaia grinned at Jack and Jett. "Can you believe the supermarket made the whole dinner, and all I had to do was pick it up?"

"A brilliant idea." Jett polished off the last of his mashed sweet potatoes. "And that was just so cool of you, Dyfan—I mean, Jack, for coming up with this idea. My parents were sort of pissed that I wasn't coming home, but I don't care. As long as my precious little sister is there, they'll hardly notice. This is way better."

"I dreaded the idea of going home and listening to my parents fight the whole time," Jack admitted. "You two have become family to me, along with the rest of the group. Too bad they can't all be here."

Gaia reached over and cut the pumpkin pie with a plastic knife. She shook the can of condensed whipped cream. "Who wants this on their pie?"

"I do." Jett accepted a paper plate, balancing it against the weight of the pie.

Gaia cut pieces for herself and Jack as well, and passed them out. As if speaking to herself, she muttered, "Chloe went home with Thomas again."

"Her home life sounds as dysfunctional as ours," Jett noted. He waited to swallow a bite of pie before continuing. "Her mother isn't even home for the holiday. Thomas seems to be the only one with a normal family."

Gaia gazed off into the dark trees surrounding them and nodded. "Almost too normal, if you ask me. Totally normal mom and dad, admired older brother in the army, adorable younger brother, quirky grandmother who thinks the sun rises and sets on Thomas. Why was he lucky enough to be born into that, and we weren't?"

Jack narrowed his eyes and stared at the altar stone. "Yeah, some people really luck out."

"Thomas doesn't think his little brother is so adorable." Gaia squatted back on her heels against the rock where she sat for the Druid meetings. "Chloe told me he tried to sacrifice a live rabbit on the altar stone at that ancient rock formation near their town. I guess Thomas stopped it at the last moment and freed the rabbit."

"Thomas has a soft heart." Jett began picking up the remains of their dinner and dumped it all into a black plastic trash bag. "Maybe that's what Chloe sees in him. She's an artist, and he's *so sensitive*."

Gaia laughed. "Chloe says Mike has another version of it. He told her when they were playing some video game. He and his buddies think there was a ghost there. They didn't stick around long enough to find out."

"Interesting," Jack mused. "I don't think Thomas will like what we're going to do for the Winter Solstice celebration. I don't think he even liked the bonding ceremony. He's not totally into this yet. He's sensitive, yes, but he also has a lot of psychic strength, which he doesn't even realize. We're going to have to work harder on him"

Gaia nodded. "Jett and I know what to do, Jack. Those techniques you taught us, along with the mental focus, are really effective. If they start pulling away again, we'll just draw them back in. I'm already planning to take a class with Chloe next semester to keep her in line."

He nodded his approval. "Excellent."

She gazed up into his dark eyes. She wondered if he had used the same techniques on her and Jett. Probably, but she didn't care. He was like the father or older brother she'd never had, and the group felt like family. She'd been cheated out of all that when her parents died in the car crash, and she'd been passed on to a cold, reluctant aunt. People who came from close, warm, families like Thomas' never realized the aching emptiness that people who didn't have that experience carried with them. She'd found family with the Druids, and she didn't intend to give it up. To keep it, she'd go along with whatever Jack wanted.

Jack stood and extended a hand to her. "What I want," he began, as if poking his finger into her thoughts, "is to start off slowly with the sacrifices. We'll start with a bird, say we found it injured, go on to a rabbit, then maybe a deer..."

Jett turned an incredulous look on Jack. "How are you going to catch a deer?"

"Crossbow." Jack smiled. "I can do that. I have done that."

Gaia stared at him adoringly. This was no sensitive wimp. What had she ever seen in Thomas, anyway? This guy wasn't afraid to experience life to the max, and that's what she wanted, too. There was something reckless within her, urging her on, pushing her, daring her to let her emotions take her as far as she could go. She wanted to feel as deeply as it was possible to feel. If it was love, she wanted the ultimate in that. If it was hatred, she'd take that to its climax as well.

"What's after the deer?" Jett twisted the neck of the trash bag shut, and faced Jack.

"I'm not sure you're ready for that. In good time, I'll tell you." He leveled his dark eyes on both of them. "I will promise you, though, you will both participate fully, and it will be the highlight of your lives." Jack gestured to them to follow, and led the way out of the woods.

Gaia felt a thrill run from her head to her toes, and neither she nor Jett pushed for an answer. Gaia took his hand as they sloshed through the snow back to where Jack's car waited. She thought she knew what the sacrifice would be after the deer. That would be the ultimate thrill, the mountain-top experience that would mark her life as different from everyone else's as long as she lived.

Vala, the chosen one. She was sure Jack hadn't picked that name for Chloe for no reason.

~ * ~

The Thorn parents and Mike opted to retire early, after their heavy dinner, the football game on TV, and a most satisfying and congenial day for all. Thomas, looking forward to hitting his own bed and waiting for Chloe to tiptoe down the hall and join him, stood up and extended a hand to her. "My grandmother's still up. Let's go have a nightcap, the inevitable margarita, with Ivy."

Chloe laughed. "After a feast like your mom put on, I could use a cup of hot cocoa."

They headed toward the kitchen, where they were met with the aroma of chocolate, which washed over them like a wave.

Chloe let out a squeal of delight. "Oh, Ivy, how did you know?"

Ivy sounded a little testy when she answered, but her eyes twinkled. "I wasn't born at seventy, you know, Missy. There were times in my life when I didn't drink just margaritas."

Amid the laughter, they seated themselves at the kitchen table and Ivy poured the cocoa from an antique hot chocolate pot.

Ivy flicked a glance at them. "I laced it with something good."

"You must have read my mind." Chloe sipped from her mug.

"Don't even joke about mind-reading," Thomas said, winking at her. "Ivy knows more than she can possibly know about everyone—we always accuse her of being able to read our minds."

Chloe shivered. "I sometimes think Dyfan can do that, too."

Ivy's eyebrows shot up. "Who in the world is named 'Dyfan'?"

"Oh, he's the self-appointed leader of a group of kids on campus who decided to form a weird club patterned after the ancient Druids." Thomas didn't want to get into that over such a pleasant visit home. "You don't want to hear about that, Ivy."

"Indeed I do." Ivy set her cup down with a firm thump. "What's the group all about? Already I don't like the sound of it."

For the first time, Thomas felt annoyed with Chloe. Why did she have to bring that up? He had a definite feeling Ivy was not going to approve, and she wouldn't be shy venting her thoughts about it either.

Chloe seemed oblivious to Thomas' reservations. She launched into a description of the group, its self-anointed high priest, Dyfan, its Druid principles as well as she understood them, and the ceremonies around the altar stone. When she began to tell about the bonding ceremony, Thomas interrupted her.

"Chloe. One of the tenets of the group is secrecy, remember?"

Ivy threw him a knowing smile. "Which you don't really give a hoot about, but you don't want me getting into this, right?"

Chloe looked at him in surprise. "I thought you didn't take the whole thing seriously at all anyway. So what's the harm in telling Ivy?"

Ivy ignored Thomas' protests. "Tell me about the bonding ceremony, Chloe."

Thomas sat in silence, knowing what Ivy's response to all this was going to be.

"And this stone circle is modeled after the real Stonehenge in England?" she asked when Chloe paused.

Chloe nodded.

Thomas watched as Ivy drained her cup of cocoa, which had cooled while she listened to Chloe. Her face took on a serious look. He winced. Oh, oh, here it comes!

"Our local pile of rocks at Mystery Hill is called 'America's Stonehenge.' Did you know that?"

"Well, yes, Thomas told me that."

"Terrible things have happened there. Evil things."

Thomas broke in. "Oh, come on, Ivy. You make it sound like the site itself is evil. There were people who did terrible things, but nothing's happened in modern times. Centuries ago, yes, but these more recent things are just stories, nothing more."

She threw him a warning look. "Those stories are chronicled in books, Thomas, written by reputable people from sources who experienced them."

"So are stories about UFO sightings," he tossed back at her. "But I don't personally know anyone who has ever seen one, have you? Or anyone who claims to have been abducted?" His feelings of annoyance increased. Why did Ivy have to spoil this perfect day, which he had hoped with all his heart would end in a perfect night, with Chloe beside him? He stood and stretched. "Chloe, I think we should say goodnight."

She didn't get up.

Ivy continued. "Those formations, although built by humans, grow a power of their own. It may be possible for the rocks to actually absorb some of the vibrations of the people who lived there over time. Add a strong personality with evil intentions..."

Thomas couldn't conceal his impatience. "Ivy, this is nuts." He shifted from foot to foot, anxious to leave.

Chloe ignored him. She stared at Ivy. "How can that be?"

"Over the centuries, the energy increases, giving off vibrations that some people can actually feel. *I've* felt it."

In spite of the warmth of Ivy's kitchen, Thomas felt a sudden chill sweep over him. Something prickled in his mind, a half-memory, but something he didn't want to remember. His words came out harsher than he intended. "And some people think that's a load of crap."

Ivy's voice rose as she leaned toward him. "Thomas, you're in denial. Those places can be—and often are—breeding grounds for evil spirits. What I am trying to say, and not very well, I guess, is that a person with evil intentions will feel his power increased in sites like that." She turned back to Chloe. "That's why I asked you what you felt when you were there. It's nothing to fool around with."

"Even our little homemade version?"

"Don't you think there is some ulterior motive in Dyfan's doing that? The more those places pretend to be sacred, the more evil creeps in."

Thomas reached for Chloe's hand again. "I don't want to hear any more about this. Let's go upstairs now."

She pulled her hand away. "No, you go, if you want to. I want to hear what Ivy has to say."

"She can always stay over in my guest bedroom," Ivy said. "We might talk into the wee hours, if she's interested."

Thomas gave a reluctant sigh. "Suit yourself." The house was chilly, winter in New England. You had to expect that in these old farmhouses, but he had hoped to have a warm body beside him to ward off the chill.

He sighed. He didn't think that would be the case tonight. Chloe's guest bedroom across the hall would probably remain empty.

~ * ~

Thomas peered into the camera, looking at the picture Chloe seemed so excited about.

"Look at this! It's just what Mr. Walsh wanted. We have to go to CVS and get this printed off. I brought a canvas and paints, and can't wait to get started."

After the heavy meal and frivolity of the previous day, all Thomas wanted was a quiet day, watching sports on TV and no annoyance from Mike, who had gone sledding with his buddies, Glenn and Brendan.

Thomas wandered around the store while Chloe printed out the pictures she wanted. He stopped to look at the magazines and paperback books, thinking he might pick up a James Patterson or Dean Koontz to read. It would be a refreshing change from the textbooks.

"Oh, excuse me." He turned to apologize to the person he had accidentally bumped into. She looked familiar, a fortyish woman with blond hair, trailed by three young children.

She smiled at him. "It's okay. There's room for both of us."

"You're—you're Donna from IHOP in Middleton, right?"

She raised her eyebrows in surprise, but nodded. "Oh, yeah, I remember your group. You came in really late one night. Is this your home town?"

He nodded. "Yours, too?" He noticed that she was really quite a pretty woman without the lines of exhaustion dragging down her face. Chunky, but pretty. Her three little ones, bundled up in snowsuits with fur-lined hoods around their rosy faces, stood in a row and stared up at him, like a group of little Eskimos.

"No, actually, we're from Concord, nearer Middleton. But my husband died last year, and my sister invited us here for

Thanksgiving. My kids love getting together with their cousins, and it helps to be with family."

"Sure does," he said, and meant it. Out of the corner of his eye he noticed Chloe beckoning to him. He tossed Donna a grin. "Nice to see you again. Gotta go."

"Who was that?" Chloe asked, but it was a rhetorical question. She couldn't wait to show him her pictures. "Look at this, Thomas. Everything Mr. Walsh wanted. It's going to make an awesome painting."

He took the print from her and examined it. "Yep. Values and negative spaces, too. It has it all."

She laughed at him. "You're so easy to be with, Thomas. I've never had a relationship like this. I like it."

"Neither have I, and I like it, too." The little déjà vu voice whispered in his ear that once before, long ago, he did have a relationship just like this one. Thomas shook his head. Something lurked at the edge of his mind, but he couldn't remember just what it was.

Chloe couldn't wait to begin her painting. In late morning, Thomas settled down with his parents in their cozy den to watch a football game, while Chloe set up her small, portable easel on the kitchen table and got out her canvas and paints. Ivy, who had spent the night in Charlie, Jr.'s vacant room, as she sometimes did, came down still wearing her leopard print pajamas with a matching light, silky robe. She took a seat at the table with Chloe, drinking her black coffee.

Chloe quirked an eyebrow at Ivy. "Too early for margaritas?"

Ivy nodded. "Do you mind if I watch you paint?"

Chloe shook her head. "Why don't you tell me more about Mystery Hill?"

"You tell me," Ivy countered. "What did you feel when you were there?"

Chloe collected her thoughts as she squeezed dabs of acrylic color onto the paper plate she used as a palette. "It was eerie, mysterious. It was obviously built by someone, and for some definite purpose."

She felt Ivy's eyes on her. "Did it feel as though you'd been there before?"

"You know I didn't see it last time. We were in the gift shop when Thomas got the call about your fall, and we came right here."

Ivy sipped her coffee. "I don't mean then. I mean before then."

Confused, Chloe raised her eyes. "I've lived all my life in Florida. I'd never been in New England before I came to college here. When could I have been here…before?"

Ivy mouthed a secret little smile, but didn't answer.

"Oh." Chloe spread white paint on a large brush and began to coat the canvas. "Thomas told me you believe in reincarnation. Is that what you mean?"

"If it felt familiar to you, you might well have been there in a previous life."

Chloe laughed. "Oh, Ivy, I'm not sure I believe any of that. It seems to me that one life is enough. Why would we ever want to come back?"

As was her way, Ivy answered her with another question. "Would you think you had all the education if you stopped learning after second or third grade? Would you have learned everything you needed to know and experience to become a complete person?"

Chloe paused with her brush in the air. "Of course not. Why in the world would you ask that?"

"One life is like kindergarten, or first grade, or second grade, depending on where you are in your soul experience. People like Ghandi and Mother Theresa have graduated from college. They don't come back unless they want to. Unless there's a need for a spiritually advanced soul to return and show us the way—again."

"So, you think if I felt something at Mystery Hill, it's because I was there before, in another life?" She giggled. "Maybe I was an Indian maiden, eons ago. The Algonquin tribes were here, weren't they?"

"The Pennacook, or Pautuckets, were in this part of New Hampshire," Ivy said. She paused before continuing. "You are an old soul, Chloe, but you have been sleeping for eons."

"Like Sleeping Beauty?" Chloe asked lightly, self-consciously making a reference to her Disney World costume. She wanted to laugh, but Ivy seemed so serious. "And Thomas is the prince who came to wake me up?"

Ivy stood and put her empty coffee cup on the counter. "Thomas is an old soul, too, and you are both back to advance to the next grade." She waited a few seconds, gazing at Chloe. "In other words, old hurts need to be soothed, old scores settled, new lessons learned."

Chloe looked up from her painting. "Old hurts? Old scores...?"

"Think about it, Chloe. You lived all your life in a warm, sunny laid-back atmosphere. Why did you ever decide to attend a little-known junior college at the other end of the country, in New Hampshire, of all places?"

Chloe opened her mouth to answer, but Ivy was gone in a swish of leopard-printed silk.

Thirteen

"I thought you didn't want to go there anymore." Thomas brushed the snowflakes from Chloe's cheek as she looked up at him. "Remember—you said you felt the 'evil' there, and after what Ivy said…"

Her bright eyes sparkled. "Oh, that was probably my imagination running away with me. And Ivy, well—your grandmother has a lot of fixed ideas about things."

"I think Gaia's been at you again." Thomas gazed down at her with concern. He would go if Chloe honestly wanted to go, but he didn't want her brainwashed by her so-called best friend. He didn't trust Gaia—not one bit.

Chloe pulled the collar of her parka up around her neck. "She just told me that it's the Winter Solstice, and a total eclipse of the moon to boot. That only happens once in several centuries. She said we should go and celebrate it, and for once I agree with her."

"We can do that right here," Thomas pointed out. He gestured around the campus. "Everybody will be out here partying—lots of beer. Better than one of Dyfan's lectures."

"I think we should be with the Druids. It'll be more meaningful."

"It's going to be cold out there in the middle of the woods. It's supposed to snow all night long. A couple of feet by morning."

She laughed up at him. "Oh, so now the New Hampshire boy is afraid of snow? I'll bundle up, and we'll have those robes over our jackets. We won't be cold."

He melted, looking at her and thinking how much he loved her. If she were going with him or without him, he'd go with her. He relented. "Okay. But we'll drive *my* car. I don't want to go with Jett and Gaia."

"All right. By the way, did you get the assignment Dyfan gave us, to bring something to sacrifice? It has to be personally meaningful."

"Oh, yeah, Jett told me."

They paused in the courtyard of the art complex where Chloe 's next class was held. He leaned down and planted a kiss on the bridge of her nose. "I hope Professor Walsh likes your Mystery Hill photos. I thought they were awesome."

"Thanks. I'll see you later." She threw him a smile and a wave and disappeared into the building.

~ * ~

"These are just wonderful, Chloe." Professor Jim Walsh shuffled the pictures in his hand, and looked closely at each several times. "Mind if I share them with the rest of the class?"

She shook her head, embarrassed, but pleased at the same time.

Chloe busied herself setting up her easel and putting dabs of paint on her palette. She would use black and white, of course, and a lot of gray, which she would tint with blue, green, brown, pink and lavender. There were hints of rust and an odd gray-green in the photos as well, so she mixed shades of paint for those.

Walsh cleared his throat, and the chatter ceased as the students halted in their preparations and turned toward him.

He held up the photographs. "I'd like to pass these around, and have everyone take a look at them. Chloe took these out at Mystery Hill, near Salem, and they are everything I asked for in your assignment."

"Oh!" A boy with red hair and an acne-covered face spoke up. His voice squeaked like that of an adolescent. "So you didn't like my pictures of trees in the snow I showed you?"

"I liked them, Jeb, but I didn't love them. Do you remember what the assignment was?"

Jeb's right hand clutched his easel as he replied. "Yeah, sure. Shapes, forms, colors that make a composition without looking like anything in particular..."

Walsh nodded. "And your pictures looked like trees in the snow. How much better they would have been if you had waited until evening, and taken shots of the shadows of the trees on the snow."

Jeb glared at the professor and didn't answer."

"You could still do that." Walsh handed Chloe's pictures to the student nearest to him. "Don't start painting today, Jeb. Take some more pictures tonight, as the sun goes down and get the shadows. Shapes, not objects."

"I have something else to do tonight," Jeb muttered, turning away to stare out the window.

A tall girl with a long, pale braid falling down her back raised her hand. Her name was Ingrid, and she looked Nordic to fit it. "How about my photos of all those birds sitting on the telephone wire? Are they okay?"

Walsh's voice took on a note of impatience. He held up his hand. "Look, I will come around and consult with you all individually. If I don't feel your pictures will work for this assignment, you can take the rest of the class off and go take some more."

Chloe struggled with her easel, tightening the screws so her canvas sat at just the right height for her to work comfortably. That done, she took a wide brush and began to apply a base coat over the canvas. It didn't take long, but she could not proceed until the surface dried, and besides, her pictures had not made the rounds of the classroom yet.

As she worked, several students put their materials away after the conferences with the teacher and left the classroom, ostensibly to take more acceptable pictures. She might as well take a break, and get a Coke from the soda machine down on the hall, outside the door of the gallery.

The tall blond girl was ahead of her at the drink machine.

Ingrid fished her soda from the clutches of the dispenser, and turned as Chloe approached. She tossed back her pale frosty braid, and smiled. "Hi. I thought your pictures were amazing." She moved aside, and Chloe fed her change into the machine.

"Thanks. I'm anxious to get started."

Ingrid turned slightly, looking up and down the hall before she spoke again. "Are you going to the meeting tonight?"

Chloe pretended not to understand. "Meeting? What meeting? Is there something happening on campus?"

Ingrid laughed. "The meeting in the woods that we both go to, *Vala*. I've seen you there. It's an important night. Will you be there?"

"Oh." Chloe gave Ingrid a sideways glance as they walked back down the hall toward the classroom. "I'm sorry. I never recognized you. Here we've been in the same class all semester, and I never knew that. Yes, I'm going."

Ingrid paused at the door. "Jeb's part of the circle, too. Did you recognize him?"

Shocked, Chloe shook her head. "You know, in that dim light and those hoods that almost cover the faces, I didn't recognize either of you."

"I'm Seyine. He's Drakthul. Watch for him tonight when Dyfan calls attendance."

Chloe caught Ingrid's arm and pulled her back from the door into the hallway again. "By the way, have you ever seen Dyfan around the campus? Do you know who he really is?"

"No." The other girl shrugged. "I've wondered, too, and I keep looking, but I never see him."

Chloe shook her head, puzzled. "I've looked for him in the dining room, around campus when I walk to classes, even at the Elk Horn. I've never seen him anywhere, except at the meetings. And even then, I can't ever seem to get a good look at him."

"I know," Ingrid agreed. "It's always dark, and those hoods..." She opened the classroom door, and Chloe followed her in.

Chloe was gratified to find her base coat dry and the canvas ready for painting. She looked around for her photos sure the last student to look at them would have put them back on the small table near her easel. They weren't there. After a few moments of searching, she called out, "Hey! Does anyone still have my pictures?"

Several students turned toward her and shook their heads. Professor Walsh raised his voice and asked the same question. "Who has Chloe's photographs?"

Everyone looked up and around at each other, shaking their heads and shrugging their shoulders.

Walsh looked concerned. "Who was the last person to see them?"

A short, small-boned Asian-looking boy raised his hand. "I put them back on her table," he said. "Right beside her paint box."

Walsh shifted his gaze to Chloe. "And you didn't find them there?"

"I went out for a Coke." She raised the can in her hand. "They weren't there when I came back."

Walsh's face took on a serious expression. "Class, if this is a joke, it's not funny. If anyone has Chloe's pictures, I want them returned to her right now."

The only answer was silence.

Walsh hooked his thumbs into his jeans pockets. "Look, this is not junior high. I take a very dim view of this kind of thing."

"Never mind. I can get reprints made," Chloe said in a low voice behind his back. She wrapped her palette in foil, clapped her paint box shut, grabbed her canvas and fled the classroom.

~ * ~

Dyfan waited for his congregation, looking almost like a ghost in his white robe, the snow falling all around him. Chloe noticed the black metal vessel on the altar stone. She guessed it was the top of an old grill. Glowing coals burned in it, a thin wisp of smoke sending an eerie signal skyward. Wondering why the snow was not falling into the coals and extinguishing the fire, Chloe looked up. She was amazed to see that a natural canopy of pine branches appeared to have laced themselves together far above the altar, and no snow fell through them

She struggled into her robe, glad she had worn a warm jacket and leggings under her jeans. The weather had turned colder, as Thomas had predicted, but she was sure the robe would keep her warm. Trying not to be obvious, she looked around for Jeb and Ingrid. She couldn't isolate Jeb from the others, but she caught a glimpse of Ingrid, who sent her a little wave. Chloe returned the gesture, and realized that with Ingrid's tall, muscular build, she might well have assumed she was a boy.

When they were all robed and standing in silence in front of their chosen stones, Dyfan, as usual, called their names, and all replied, some in clear voices, others hardly able to be heard. Chloe listened for Drakthul's name to be called, and took note of the Druid who replied, recognizing Jeb's squeaky voice, now that she knew he was among them.

Their high priest said nothing for another moment, but stood at the head of the circle with his head bowed, as if in silent prayer. He raised his head and looked around, trying to lock eyes with each one in turn. As all the Druids watched, he walked with a slow, deliberate gait to the altar stone, coming to a stop in front of Gaia, to Chloe's left.

"Nature has provided us with an acceptable sacrifice," he intoned. He reached into the folds of his robe, and with both hands, held up a small brown bird. It fluttered its wings against his hands, and made a sharp, terrified sound. One leg dangled limply from its body, while the other scraped at the air.

"It is injured," Dyfan said. "It would not live long in this cold and snow. It is better off this way."

Chloe stifled a gasp as Dyfan gave the bird's neck a deft twist, and the offering died in his grasp. He placed it in the center of the embers with a show of reverence, then stepped back. "As I have offered a sacrifice from nature, so will each of you now in turn place your offerings in the fire."

Chloe shivered in the depths of her robe, but she had to agree with Dyfan about the bird's fate. It would have frozen to death before the night was over anyway. Better a quick, meaningful death than a slow, frigid one. She watched, fascinated, as Jett stepped forward and laid what looked like a metal sports trophy next to the bird, whose feathers had caught fire and begun to burn. They gave off a sickening odor, damp and sour. Jett stepped back and Gaia took his place. Chloe caught her breath, and heard a couple of murmurs from others as Gaia held up a crucifix. It gleamed golden in the firelight, as she dangled it by a long chain, then dropped it on top of the bird.

Chloe took her place, and wondered in a moment of panic if her offering was good enough. Clearly, a sports trophy and a crucifix were important symbols, and all she had brought was a letter to her mother which she had never sent. She had written it before Thanksgiving, when she found out her mother would not even be home, and did not seem to care where Chloe went for the holiday, or didn't go anywhere at all. In it she vented her feelings, being honest about the closeness she had always wanted with her mother, and how she'd always felt left out. She would be coming home for Christmas, she had written, and she really hoped things could be better between them.

She never mailed it. Now, she was giving up this hope. She raised the envelope into the air, as Gaia had done with the cross, then dropped it into the fire. It caught right away, and Chloe with both misgivings and relief, watched it burn. Her relationship with her mother would be whatever it was.

Thomas took one long step toward the altar, and with no show of ceremony at all, dropped two large Snickers bars into the fire. Chloe choked back a laugh. They were his favorite candy bars, but did he consider this an acceptable sacrifice? Were they that personally meaningful to him? He poked her arm with his elbow as he stepped back into place, and ignored the hard glare Dyfan turned on him.

The rest of the Druids took their turn bringing their offerings to the altar. Chloe's stomach began to churn as the smell of the roasting bird mixed with the aroma of scorched chocolate. She leaned up against Thomas, who put his arm around her. A few minutes later, all but one robed form had approached the stone. Drakthul. Chloe, feeling relieved that the ceremony was almost over, watched as the last participant raised his hand above the fire and let a handful of paper fragments fluttered downward. They caught fire instantly as they touched the coals, but not before Chloe recognized bits and pieces of her Mystery Hill photographs.

Fourteen

Dyfan retreated to his post and stood in front of the largest tree in the circle, a massive oak, lonely without its leaves. He bent and retrieved a black bag from behind the tree. The Druids watched, the silence of the night broken only by the whining of the wind.

Reaching into the bag, Dyfan drew out a ball of yellow cord. Thomas watched, his amusement giving way to a nervous apprehension. What did Dyfan intend to do—tie them all up, bind them all to each other in some sort of 'togetherness' ceremony? Whatever it was, he already didn't like it.

Dyfan passed the yellow ball to the Druid on his left, and gestured that he should pass it on. Balls of twine, each a different color, made their way around the circle, until the yellow ball came back to Dyfan. Thomas' string was copper-colored, almost a perfect match for his hair, and Chloe's was blue, which he knew was her favorite color. His mind blinked in confusion. This could not just be coincidence...or could it?

Dyfan circled around the large oak with his ball of cord, and tied the loose end to the rest of the skein, making a yellow line around the tree. In a few seconds, Thomas could barely make it out, as the swirling snow settled on the lightweight rope, masking its already pale color.

"Each of you will do the same," Dyfan said. "Tie your cable around the trunk of the tree directly behind your stone. Be sure you knot it tightly."

The Druid holding a lime green ball of twine spoke up. "What're we doing with this?" The squeaky voice held a tinge of fear.

Dyfan continued as if he hadn't been interrupted. "This is a test of faith and trust in your fellow Druids. Walk straight into the woods—you will all be fanning out in a great circle, which is symbolic of our being anchored together even when we are apart.

"Walk for ten minutes, then stop, look around you and contemplate the awe and mystery of nature."

"How do we know when..." The same squeaky voice. Thomas shifted from one foot to another. If he hadn't liked this activity in the beginning, he liked it even less now. No way was he letting Chloe walk even one minute into the dark woods alone.

"I have a whistle. It sounds like a wolf howl. When you hear that, it will be the ten-minute mark. Stop and contemplate. I will blow it again in two minutes. Follow the yarn trail you have made and come back home to the circle."

Thomas balked. "Look, Dyfan, I don't like this..."

All the hooded faces swiveled toward him. Dyfan's dark eyes pierced his across the clearing. Something shifted inside. He felt Dyfan's presence, and sensed the power of his mind. He tried to outstare Dyfan, but the high priest's gaze never wavered—and there was something else, something intangible but forceful that reached Thomas across the clearing. His resistance ebbed.

"Don't go around any trees. Keep on a straight path so your cord doesn't get tangled. There is nothing to fear. These woods are safe." Dyfan raised his arms like a priest invoking a blessing. "When you all return, we will drink to the sanctity of nature—the Great Mother of us all—and view the eclipse of the moon. Go now."

Thomas turned and tied his copper-colored twine around the tree behind him. He felt like a whipped dog, but he could not summon the strength of will to fight back. What was this power Dyfan had over them? As he wrapped the cord around the tree, he vowed to find out how to fight the high priest's strength of will. Or better yet, he and Chloe would never return to the circle. His cold fingers fumbled with the cable still wrapped around the ball; it seemed to be snagged somewhere, and he could not get it to unroll. Finally, he jerked it loose, and looked around for Chloe. She had vanished, and all the others in the circle were gone as well. Only Dyfan stood there, a white statue in the night, staring at him. With an effort, Thomas tore his eyes away, turned and stumbled into the woods.

~ * ~

Ivy jerked awake as if she had been slapped. She'd intended to wait up to see the eclipse of the moon but had fallen asleep in the comfortable padded arm chair in front of the electric fireplace, where she often sat and read in the evening. Something was wrong—she could feel it all through her body.

Her first thoughts were for her daughter, Sharon, and Charlie Sr. and Mike. But the sensory messengers didn't respond as she fixed her mind on them. She got up, groaning a little. Oh, these achy muscles. I feel so young at heart that I forget my body is old. So much older than I really am. As they say, getting old is not for the timid.

She walked the short distance to a window and gazed out at the Thorn home across the covered pool. She could barely make it out through the snow, which had begun to fall in the early evening. No—she was sure nothing was wrong there. What then? Charlie Jr. over there in Iraq? Her breath caught in trepidation. Had something happened to Charlie? Again, there was the sense that everything was all right there. What then? A sudden picture of Thomas and Chloe rose in her mind. She saw them as clearly as if they stood outside her window.

She concentrated. Thomas or Chloe—or both? She realized then, that she saw each of them separately. There was a division between them—like two different snapshots. They both wore robes, Thomas in a brown one, Chloe in blue. The sliver of a red moon shone behind them. Thomas looked almost drugged—perplexed and uncertain as his eyes shifted from one point to another. Chloe's eyes, however, looked out at her directly, through time, through space. As Ivy watched, Chloe's body sagged, as if with fatigue, and her eyes closed. Ivy watched her slump to the ground and lie still, as the snow began to cover her body.

The vision faded. Ivy stared at the puddle of red moon, the same one she had seen in her mind. She staggered back to her chair and fell into it, her hands over her eyes. It all came together in a rush of knowledge—the eclipse, the Winter Solstice, the Druid group Thomas and Chloe had joined. The evil force she had warned them about had risen and shown its fangs. She knew how to meditate, and she had reached the minds of others using this method several times in the past. The difference was, they hadn't known it. This time she had to make Thomas conscious of what she knew. She took several deep breaths and forced herself to relax. Starting with her toes, she concentrated on each part of her body, making it go limp, moving upwards until she had covered it all. When she reached the right physical state, she felt bodiless, as if she were floating on air. She closed her eyes and thought of nothing but Thomas, picturing his face, trying to hear the sound of his voice. Unless she succeeded in making contact with him, she knew that Chloe would die.

~ * ~

Thomas staggered on through the snow, avoiding going around trees in order to stay in a more or less straight line. He unwound his red-brown cord as he walked. For perhaps fifty feet or so, he had walked parallel with Chloe's blue line, but she had started out before him, and it wasn't long before he'd lost track of her, and the blue cable veered off to the left. He couldn't continue alongside it, as a line of small blue spruce prevented him from going in that direction. He plodded on until he became foggily aware that five minutes must have passed. He stopped and turned back in the direction he had come, waiting for the sound of Dyfan's wolf whistle. He listened for a moment, then said out loud, "Maybe I just didn't hear it and went too far. I'm probably beyond the sound of it now. I should turn back."

The sound of his own voice vibrating against the stillness of the woods helped his mind to clear. He took a few steps, re-rolling the rope onto the ball, and headed back toward the circle. He could barely see through the snow. His yarn snagged on the branches of a bush and he gave it a tug—he knew at once by the sudden relaxed feel of the string that it had broken. He untangled it from the bush and reeled it in. With a sinking feeling, he looked at the line and knew it hadn't broken on the bush. The end was not frayed; it was clean-cut, as if snipped with scissors.

Disconcerted, he continued walking, but he was no longer sure of the direction. His mind reeled; who disliked him enough to cut his cord so he might not find his way back? Gaia? Dyfan himself?

And what about Chloe? Had someone cut her rope, too? Panic rose in him. He had been a fool ever to agree to this—walking off into the forest tethered by a mere string to a tree half a mile away! The snow was blinding, and even in long, coarse robe, the cold seeped in, stiffening his arms and legs. What if she were lost, her string cut; she would never be able to find her way back.

A movement, a color, caught his eye. He shaded his eyes and tried to see what it might be. A figure stood between a couple of trees, but as he started toward it, it moved away from him. He stopped; it stopped. It walked stiffly, like Ivy, but that certainly couldn't be. He called out, "Who is it?"

There was no answer, but the shimmering figure seemed to be waiting for him. When he struggled toward it again, it moved away, slowly, so that Thomas could keep pace. When he stopped, it stopped. He remembered the account of the hunter who'd seen the silvery mist leading a procession up the hill. The message was clear; he was supposed to follow.

As his mind cleared, the snow swirled around him, but he began to think more clearly. An image of Chloe filled his mind. He saw her sprawled in the snow, her hood thrown back so her honey-colored hair fanned out on the white carpet that was fast covering her.

"Thomas! This way." It *was* Ivy's voice; he'd know it anywhere, but how could it be? The snow had become so heavy that the shimmering figure was lost to him, yet the voice that sounded like his grandmother's came from the same direction. He plowed on, more exhausted with each step.

Time passed and he forced himself to follow the voice which called to him each time he thought himself too tired to go on. Although the trees in the forest were evenly spaced, for the most part, with a lot of space between, there were sections that grew more densely, as if separating one part of the woods from another. He came to a small copse of trees, and began to push his way through it. The wind blew the snow away from him and he spied a figure through the intertwined branches.

"Chloe!" His voice was hoarse, and not as loud as he tried to make it.

The figure halted and turned toward him. His heart sank as he made his way through the brush. It wore a robe, but not Chloe's blue one, and the figure was too tall to be her.

He staggered toward the figure, and it held out its mittened hand to him.

"Ingrid," she said, and he recognized the Druid Dyfan called Ceyine. "Someone cut my cord. I'm lost."

That bastard. *Chloe might be dead here in these frigid woods, and if she is, I will kill him. Just like I killed that snake, Askook...*He gasped and shook his head. Where had that come from?

"I have to find Chloe. Come on, I think she has to be over this way. Come on."

"I've just come from that direction. I didn't see her."

Ivy's voice called to him again, and there was that faint shimmer of—something among the trees farther on.

He pulled at Ingrid's arm. "Come on. She's this way, I know it."

They nearly missed her body curled up between two logs, almost covered with snow. If the wind hadn't shifted at the very moment they were passing her, they never would have seen her. If that strange shimmer hadn't been right there, hovering over her for just the blink of an eye—but fate, karma, or whatever it was all worked together and the timing was just right.

She seemed to be asleep, or unconscious, and didn't respond to their voices or their cold hands rubbing her colder face and arms. Thomas and Ingrid picked her up, shifting her weight between them.

Ingrid looked around her in confusion." Which way is back?"

Thomas saw a few inches of Chloe's blue cord in the snow. "This way. We'll follow it back." He picked up the end of it and tugged. It came easily, and he understood that her tether, too, had been cut.

But—it did lead back to the circle. He gestured to Ingrid. "Come on. We'll follow it back anyway."

After what seemed an eternity, snow blowing in their faces, the temperature dropping minute by minute, the splash of red moon seeming to dart between the branches of the trees as they fought their way back, they came into the open space of the circle.

Dyfan stood in his usual place. All the Druids had returned, and stood pale as sheets, cold and silent, shivering in the circle.

"Welcome back, Ceyine, Vala, Lochlan."

Thomas didn't favor him with a glance. He and Ingrid carried Chloe around the circle, and toward where they had left the car.

"Lochlan. Take your place back in the circle."

Thomas didn't answer.

"Ceyine, take your place in the circle."

Ingrid stopped short, almost causing Thomas to drop Chloe. As if in a trance, she turned and looked back at Dyfan.

"Ingrid—come on." Thomas tugged at her parka. "Let's just get out of here."

He watched in disbelief as a different expression came over Ingrid's face. She carefully disengaged herself from him and Chloe and walked back toward the Druids as if in a trance.

"Ingrid!" She didn't look back.

Thomas shifted Chloe's limp body in his arms. Exhausted as he was, he could carry her to safety, and he would. He had made up his mind. He was through with all of it, with Dyfan and the Druids, with Gaia and Jett, and if he had anything at all to say about it, Chloe would never set foot in the Midstate Stonehenge circle...ever again either.

Fifteen

"Chloe really wanted to go home for Christmas." Thomas gazed into the electric flames of Ivy's fireplace, and wished they were real. "She wanted to talk with her mother about their relationship."

"And I just bet she needed a break from Midstate and everything that happened a couple weeks ago. It's a wonder she didn't catch pneumonia."

Thomas' mouth tightened. "I could kill that bastard, Dyfan, and not feel an ounce of remorse."

Ivy threw him a small, wry smile. "Well, best you didn't, but I hope you and Chloe will stay away from the group from now on."

"We intend to. And away from Jett and Gaia, too. I've moved out of the dorm and rented a small apartment for us. But..." He leaned toward her, his chin in his hand. "I just can't figure out what power he has over the Druids, and how he controls them."

She sighed, and he thought how much Ivy had aged since she had broken her arm in the fall. She'd recovered quickly, but that edge she'd always had, that spark that set her apart from most other people her age, had dimmed a bit. She picked up her margarita, just an ordinary strawberry one this time, and her hand shook a bit as she raised it to her mouth.

"I told you these things develop their own evil power. Like Mystery Hill here. Too many stories of odd happenings there to discount them all—screams in the night, strange visions, ghosts..." She shook her head. "The most rational investigators can't come up with any explanations that make sense. You have to come to the conclusion that something called 'evil' exists on its own, and it often makes its home in places like that."

"Hmmm. Evil exists on its own. Do you really believe that, Ivy?"

"I do. How else do you explain Hitler, or Charlie Manson—or some of the things that are going on these days, the terrorists, and so forth."

"And because terrible things happened at Mystery Hill over the centuries, evil will always be there?"

Ivy rubbed a hand across her eyes, then shook her head. "No. Rocks are rocks. But I believe that the spirit of what happened there lingers on...but it could be erased by the spirit of someone with enough strength of good will..."

She was obviously tired. Thomas didn't reply for a moment. He supposed if he'd asked his parents the same question, they would have shrugged, shaken their heads, said no one could answer questions like that, and would he like to order a movie to watch on TV tonight? It's not that either Sharon or Charlie was a shallow person, but they were content with their lives as they were, and preferred not to have them disturbed by disruptive ideas. Ivy seemed to have a deeper interest in why things happened and the forces that moved them.

"I think I might go up there, to Mystery Hill, tomorrow and look it over again."

Ivy glanced up at him, surprised. "Why do you want to do that? You've been there plenty of times."

"I remember a field trip in high school, when some noted archeologist who was doing some work on the site, showed us around and explained to us various theories on who built what and why."

A flicker of amusement crossed Ivy's face. "You remember that? What year was it, do you think?"

All of a sudden, he wasn't sure. "Uh, junior or senior year, I guess. But it was fascinating, and I'd like to look at it from that point of view again. I'll take Mike along."

"Who was the teacher of that class?"

He searched his memory. "Uh, Mr. Jackson, I think, but maybe it was that guy who only taught at the school for one year—I can't remember his name."

Ivy decided not to push it further. She had given him just enough to tease him, if he thought about it again.

"Just be careful." She stood up and moved to hug him. He felt her thin body against his, and he hugged her tightly, grateful that whatever life force arranged things had included Ivy in his life.

He stepped back and locked eyes with her. "I felt you out in the snow, when I was lost and looking for Chloe. I heard your voice. You helped me find her."

She nodded. "The mind is an amazing force, Thomas. There's no end to what it can do, if people would just learn to use it."

She watched as he put his head down and headed across the frozen lawn toward the house. She sighed. "I'd better write this down in my journal. The older I get in this life, the more it slips away from me. But—every day, I remember more of what once was, all the way back to when I was Tihana and—I'm starting to believe Chloe was Kanti."

Again something pricked at the edges of her mind. Could it really be…?

Ivy picked up her pen and the worn leather journal, and sat in her easy chair. Her pen dropped into her lap as she leaned back in her chair, closed her eyes and allowed her mind to drift.

~ * ~

The beautiful young girl had tears in her eyes. Her hands clutched her stomach as she stammered out her news. "Grandmother, I am with child."

"Does the chief know?"

"Yes. He is angry. His son thought we could join if he knew, but he has refused his blessing on us. He will not speak to me. He turns a hard face to Achak."

"Then I can do nothing, my child. If you had come to see me first…"

"You must help me! Hide me, show me where to go! They will offer me up for a sacrifice."

"They will say you have defiled the chief's bloodline."

"We did nothing but love each other. Help me, I beg you."

It was too late. Two muscular warriors appeared at the cabin door. Kanti screamed. Tihana pushed Kanti behind her. "Please don't take her. She is an innocent child."

They pushed her aside as if she were as inconsequential as a branch of a willow tree, and she fell to the ground. The taller one seized Kanti, none-too-gently either, and threw her over his shoulder like a sack of grain. Tihana, struggling to get back on her feet, heard the young girl's screams of terror until they suddenly ceased.

~ * ~

To his surprise, Mike didn't give Thomas a hard time about accompanying him to the Mystery Hill site. He seemed almost grateful to get out of the house.

The road was plowed as far as the small wooden structure which housed the gift shop, where tickets were sold. However, no other cars were parked there, except a black Jeep huddled next to the cabin.

Thomas paid the admission fee and they left by the back door. The woman named Annie was still there, and she gave Thomas a brief nod, as if she recognized him. The trail to the site itself had not been cleared, although other people had trudged up the hill, so there was a footpath broken through the snow.

Mike plowed along ahead of him, kicking at the snow as he walked. He looked back over his shoulder at Thomas. "What do you expect to see here? Everything's covered with snow."

"I don't expect to see much of anything. I just want to get a feeling for the place."

"A feeling? What do you mean?"

"Well, Ivy says that places have personalities, or particular traits, just as people do. I want to see if I can feel anything like that here."

Mike packed a snowball and threw it at a small brown bird huddled on a low branch of a tree. The bird squawked and flew to a higher branch. Mike laughed. "I sure wouldn't believe anything that crazy old lady says."

Thomas grabbed Mike's shoulder and jerked him around to face him. "I don't ever want to hear you talking about your grandmother that way again. Ivy sees and knows more than anyone else I ever knew. She's a very wise woman. You need to respect her, and listen when she tells you something."

"Ow!" Mike shrugged away and backed up a few steps. He bumped up against the stone wall on one side of the path. "Jeez, Thomas, you used to be sort of fun. Now, since you went to college, you're like all the other grown-ups. All they do is pick on me."

"What do you know about having fun? You're just a kid. There are different kinds of fun when you grow up." The path they had followed ended at a small stone structure. In an effort to divert Mike, he asked, "What do you suppose this was used for?"

Mike kicked at the rocks. "Dunno. Why don't you tell me, since you know everything?"

Thomas tried for patience. "Some people think it might have been a guard house, you know, for a sentry to keep watch over the place."

"For what? Attacking buffalos?"

He kept his voice even. "No, for enemy tribes or spies, I'd guess." He pointed at the path which led up a hill. "It might have been the lead-off place for ceremonial walks. This path leads up to a site where they might have had religious ceremonies." He began the trudge up the hill with Mike following.

"Yeah, there's an altar up there." Mike sounded a bit more enthusiastic. "Did they have human sacrifices there?"

"Some scholars think so, because there is a groove cut around the edge of the altar rock, for the blood to run into. Then there's a sort of stone pit built into the ground where all the blood collected."

They arrived at the center of the site. Thomas looked around, appreciating the work the ancient builders had put into the design. Or what was left of it. The following civilizations had taken their toll, removing some stones, adding others. Old trees had died, and others like the gigantic pine they stood beside had taken their place. Others had been cut down for timber. He realized it probably didn't look much like the original site, but it was still all very mysterious.

"Look." Thomas pointed to one of the larger structures. "What do you think that might have been used for?"

Mike seemed bored again. "Dunno."

"Probably for grain storage, if the tribe spent the winter here," Thomas explained.

"Hooray for them." Mike looked around. "I don't feel any 'evil' here. How can a bunch of rocks be 'evil?' This is boring. Why don't you tell me something interesting?"

Thomas stifled a sigh. "Like what?"

"How it feels to screw Chloe, for instance?"

"What did you say?"

Thomas couldn't believe his ears. He stared at Mike as if he had never seen his little brother.

Mike seemed to realize he had gone too far. "I—I didn't mean to say that, Thomas. I was thinkin' it, but I didn't mean to say it." He backed away from his brother and fell over a rock that was covered by snow.

Thomas grabbed the front of Mike's parka and hauled him to his feet. His anger surged like a tide. "You know, you're out of control, kid! I don't ever want to hear..."

With half an ear he heard the branch of the giant pine crack and give way. His quick reflexes cut in, and he swung Mike out of the way, throwing him as far as he could into a snowdrift, as he stumbled backward himself. The heavy branch crashed down, and landed where they had stood, its split from the main tree sounding like a series of gunshots in the wintry silence.

Sixteen

Thomas, finished with his Christmas vacation homework assignment for English, lay back on his bed, his arms behind his head. Instead of writing a traditional essay, he'd dared something different: an imaginary dialogue between the poet Robert Frost and a down-to-earth dairy farmer up in the Green Mountains of Vermont. He had included all the information about Frost's life, plus excerpts from his poetry, so why should Dr. Harris care if he took liberties with the format? Well, he surmised, as he turned his head to stare out the window at the still-falling snow, he'd either get an A+ or an F. That's usually how it went when you ventured off the beaten path. However, remembering what Ivy had told him about his loving Chloe in a previous life, he'd ended his paper with a variation of his own on the famous lines from Frost's "The Road Not Taken."

Two loves converged in an age, and I—
I chose the one that would not die,
And that has made all the difference.

Thomas smiled to himself. He'd like to see Dr. Harris argue with that.

The aromas of dinner wafted up the stairs. Something smelled delicious, something Italian with lots of garlic. Sharon always made something special, a dish she knew he loved, on the last night he was home. The food on campus was good and plentiful, but it couldn't compare with his mom's cooking.

The phone on the bedside table rang and he reached over to pick it up. Before he even got it to his ear, he heard Chloe's frantic sobbing.

"Chloe! Sweetheart, what is it? What's happened?"

He barely made out her words. "My mother—she's dead!"

"What?" He sat up so fast the book of Frost's poetry fell off the bed onto the floor.

"Oh, Thomas, she took her own life. She overdosed. I went out to meet an old friend for lunch, and I just came back and found her. The medics are here—"Oh my God, Thomas, I just don't know what to do."

"Do you want me to come down? I'll hop on a plane tonight, if I can get a flight. Tomorrow for sure."

"I do—but no, Thomas, I don't think you should. My aunt and uncle are here. They live just around the corner. They'll take care of everything, but..." She broke down into sobs again. "We had such a lovely Christmas. We talked and talked, and seemed to relate for the first time in I don't know how long—maybe since I was a little girl. Then I came home—to this."

"Chloe, what can I do?" He'd never felt so helpless. A lot of good his quick reflexes and intelligence could do in this situation. Chloe's voice grew fainter; he heard her talking to someone else.

"Thomas, my Aunt Alice, my mom's sister, wants to talk to you."

"Sure." He waited, curious to hear what a relative he'd never met would have to say to him."

"Hello, Thomas," the voice, a more adult echo of Chloe's, said. "This is Chloe's aunt, Alice Craig. "We've heard a lot about you this past couple of weeks. Chloe seems to think a great deal of you."

Thomas decided not to beat around the bush. "We've spent a lot of time together. I love her."

Aunt Alice gave him the typical adult response. "Uhm, yes, well you two are very young. Everybody falls in love in college. That's not to say it's a forever-thing, Thomas."

Thomas bristled. "You may not think it's the real thing, Mrs. Craig, but we do. We are very sure."

Her voice softened. "Thomas, feelings come and go, and sometimes life forces us to go in a direction we didn't intend to."

"What are you trying to tell me, Mrs. Craig?" He already knew. His stomach had opened into an empty pit and he waited for her words.

"Her uncle and I think it best for Chloe not to go back to college in New Hampshire. It's such a long way from here, and she's going to need family around her now."

Thomas found it hard to breathe. He passed his hand over his forehead. "She has family here," he protested. "My parents love her like a daughter. She can be here with us whenever the college is closed."

Aunt Alice's voice held sympathy, but also determination. "I'm sure they do, Thomas, but she belongs here with us. My husband will call Administration tomorrow and withdraw her from the school. There are good colleges here, too. She can transfer to one of those."

"No! No!" Thomas shouted into the phone. "Let me talk to her."

He held onto the phone as if it would fly away if he relaxed his grip. After what seemed like a long wait, Chloe, her voice thick with tears, whispered, "Thomas?"

"Chloe—you can't stay there. What about us?" He heard the quaver in his own voice, but he didn't care.

He couldn't understand what she was trying to say as she tried to speak through her sobs. He managed to make out, "I-I'm just too upset to talk now. I just can't decide anything right now."

"Chloe! I'm coming down there. What's the address? What airport do I go to?"

Aunt Alice came back on the line. "Thomas, please do not come here. Chloe needs rest and quiet and a chance to adjust to all that's happened. She needs her family—us, right now. Maybe in a few months..."

"No." Thomas attempted to reason with the aunt. "I can come down, be with her..."

Aunt Alice's voice was quiet and determined. "Not now, Thomas. Can't you tell she's falling apart? She is very distraught by my sister's..." she hesitated over the word... "suicide. She needs quiet time to heal. She doesn't need conflict and confusion."

"Mrs. Craig, please..."

"Thomas, I'm going to hang up now. Please don't call her. I'm sorry, Thomas, but this is how it has to be right now. Goodbye, Thomas." The phone clicked on the other end.

He dialed the number again and again, only to receive a busy signal every time. He tried his cell, calling Chloe's cell. It offered to take a message.

Thomas jumped up and raced to the closet. He threw shoes and boxes out of the way as he searched for a small, overnight bag. He found one, and although the leather was scratched and discolored, he decided it would do. He snatched a couple of lightweight shirts and tees from a drawer, a pair of shorts and a pair of khakis. He went into the bathroom and swept his toiletries off the sink and into the bag. He zipped it closed and headed downstairs.

His mother turned as he entered the kitchen and gave him a big smile. "Dinner's just about ready—oh, Thomas what's the matter? You're not going back to Midstate tonight before dinner, are you?"

His mouth tightened. "I'm sorry, Mom. I have to go to Florida. Right now."

Her blue eyes opened wide. "Thomas, whatever for? You'll never get a flight tonight in this weather."

"Then I'll sit in the airport 'til I do get one." He told her briefly about Chloe's mother's death, and his conversation with Aunt Alice. "She said not to come, but I have to."

He set the bag on a chair, put his arms around her and hugged her. "I'm sorry, Mom. Dinner smells amazing, but I can't sit here when Chloe needs me. I'm going to bring her back. That's okay with you, isn't it?"

She nodded. "Of course it is, Thomas, but is that the best thing for Chloe? She's had quite a shock. Maybe she just needs quiet for a while."

He shook his head. He wasn't going into this argument again if he could help it. "I'll go say goodbye to Dad and Ivy, then I'm off. I'll call you when I get there."

~ * ~

Ivy didn't think he should go to Florida, either. Thomas felt disheartened, as he had counted on her support.

"But she needs me. I have to be with her."

"No, Thomas. What she needs is time to get over her mother's suicide. It isn't that you wouldn't comfort her, but she needs to come to terms with this by herself. They don't want you to come, so you should respect their wishes."

"The aunt hung up on me," he said. "When I called back, there was no answer. I think they took the phone off the hook. Chloe didn't answer her cell, either."

"That should be enough to convince you," Ivy said. Her face showed her sympathy, but she was adamant in her conviction that Thomas should not go where nobody wanted him.

Everything in him protested, but little by little with stubborn resistance, Thomas finally conceded her point. He threw his parka on a chair and accepted a dark-colored margarita. "What flavor is this?"

Ivy smiled. "Mulberry."

"Mulberry? Where the heck did you get mulberries?"

"This little esoteric market I visit sometimes had them. I bought them last summer and froze them...for an occasion just like this."

"For a non-celebration?" He took a sip. "Not delicious, Ivy... but interesting."

"Well, Thomas, Chloe told me about your sacrifice at the Druids' ceremony. If Snickers grew on bushes or vines, I would be glad to make you a Snickers margarita."

For the first time in that long, dreary day, Thomas laughed.

~ * ~

"Thomas, it's for you." His mother poked her head into his bedroom.

Thomas had heard the phone ring, but ignored it and turned over in bed, thinking it couldn't possibly be for him. The only person he wanted a phone call from wasn't going to be on the other end.

He picked up the phone from the end table. He didn't recognize the voice.

"Thomas, this is John Rigozzi. I'm sorry, but I have to reneg on the apartment I said I would rent to you. My sister-in-law has had an emergency, and I need to put her and her two children up there for a while. Maybe when things calm down, I can let you have it—later in the year. And I'll give you a discount for the inconvenience."

Thomas gave an inward groan. This seemed like an unpromising start for yet another frustrating day. "Okay," he said. "I respect that you need it for family."

"I'll send you back your deposit." Rigozzi didn't sound any more cheerful than Thomas felt. "And thanks for understanding."

Thomas hung up and swung his feet over the side of the bed. Basketball practice began again tonight, classes tomorrow, and he had to find a place to live. After a series of disappointing calls to the college, where admissions and housing representatives assured him there were no vacant rooms on campus, he made anther call he didn't want to make.

Jett sounded alert and cheerful. "Sure, Thomas, I'd be glad to have you back. They didn't assign me another roommate yet, so, sure, that's cool."

"Fine. See you in a few hours then."

A few minutes before three, Thomas pushed open the door to the dorm room he had shared with Jett, and threw his luggage on the bed. Here he was, back in the room with Jett, and there was nothing he could do about it. He set up his computer on the same desk he had used before. Resentfully, he replaced his books in the bookcase, unpacked and put his clothes away.

He looked at his watch. The dining hall wouldn't be serving until five, and he didn't feel like going to the Elk Horn, although he was pretty sure that's where Jett would be hanging out. He knew all too well that the gnawing in his stomach was not for food, or for a bottle of beer, either—it was for Chloe, and that was the one thing he couldn't have.

After all these months, he found himself right back where he'd started, but without the upbeat feelings with which he'd started at Midstate.

He heard voices and footsteps in the hall outside.

Jett pushed open the door and came into the room, followed by another student.

"Hi, Thomas, welcome back." He gestured to his companion. "You already know Jack Wayland."

Thomas looked at Jack, puzzled. He was of medium height with dark hair and eyes, a thin face with angular cheekbones and a sharp nose. He'd never seen this guy around campus, or hadn't noticed him. He'd never seen him with Jett.

"No, I don't think I do." He held out his hand and Jack met it with a smack across the palm.

Jack laughed. "Sure you do, Thomas, but you know me better as Dyfan."

Seventeen

Thomas took a few steps back, clenched his fists, and fought for self-control. He wanted to punch out Jack Wayland, alias Dyfan. He wanted to make him hurt physically as much as he himself hurt emotionally.

He glared at Jett. "Why the hell did you bring him here, after what he did to Chloe?"

Jett flopped down in the chair at his desk, and unzipped his jacket. Jack took Thomas' chair as if it were a throne and he were entitled to it.

Thomas fumed. "I'm not going to stay in the same room with you." He grabbed his parka and started for the door.

"What did I do to Chloe?" Jack's voice was calm, friendly.

Thomas wheeled around, his hand on the doorknob. "I can't believe you! You cut her rope and she almost died in that snowstorm."

"Sit down, Thomas. I'm going to explain all that." Jack gestured to the bed, which was the only place left to sit.

Infuriated by Jack's tone, Thomas took a few steps toward him, with every intention of delivering a hard blow to the bastard's face.

Jett jumped up to intervene, and stood between him and Jack. He took his arm and pushed him toward the bed. "Sit down and listen, Thomas."

"I'm not listening to anything he has to say. I almost lost Chloe, and if it hadn't been for..." He broke off, as he watched the change in Jack's eyes. They became Dyfan's eyes, and he found himself trapped by his gaze, just as he had been at the Druids' gathering. "No, no," he gasped, fighting for control. "Get out of here, Jack—Dyfan, whoever you are."

"Sit down, Thomas," Jack repeated.

"No." He reached for whatever strength of will he still possessed and turned away, staring out the window at the snow. Ivy's face flickered before his eyes. Her lips moved, as if she were trying to say something, but the image faded before he read it.

"Thomas." That voice. His defiance ebbed away. Still fighting it, but knowing he had lost, he turned back to face Jack.

Something shifted inside him, as it had before under Dyfan's stare. He backed up and sat on the bed, feeling his resolve to get out of the room fade away. One part of his mind still screamed at him to leave, but the rest of it seemed numbed to his own decisions.

Jack leaned forward toward Thomas, pinning him with his black stare. "You said 'if it hadn't been for...' Thomas. What did you mean by that? How did you find Chloe?"

Thomas shook his head and tried to break the lock Jack had on his eyes, but he could not look away.

"Tell me. Who—or what helped you find her?"

He couldn't hold the words back. "Ivy—my grandmother."

"How did she help you?"

Thomas' mind replayed the shimmering light he had seen in the snowstorm, the voice that had called to him. Although what was left of his conscious mind screamed at him not to, he heard himself tell Jack about Ivy's psychic powers. "She saw Chloe in a vision. I heard her voice, I saw something through the snowstorm, and knew I was supposed to follow it. I did, and it led me to Chloe. If I hadn't found her, she would have died."

Jack sat back and seemed to relax. "No, she wouldn't have, Thomas. That's what I wanted to explain to you."

"You cut her cord!" The words were hard to get out, and he choked saying them. It felt disloyal to be accusing Jack—Dyfan—of an evil intention.

"Yes, I did. I cut everyone's cord. It was a test of faith. But I, and Jett and Gaia, knew where everyone was at every minute. And everyone made it back, alive and in good shape. That was the point, Thomas, trust. And you failed that test."

"And you took Chloe and left," Jett added.

"You ridiculed the sacrifice," Jack continued. "But the day will come when you will make an acceptable sacrifice."

There was a part of Thomas' mind which knew he had fallen under Jack's control. His head felt as if it were filled with cotton. He made an effort, but he didn't have the mental strength to fight it. He felt a wave of contrition. "I—I'm sorry," he stammered.

Jack maintained eye contact. "Do you have a picture of Ivy?"

"No, not with me. But there's a couple of her on my camera."

"Where is your camera?"

"In my desk."

Jack exchanged glances with Jett, and Jett nodded.

"Very well." Jack stood and stretched his arms above his head, clasping his wrists. "Now, what did you intend to do this evening, Thomas?"

"Basketball practice, after dinner."

"I don't think so, Thomas. Before we go to dinner, you will call the coach and quit the team. Where's your cell?"

Thomas pulled it out of his pocket.

"Is the coach's number stored in there?"

Thomas nodded.

"Call him and tell him you will no longer play."

Thomas did so, repeating over and over against Coach Walsh's incredulous protests, that he simply did not have the time or interest to play anymore. His grades were suffering; he had to get them up. He'd lost all interest in the game. He thought he'd take up something more intellectual, like chess. When Coach sounded incapable of taking 'no' for an answer, Thomas hung up on him.

Jack nodded his approval. "Well done. Now you will have more time to participate in the spiritual life we offer, and you will learn that it is the only life that counts. It's the road less traveled."

Something familiar echoed in Thomas' mind, but he nodded, feeling emptier inside than he ever remembered feeling.

"One more thing." Jack's eyes bored into Thomas. "You will remember none of what I have told you to do. You will think the decision to quit basketball and hang out with Jett and me, and your desire to attend all Druid meetings are yours and yours alone. Do you understand?"

"Yes."

"Very well." Jack waved his hand in front of Thomas' face. Thomas blinked. The thought passed through his mind that he had enjoyed meeting Jack, and the three of them had just had a great conversation. At the same time, the feeling didn't seem quite genuine. It was as if behind the thoughts at the forefront of his mind lurked a hollowness he could not even comprehend.

He grinned at Jett. "Man, I'm glad I called Coach and quit that team. I'll have so much more time to hang out with you guys."

Jett stood up, zipped his jacket and smiled back at Thomas. "Okay, Buddy, let's go to dinner."

~ * ~

Jack suggested going to IHOP. "Let's bypass the caf tonight. It'll give us a better chance to talk without interruption, and I have a weird yearning for French toast for supper."

"That sounds great—I'll have that, too."

Jett laughed.

"What's funny about that? I love French toast."

"That's good," Jett said, smiling at him. "Very good, as a matter of fact."

IHOP seemed nearly deserted, the supper crowd evidently having gone elsewhere to eat.

Jack led them to a booth near the back of the restaurant. A soon as they wrestled out of their heavy jackets and hung them on the coat hooks at the end of the booth, their waitress showed up, order pad in hand.

"Good evening, guys. Good to see you back. What can I get for you this evening?" Donna smiled at them.

Thomas recognized her from one of their previous visits, and also running into her in Salem. "Hi, Donna. How are you?"

"Oh, fine." She wouldn't meet his eyes, but stared at her pad. "These are our specials this evening…"

Thomas didn't hear about the specials. Donna didn't look so good. The fatigue lines etched permanently into her face seemed even deeper, and a suspicious blue-black bruise lingered under her left eye. She'd tried to cover it up with heavy makeup, but it still showed.

Jack ordered for all of them.

Jett sighed. "I'd really like a beer with this," as Donna placed a pot of coffee on the table, along with three mugs." Jack poured coffee for all three of them.

"You can go to the Elk Horn later." Jack piled up the menus and slid them to the end of the table. "It would be good for Thomas to cut loose, enjoy himself for once, instead of worrying about everyone and everything."

Thomas reached for the jar of jam on the table and turned it in his hand. "Chloe couldn't eat this strawberry jam. She's allergic to strawberries. Did you know that?"

That seemed to open the door. Jett leaned forward. "How is Chloe? Is she back from Florida yet?"

Thomas blinked. It seemed unbelievable to him that everyone didn't know what had happened. "Chloe's mom committed suicide. She's not coming back."

"*What?*" Jack set his mug down with a thump. "What do you mean, she's not coming back?"

"Just what I said." Thomas sipped at his coffee, wishing like Jett that he could have a cold, frosty beer instead. "She's falling apart emotionally, and her relatives down there are insisting she stay there with them."

Jett turned an expression of disbelief on Thomas. "And you're okay with that? Didn't you talk to her yourself?"

"Of course I did." Thomas felt the emptiness sweep through him again, but it was more like something he remembered feeling than what he actually felt at the moment. "She said she couldn't deal with any decisions right now. About coming back or about us."

Jack and Jett exchanged glances.

Donna arrived with their order, and set the tray down on a small folding table while she delivered the plates to them. As she placed the food in front of him, the end of her long-sleeved blouse rode up a bit, and Thomas noticed the darkening bruise there. He flicked her a questioning look, but she refused to meet his eyes.

"Uhm, this looks great." He picked up his fork, but halted in mid-air as Jack grasped his wrist. "Thomas."

"Uhm, what?"

"Chloe has to come back. You have to get her back."

Thomas lowered his fork. "I can't do anything about it, Jack. It's out of my hands. She doesn't answer my phone calls. Her aunt is very possessive."

Jack's grip tightened around his wrist. It hurt, but Thomas thought it would make him look like a wimp to protest. "You're going to Florida, Thomas, and you're going to bring her back."

"No—I can't do that..." The grip tightened. Thomas winced, but made no effort to shake him off. Jack seemed amazingly strong for a guy his size.

"Yes, you can. And you will."

"She doesn't want me..."

Jack's black eyes pierced his. "Sometimes what one person wants is not what the group needs. The Druids need Chloe to complete the circle and their mission."

Again, Thomas' will seemed to erode under Jack's gaze. He managed to ask, "What mission is that?"

"The Druid's ceremony of thanks we will hold at the end of the school year. It will be the most meaningful moment of your life, believe me, Thomas. And of Chloe's, I promise you." He let go of Thomas' wrist.

"And we're going to hold it at the North Salem place," Jett put in. "The New Hampshire Stonehenge near where you live."

Thomas rubbed his arm. Pictures of the rock formations rose in his mind, along with an overwhelming feeling of deep reverence. "Mystery Hill? Why there instead of our own Stonehenge?"

"It has a history, which our meeting place doesn't."

"Ivy says there is an evil history there." Thomas said, almost to himself.

"It's only evil if you think it is," Jack replied. "Your grandmother has an untrue bias. To me it is a place that has a deep spiritual significance. You and Chloe are part of the circle, and for the most spiritual benefit to all, we need you there."

That made sense to Thomas. He nodded. "I will go to Florida and bring her back."

"Yes," Jack agreed. "You will. And, to make the ceremony even more meaningful, I will perform a joining for you and Chloe, if you wish."

A wave of joy shot through him. Thomas didn't think it would be possible to feel any happier. Joined with Chloe! Her aunt didn't think they had a forever-thing between them, but Jack understood. He felt profound gratitude toward Jack. He would do anything for him.

As they left IHOP, Thomas spied the waitress, Donna, wiping down one of the tables near the door. He signaled to Jett. "Go ahead. I'll be right with you."

She looked up as he approached. "Hi. Thomas, isn't it? We keep running into each other."

"Yeah. How are the kids?"

"Oh, fine, thanks." Again, she looked away, refusing to meet his eyes.

"Look, Donna, is there anything I can do to help? It looks to me like you might be having a rough time."

Embarrassed, she shook her head. "I left my husband. I moved into a small place my brother-in-law owns, temporarily, at least.

The manager called from behind the counter. "Hey, Rigozzi. Can you give us a hand back here?"

Thomas gasped in surprise. "Your brother-in-law's name is Rigozzi? You took that apartment on Maple Street over the pharmacy?"

"Oh, are you the student who rented that and John had to reneg on you? I'm so sorry, Thomas—we might be out in a couple months."

"Oh, no hurry, no hurry. I'm back in the dorm room with my former roommate. I never should have left."

"Rigozzi!"

"I'm sorry. I have to go." Thomas watched her scurry off. He examined the developing bruise on his own wrist. He and Donna were an unlikely pair to have anything in common. He reflected that Fate had a weird way of tying people together.

He shrugged as he left the restaurant to rejoin Jett and Jack. Florida awaited.

Eighteen

The morning of his departure brought more snow. The first flight he could make left at two pm. Leaving the dorm shortly before noon, he turned up his collar, and carrying his travel valise, he headed for his car to make the short drive to Manchester.

Someone called his name. "Thomas! Hey, wait up a minute."

He turned in surprise as he saw Coach Walsh striding toward him. "Thorn, I'd like a word with you, please."

Thomas put his head down and continued toward his car. "I have a plane to catch, Coach. Can't talk now."

Walsh caught up with him and took his arm. "You can give me a minute."

Thomas stopped. He found it hard to meet the coach's eyes. Why was that, he wondered to himself. He hadn't done anything wrong by quitting the team. It was his choice, his life, not the coach's.

"I've seen you around campus with Chloe McAllister. She wasn't in my morning art class, and you've quit basketball. What's up, Thomas?"

The professor-coach actually looked more hurt than puzzled.

Thomas faltered. "It's nothing to do with you, Coach. Chloe had a family tragedy in Florida, and she says she's not coming back. Me—well, I just think I can find something more productive to do with my time. I need to put more effort into my academics."

"Chloe's not coming back? I'm so sorry to hear that, and of course, about her family. She excelled in my class in painting."

"Yes, I know, and she loved your class, too. But, Coach, I really have to go. I have a plane to catch."

Coach's eyebrows shot up. "Do I guess that you're going to Florida, maybe to try to persuade her to come back?"

"You got it."

"You know, Redfern is just around the corner. Why don't you give me a lift over there, and I'll run in and get that last painting she did. I'm sure she'd want it."

Thomas glanced at his watch. "Okay, I guess I have time for that."

He pulled his car into the circular drive, and Walsh jumped out and ran into the building. Thomas let his mind drift as his eyes fastened on one of the sculptures standing in the snow outside the building. Some enterprising students had built a snow sculpture parodying Michelangelo's David right beside it, and they had done a good job of it, too. Thomas smiled to himself. The art students' version of a snowman.

The passenger door opened, and Coach bent down to hand the painting to him.

"She wanted to do just a little more to this, but I consider it finished as is. Tell her she got an A, and if she ever comes back, I'll be glad to have her in my class again."

"I will." Thomas took the painting and laid it on the seat beside him.

"And you, too, Thomas, if you change your mind about playing basketball. The team will miss you. You'd be a star next year if you stayed with the team."

"Thanks." A shaft of guilt shot through him, and he couldn't meet Coach's eyes. He waved in his general direction, waited until he heard the door close, and pulled out of the art complex and away from the college.

The road to the Manchester airport was busier than it should have been for that time of day, or for any time of day, for that matter. Thomas had to slow his speed as the traffic stopped from time to time, and he was forced to wait, tapping his fingers on the wheel and enduring the impatient blaring of drivers' horns. He checked his watch. If traffic delayed him much longer, he just might miss his flight.

He noted an exit coming up in a half mile. It didn't lead directly to the airport, but he knew the roads around well, and he could take another route. Traffic speeded up a bit, and he followed suit. He whizzed past the exit; it looked as though he might make it after all

The Mercedes SUV ahead of him slowed suddenly and Thomas jammed on his brakes. The jolt sent Chloe's painting sailing off the seat onto the floor. It landed face-up and angled toward him. He couldn't help looking at it.

The Mercedes stopped. Thomas stopped behind it. Other cars hemmed him in on all sides. Up ahead, somewhere, he heard the sharp sirens of police cars. He wiped his hand across his forehead in frustration. This looked like a long wait, and yes, he would miss his plane. Well, he would just camp out at the airport until he could get another.

He stared at Chloe's painting of Mystery Hill. The altar stone lay in front, flat, smooth and bare. Rock formations loomed behind it, and the ceremonial trail led away down the hill. Something prickled in his mind, a vague memory of something. He knew this place well, he had grown up with it, but this seemed to be something else.

Traffic began to move again, creeping toward Manchester, but Thomas, mesmerized by the painting and the feeling that he needed to remember something lurking on the edges of his mind, didn't accelerate. Horns blared as cars growled past him.

A balding guy in a gray SUV slowed down, and his passenger side window rolled down, "Hey, jerk, get moving there." Thomas glanced up in time to catch the rude gesture that followed, but it didn't register with him. There was something else he needed to pay attention to...but he just couldn't pin it down. His eyes returned to the painting.

~ * ~

Thomas' spirit floated over the thruway, and watched while the ambulance screeched to a halt. The EMTs scrambled out and raced to the car, while a harried-looking cop blocked the lane and directed traffic around it.

I hope I'm not dead. I had something important to do, and I know I haven't done it.

He felt the presence of the Coordinator. "You're not dead, Thomas, but you certainly have messed things up. You're in a lot of trouble."

Thomas watched his body taken from his wrecked car and strapped to the stretcher. He thought he didn't look too bad. There was blood on his forehead, seeping into his hair, and one arm twitched on its own, but it didn't look nearly as bad as it might have been. The woman in the red Focus who had hit him from behind, didn't seem to be hurt. She stood shivering in the street, talking to another cop, crying and wringing her hands, as the officer wrote things down on a pad.

"Thomas, pay attention."

He shifted his attention to the Coordinator. "What trouble are you talking about?"

"You fell under the influence of evil. Dyfan."

He remembered. "Yes. I didn't have the strength to resist."

"You should have, Thomas. We provided you with a solid family, and a grandmother whose power for good is at least as strong as Dyfan's is for evil. You didn't take her seriously enough."

"How do I fix this? I have to go to Florida and bring Chloe back, don't I?"

"She'll come back on her own. She knows what to do, and she'll find the strength to do it. Your job is to build up your power of resistance."

"How do I do that?"

"Listen to Ivy. Tell her everything."

The scene below began to fade. Thomas resisted, not wanting to go back into that heavy body and experience the pain he knew would accompany that. Then, with a burst of resolution, he floated downward and entered his human body.

~ * ~

Thomas opened his eyes and blinked at the sudden shock of white all around him.

"Where am I?"

He knew the answer, of course. White walls, the IV

attached to his arm as he lay flat in bed, everything so bright, Ivy bending over him—of, course, he'd had an accident and landed in the hospital.

"Elliot Hospital, Manchester. How do you feel, Thomas?"

He lifted a hand and explored the bandage on his head. "Not too bad, considering. Am I hurt badly? Where are my parents?"

"You have a concussion and a few bruises. You were lucky. And Sharon and Charlie ducked out for a bite to eat. You've been out for hours."

He groaned as he felt the pain in his head cut in. "How's the car?"

"Totalled. But don't worry about that. You can have mine. I always have Sharon or the guy down the street to take me where I need to go."

"When can I go home, and back to school?"

"This afternoon. You need to rest for about a week, but there's no lasting damage. We think it's best if you stay with me, in my tiny spare bedroom, so you won't have to climb up and down stairs. You need to save your legs for basketball."

"Oh, Jeez." He winced as it suddenly all rushed back. "Oh, Ivy, I quit basketball. What have I done?"

Ivy's eyebrows registered a hint of surprise. "You quit basketball?" Her expression turned serious. "I think more is going on than you've told me, Thomas. Is it that Druid group Chloe told me about?"

"Yes. The head of it, a guy named Dyfan..." his voice trailed off.

"What about him?"

He groaned. "He has some sort of power. I don't know what it is, but when he and Jett and I get together, he seems to take over my mind." He squinted up at her. "You know how I hate French toast?"

"Yes. You never would eat it, even as a kid, not even drowning in maple syrup."

"Well... I know this is a stupid example, but he convinced me that I love it. We went to IHOP and I ate it." He shuddered. "Ugh. Far as I'm concerned, I might as well eat soggy cardboard..."

Ivy interrupted him with a laugh. "I know, but I hardly think that's the real problem, is it?

"Well, look who's awake." His dad grinned down at him. "Ready to go home, son?"

Thomas nodded, feeling his head throb as he did so. "Where's Mom?"

"Coming right along after me. She's talking with the doctor and getting a couple of prescriptions for you. You'll be going home this afternoon." He walked to the door and peered out into the hall, as if looking for Sharon and the doctor. "You'll be back on the basketball court next week."

Thomas met Ivy's eyes, and she leaned down close enough to whisper to him. "Back on the court, yes, but first we're going to have a week of another kind of class. Just call it "Resistance to Evil 101.""

Nineteen

By midweek, Thomas' aches and pains, as well as the throbbing in his head, faded to an unpleasant memory. His arm looked bruised, and had some lingering soreness, but the doctor assured him it would soon feel normal, with no lasting ill effects. Best of all, his mind felt clear and clean, almost as if it had taken a shower. He grinned at his own analogy.

He sat in the Hitchcock rocker across from Ivy in her small, not-so-neat living room. While he slept, she'd spent the morning rolling beads from triangular shapes she cut from colorful magazine pages. All her materials, including the pot of wax she dipped them in to seal them, littered the small card table.

He shook his head in amazement. "I can't believe what that guy did to me. And Chloe, too. No wonder she decided to stay in Florida."

Ivy nodded her head in agreement. "She'll be back, Thomas. I know she will."

He leaned in toward her. "Ivy, how do you know? I've called her cell every day, and it's always 'leave a message.' It's killing me to hear her voice, but not be able to talk to her."

Ivy bit her lip and shifted position to favor her injured arm. "There are some things I just know. I have dreams, I have intuition, I have awareness...and sometimes I have absolute conviction about one thing or another. Sometimes I have—well, memories are what I have to call them, about events in the past that just surface in my mind. I see the events as clearly as if they were movies playing in front of me."

"And they are sometimes about me? And Chloe?"

"Very often. I think that's why I was placed here, in this time and space—to guide you, help you and protect you, if necessary."

He sat back and rubbed his hand over his chin. He hadn't shaved since his accident, and had a rough growth of stubble. He regarded her, wondering why he needed a protector, and if he did, who had arranged that.

"What do you mean, you were placed here? And who would it be who decided all that?"

She sighed. "Thomas, life is not at all what you think it is. We all live many times..."

He laughed. "Now you're sounding like one of those wacko psychos. Come on, Ivy."

She smiled and nodded. "Maybe those so-called wacko psychics and I have more in common than you think. But, I'm not going on unless you take this seriously."

His cell phone rang. It might be Chloe, finally calling him back. He dug it out of his pocket and scanned the window. "It's Jett. He's called about fifty times. I probably should tell him what happened and that I'll be back."

Ivy leaned forward, grabbed the phone from him and tossed it onto the sofa, where it continued to ring and vibrate. "Don't answer that, Thomas. Don't call him back. And you are not going back to room with him. Now, getting back to the main question. You don't believe you've lived before? You don't think your life is being guided somehow?"

"I-I never gave that much thought, except that when I left for college you told me I'd meet a girl named Chloe and I did."

"And you think that was an accident?"

He felt a flash of annoyance. Maybe he was spending too much time with his grandmother, if she were beginning to get to him. "I don't know. I admit you have uncanny knowledge about things from time to time, but this stuff about past lives and destiny—well, I can't take that seriously at all."

She gazed off into the distance, and didn't respond.

Oh, oh, maybe she's getting a message from outer space, or wherever it is her ideas come from. Again, Thomas smiled at his own thoughts.

Ivy seemed to come to a conclusion. She got up from her chair with an agility that surprised him, and stood looking down at him. "Okay, kiddo. Here's your first assignment. I'm going to give you the journal I've kept over the years. You read it. That should keep you busy for a while." She headed for the antique desk where she kept her papers and files.

He fingered the worn, brown leather book. It had a gold ribbon page marker, and looked more like a Bible than a diary. Just the size of it made him feel tired. He glanced back up at her. "And what are you going to do while I'm reading this tome?"

She struggled into a tan suede parka that had sheepskin cuffs and collar and a lined hood. She dug red mittens out of her pocket and pulled them on. "I'm going down the street to see Russell."

He raised his eyebrows at her. "In the middle of the afternoon?"

She arched one shoulder in a provocative-looking shrug. "A woman has her needs, Thomas. When I get back, we'll talk."

~ * ~

Ivy had termed it "Resistance to Evil 101, and Thomas' head spun with all she had taught him. His feelings ran the gamut from frustration to disbelief. What if he didn't want this assignment—was he free not to do it, or not? Would disaster fall on him, if he simply decided to go his own way, and if Chloe never came back to him? He still could not comprehend, or even fully believe, all he'd read in Ivy's journal. It seemed so fantastic that he had decided on his own, after centuries of waiting, to be inserted fully grown into this family, with a full-blown destiny sitting in front of him, to save an ancient love from death in present time. Could this possibly be true, or was it just Ivy's overactive imagination? That bit about Achak and Kanti—they were he and Chloe a couple of thousand years ago? He fiddled with his mother's excellent pot roast, and shook his head.

Sharon laughed as she shoved a bowl of mashed sweet potatoes in front of him.

"I haven't asked you yet, Thomas. Have some more sweet potatoes. I know you love them."

He switched to a nod, and took the dish. "Yes, I will have seconds, thanks." He helped himself to a generous scoop. They smelled so good, so real. After reading Ivy's journal, and subjecting himself to hours of her intense anti-evil training, he felt more confused than ever. What was real, what wasn't?

His younger brother interrupted his thoughts. "Boy, you're weird tonight, Thomas. What gives? Ivy put a jinx on you?"

He reached over and rumpled Mike's coppery hair. This kid was real, anyway, no matter what else was or wasn't. "I know. I'm just tired, Dude. But I'd love to play that video game with you later. Take me on?"

Mike's face lit up as he grinned. "You bet. But I always win."

"That he does," Charlie Sr. agreed. "I can't beat him."

Dinner evolved into a normal family meal, and Thomas finally relaxed. Whether he had been born to them, or assigned to them, Sharon took good care of everyone, kept a warm, attractive home and prepared comfort-food meals. Mike was a pain-in-the-ass, but a totally acceptable little brother. Big brother Charlie called and wrote regularly from Iraq. His mild-mannered father sat at the head of the table, and surveyed his domain with contentment. Then there was Ivy, the wild card. Where in the world, or *worlds,* had she come from?

Charlie put down his fork and pushed his plate away. "We got a letter from Charlie today, with some interesting news." He pulled a blue envelope from his shirt pocket. "I thought I'd read it to everyone, before we scatter for the evening."

Mike jumped in his chair. "Is he coming home? Oh, boy, I can't wait."

Charlie smiled. "No, not that. Something else."

"We have twenty minutes before the news," Sharon said. "Time for dessert first. Mike's favorite tonight."

Thomas watched with amusement as Mike attacked the dense, dark chocolate pie his mother produced.

"You'll take a slice back for Ivy? Is she feeling all right?"

Thomas nodded. "She's a little tired, that's all, and not in the mood for a big meal, but Ivy's as much a chocoholic as Mike is. It's a wonder she's hasn't come up with a chocolate margarita yet."

"Give her time," Charlie said with a wry grin.

When Sharon had removed the china and silverware from the table, his father cleared his throat and unfolded the letter from Charlie.

Thomas listened with attention and admiration as Charlie described his duties in that far off foreign country. He wondered why Charlie had opted for that path, the military instead of college. He tried to call up his brother's face in his mind. He couldn't picture him clearly, and he couldn't pin down his personality. Reflecting on what he'd learned from Ivy's journal, he wondered if he'd ever known Charlie in person at all.

That's ridiculous. He shook off the unwelcomed thoughts and focused on the letter from his brother.

"...and I've met a wonderful girl. Her name is January..."

"January!" Thomas and Mike exclaimed in unison.

Charlie smiled, and continued without comment. "...but everyone calls her Jan. She's an Army nurse, and just the best thing that's ever happened to me. She's really pretty with blonde hair and blue eyes, and so petite...she makes me feel so protective of her.

"Bet she's not as pretty as Chloe," Mike muttered.

Thomas threw him a grin, but didn't comment.

Charlie continued. "...and the best thing is she's from New England, too. She grew up in western Mass in Williamstown. I can't wait 'til we both get home and you can meet her. I know it's early yet, but Mom and Dad, I really think she's the one for me."

Thomas nodded to himself. Yes, when the right one came along, you knew, you just knew. It wasn't rocket science.

~ * ~

Thomas, fighting fatigue, wanted to enjoy a simple margarita with Ivy, and go to bed early. He often watched the tiny TV in the bedroom in bed until about to drift off, when, somehow, he had the presence of mind to flick off the remote before he fell asleep.

Ivy, however, wanted to discuss Jett and Dyfan and the Druids, but she was perfectly willing to make margaritas for both of them. "It's raspberry," she said as she handed him something pink and frothy in a glass. "I know you like that."

"Thanks. I'm not in the mood for something exotic tonight."

Ivy nodded. "Don't you understand yet what Jett and Dyfan did to you, and why?"

"Well, Dyfan yes, but Jett…"

"Jett is in league with this guy, and totally in his power, and they do not intend anything good for you. And I'm really afraid for Chloe."

Thomas rolled his eyes. "I know they used some kind of hypnosis on me, but I still don't understand why. Dyfan and the Druids are just a bunch of college kids, dressing up in robes and pretending to worship nature gods and connect with the past." He shrugged. "That's all it is. But it's silly and a waste of time, and I won't do that anymore. It's back to the basketball court for me."

"It's *not* silly." She emphasized the word. "It's dangerous. And I mean to give you the tools to fight them, so they can't control you anymore."

He sighed. "I wish I could just go to bed, Ivy. I'm tired."

"This is important. You're going back to school this weekend, and as someone once famously said, I want you *to go 'armed and dangerous.'*

He laughed and gave in. "Okay, shoot."

She pointed two fingers, symbolizing a gun at him to emphasize what she was about to say, when Thomas' cell phone rang.

"It's probably Jett again."

"Don't answer it."

He glanced at the phone, and jumped out of his chair. He headed for his bedroom. He called back over his shoulder. "The lesson will have to wait awhile, Ivy. I have to take this."

It's Chloe—oh, my god, it's Chloe.

Twenty

Her voice sounded as if she were sitting in the next room. Thomas flopped on his bed, feeling his grin stretch from ear to ear.

"Chloe, I've missed you so much. Tell me you're coming back."

"I want to. I miss you, too. It's just not that easy."

"Why not? Just grab the next plane and fly to Manchester. I'll meet you."

He picked up on the strain in her voice. "Alice wants me to stay here, transfer to one of the colleges in the area. She never had kids, so with my mom dead, I'm all she has. I don't want to hurt her any more than I have to."

He wanted to yell over the phone that it was *her* life, and her decision to make, not Alice's, but he stopped himself in time. Ivy had said she would come back, and he had to trust that, not only was she right, but that Chloe would make the best choice for herself.

"Where are you now?" Chloe asked. "In the dorm? Is Jett there?"

"No, I'm at Ivy's.

"In the middle of the week? Is she okay?"

He let out a small, rueful laugh. "Oh, yeah, Ivy's fine. But I have had some interesting developments in my life," He couldn't help but add, "which you would know about if you'd ever answered my calls."

She sounded sincerely apologetic. "I'm really sorry, Thomas. We went to Michigan for my mother's memorial service, just got back a few days ago. I've been a wreck trying to decide what to do, and Alice is like a dog with a bone. She just won't let it go."

"Listen, Chloe, I've got a lot to tell you. But first, I want to know—have you felt different since you've been back in Florida?"

She laughed, and she sounded like the Chloe he had first met. "Well, of course I feel different. I'm not buried in snow up to my neck, and putting on six layers of clothing every time I go outdoors. Is that what you mean?"

"No, not really. I mean, does your mind seem different, clearer somehow?"

He heard her gasp. "Yes! It's been the weirdest thing. At first I thought it was just because, in spite of what's happened here, I've had the time and space to think about things. But—since you put it that way, I'd have to say it's been like a fog has lifted. Is that what you mean?"

He gave out a long sigh of relief. "That's it, exactly. And do you know what—or who—got our minds all fogged up in the first place?"

"I guess that's what you're going to tell me, about those interesting developments and all, right?"

He related what had happened, beginning with Dyfan's orders for him to go to Florida and bring Chloe back. "I ran into Mr. Walsh and he gave me your Mystery Hill painting. He said you got an A+ and you're welcome back anytime."

She let out a cry of dismay when he told her about the accident. "But you're okay. You're not hurt, are you?"

"No," he assured her. "But I spent a couple days in the hospital, and now I'm at Ivy's resting up. But I need to talk to you about Jett and Gaia—and Dyfan, and why we have to stay away from them and the Druids from now on."

When he finished, he waited for her reaction. Would this be the deciding factor, the one that would convince her to stay in Florida?

"Well... I'm not going to let them scare me off, but we can't stay in the dorm anymore, can we, not if they're messing with our minds."

"I'll find a place for us," he promised. "Are you scared, Chloe?"

"No." He visualized her tossing back her honey-colored hair, and that stubborn expression crossing her face. "I'm angry that they thought they could do this to us. It makes me more determined to come back and be with you, and if we have to face them down, we will."

He thrilled at her display of courage. "Ivy's giving me some techniques we can use to prevent that from ever happening again. We'll be okay."

"I know we will," she said. "I trust you, Thomas, and I trust Ivy. I'll have a serious talk with Aunt Alice, and let you know when my flight will get in."

He decided not to tell her about Ivy's journal, and what they had discussed about previous lives. It seemed rather far-fetched to him, now that he thought about explaining it to someone else. He'd just save that for later, and tell her on a need-to-know-basis.

Nearly an hour later, they said their good nights and Thomas flicked off his phone. He relaxed into his pillow, feeling dizzy with elation. In just a few days he'd hold her in his arms again.

After a few minutes, he roused himself and went out into the living room.

Ivy looked up from her paper bead-making and smiled. She knew. "You're not tired anymore, are you, Thomas?"

He took his seat in the rocker again. "No. I think I'm ready for that lesson now."

~ * ~

The next morning, things fell into line like baby ducks following their mother across the street. His cell phone rang just as Thomas stepped out of the shower. He whipped a towel around his waist, tied the ends and grabbed the phone.

"Good morning, Thomas." It was John Rigozzi's voice. "I hope this isn't too early to call. I have a sudden vacancy, and wondered if you would be interested in renting it. You get first dibs on it."

"Oh, Donna's leaving already?"

"No, no. This is another, smaller place—my tenant skipped out a few days ago, owing me several months' rent. It's small, but furnished, and just around the corner from the campus. Are you interested?"

"Am I ever! I'll take it." Thomas couldn't believe his luck. He didn't even care what it looked like. He and Chloe would have their own digs. No Jett, no Gaia, no Dyfan interfering in their lives.

He heard Ivy moving around in the kitchen, and the aroma of bacon and toast invaded his space. He'd hardly put on his jeans and sweater when the phone rang again.

"Thomas, it's Chloe. I've got my ticket. Can you pick me up Friday afternoon at the Manchester airport?"

"Of course I can. We'll come back here and drive to campus on Sunday. Is that all right with you?"

"It is, and I can't wait. I can't wait to be with you again."

He couldn't wait, either, and his love for her surged all through him, making him feel twice as alive as he had been five minutes before.

He told her about the apartment, and felt her excitement build when she realized they would have a place together. He hung up with her, feeling as though the pieces of their lives, which had been broken and scattered around the landscape, were coming back together again.

Before he left his bedroom, his phone rang again. He hesitated, knowing that Ivy had breakfast ready for him, but when he glanced at the window and saw Coach Walsh's name, he picked it up.

"Thomas, hope I'm not bothering you, but I thought I'd make one more stab at convincing you to come back and..."

"I don't need convincing, Coach. I'll be back."

Walsh exhaled a long sigh. "That's just great. Now, do I dare ask about Chloe? How is she, and any news on that front, about her possible return?"

"She's fine, and coming back Friday. We'll both be back on campus on Monday."

The relief in Coach's voice made Thomas smile to himself. "I'll see you Monday night at practice. And, Coach, thanks for giving me a second chance."

"Everyone deserves a second chance," Walsh replied. "I hope you both make the most of it.""

"We will." Thomas hung up, then allowed himself a chuckle. 'I hope you both make the most of it.' Typical teacher remark; the best of them cared about their students and they couldn't help saying things like that. It was in their blood.

~ * ~

Thomas dug into a hearty breakfast with real appreciation. Ivy shared his good news about Chloe's imminent return. She drank her coffee from a warped-looking mug that had been a product of a ceramics class she'd taken a few years ago. She freely admitted that the set of mugs she'd produced weren't market quality, but she didn't care. She'd made them, and she liked them.

She took a sip of coffee. "Do you have any plans for something to do with Chloe while she's here?"

He raised his own mug to her in a salute. "We're right on the same wave-length. I'd love to do something really special with her, something fun after all we've been through. Any ideas?"

"I certainly do." She leaned back in her chair and gazed at him with a small smile, as if she knew something he didn't. "Thomas, do you remember the year, you were about eight, I guess, when we visited my father's dairy farm up in Candia, and all the cousins from Bedford were there, too..."

A picture began to surface in his mind. He saw the simple white farmhouse, the red barns, his plain, kind-faced grandparents, and the memory of a wonderful adventure in the snow returned full-force.

"That would be perfect, absolutely perfect. But does anyone still do that, I mean with horses and all?"

"I know someone who does. I cut this out of the newspaper just in case." She slid a four inch square of newsprint across the table to him.

He picked up the ad. The black and white ink illustration at the top, done in a Currier and Ives sort of style, told the whole story.

"Perfect," he breathed, and leveled a grin at his grandmother. "This will make a New Englander out of her if nothing else ever does. I remember that as one of the best times in my life."

"Yeeesss..." she said, drawing out the word, with a repeat of her strange little smile. "And I know you'll enjoy it this time, too. It'll be just like the first time, all over again."

Twenty-one

Chloe looked out the window at the acres of trees, red barns sitting behind plain white farmhouses and the craggy, ice-blue mountains with snow-covered tops in the distance. At one point, a black horse stood by a fence which ran along the road, and Chloe asked Thomas to stop so she could take a picture. The horse whinnied, shook his mane and ventured closer to her as she positioned herself to get her shots. He stuck his head over the fence and tried to rub his nose on her sleeve. Chloe stroked his long face, and backed up a few steps to focus on him. Thomas wished he had his camera, so he could take a picture of her taking a picture of the horse. He remembered briefly that he'd left it in his desk in the dorm, and Dyfan had shown an interest in it. Well, he wouldn't worry about that today. This day was a gift for Chloe.

"Where are we going?"

Thomas laughed. "None of your business. You'll find out when we get there." He reached across the seat and squeezed her hand. He still felt giddy from the night of love-making they'd had the evening before. Ivy, conveniently, had something she just had to tell Russell in person, and no, a phone call wouldn't do at all, so they had the mobile home all to themselves for a few precious hours.

Chloe hadn't been hesitant about making love, and had not held back. There was something almost too-familiar about it, as if he already knew the curves of her body, and what caresses pleased her most. She clearly felt that, too, as she pleasured him, and her hands and mouth knew just what to do. When they finished, they lay together, complete in each other, and Thomas thought that another piece of the puzzle had been put into place, and it fit perfectly. It had briefly flicked through his mind what Ivy's journal had revealed, that they had known each other thousands of years ago, but that seemed like such an improbable theory. Really, how could that be true?

The landscape flew by, bare-limbed trees mingled with dark green firs and blue spruce, dark against the pristine snow. They passed by a picturesque old mill, complete with an antiquated water wheel. The pond, once used for its water power, was frozen over, and half a dozen skaters flew in rhythmic circles over its icy surface.

"Oh, Thomas, please stop. I want a picture of this, too."

"Okay, but you'll have to hurry, and we can't stop any more. We have to get where we're going at a scheduled time."

She raised her eyebrows. "Oh, you didn't tell me that." She hopped out and took several pictures, not taking time to get shots from different angles, then returned to the car.

"Okay, I promise, no more until we're on our way home." She looked around as he started the car up again. "It's just so beautiful, and all these little scenes are like pictures from a hundred years ago."

He nodded. "Parts of New England are like that. The old buildings, the stone fences along the roads, the covered bridges...the past is with us all the time here."

"Covered bridges?" she gasped. "Are you kidding? I thought they were just pictures on calendars."

He laughed and squeezed her hand again. "Nope. We have them. A number of them, in fact."

She sighed and leaned back against the seat. "This is just so perfect. You and I and this amazing country scenery. I don't know how it could get any better."

Thomas didn't think it could get any better, either, and he pushed away the shadow that edged into his mind like a warning.

He smiled as he took a left off the main road, onto a much narrower stretch that looked as if it had been recently plowed. It led up a hill, around a corner and through a stretch of woods. Thomas slowed as the farm buildings came into view.

Chloe sat up, staring at the red barn with a silo, the white farmhouse with its green shutters, and another barn, gray with a wide ramp leading up to its open double doors.

A wagon filled with hay stood outside. An unpainted fence made of wooden posts and barbed wire, stretched back into an unending expanse of snow. Beyond that lay the woods.

The farmer, wearing a heavy black and red checked shirt and a knit cap, came out of the barn and waved at them.

Thomas turned to Chloe and gave her a big grin, as he drew on his fleece-lined gloves. "Put your mittens back on. We're here. Let's go meet Mr. Billings."

Jason Billings looked as if he'd always been the age he was then. It was hard to tell whether he was forty or seventy. He had a kind, weathered face, etched with deep wrinkles, but the lines around his eyes and mouth looked as if they'd been made with smiles.

"Ready?" A slow grin crossed his face. "Willard's bringing the horses out now."

True to his word, a younger version of Jason appeared, leading two horses, one chestnut, one gray, wearing thick leather harnesses.

Chloe gasped. "I can't ride a horse, Thomas. I've never even been on one."

Jason chuckled. "Don't worry, young lady. You're riding in that."

Chloe turned and looked wide-eyed at the wagon with its load of hay. Willard led the horses to the front and positioned them between the long wooden shafts attached to the wagon. With practiced hands, he girded the horses around their middles, and fastened the belts to the shafts. When the horses were hitched, they stamped their feet and tossed their manes, blowing through their noses, impatient to get going.

Willard slapped the gray horse on his neck, and glanced back at Jason. "You driving, Pop?"

The older man nodded. "Yep. Gonna do this trip myself. You can get Mac to help with the milking."

Jason stomped through the snow to the wagon, unfastened the back panel, and let it down. He gestured to Thomas and Chloe. "Okay, let's get you in here." He put his hands together to make a stirrup for Chloe's foot.

Thomas jumped in by himself, then turned and held his hands out to Chloe, and pulled her up onto the surface of the hay. They fell back into it, laughing.

Chloe started to sit up, but Thomas pulled her back down beside him. "Let's just lie here and enjoy the ride. The sky is blue just for us today."

"Giddyap!" Jason yelled, and the horses moved off, bumping over the uneven ground until they hit the road.

Chloe sighed. "Oh, this is perfect. The hay is softer than I would have imagined, and it smells good, too—so sweet and fresh. This is like being alive in a Christmas card."

Thomas raised himself up on his elbows, leaned over and planted a hearty kiss on her mouth. "This is a special New England event, just for you."

Lulled by the steady clip clop of the horses' hooves and the rhythm of the wagon, Thomas allowed his thoughts to roam as he stared up through the road's overhanging branches, crested with snow, at the clear sky above. He barely noticed when they turned off the road and entered the woods, but Chloe gave a little cry and bolted to a sitting position. "Thomas—why are we going off into the woods?"

He sat up, puzzled by her reaction. 'What—why are you afraid of the woods?"

He threw his arms around her as he remembered. "Oh, Chloe—of course, I should have told you. There's no reason to be afraid. This is a *good* thing, not like what happened with—uh, the Druids." He hated saying their name.

He rubbed her back, trying to control her trembling. "You have to trust me, Chloe. This trip is nothing like that."

Little by little she appeared to relax, but he kept his arm around her. He sensed her deepening fear, however, as they went farther and farther into the woods. Her face tightened, and her wide eyes glazed over. She clung to him.

"We're not getting out of the wagon, are we?" she asked. "I don't want to get out."

"Hey." He tipped her chin up so she had to meet his eyes. "Remember what you told me over the phone—that you're angry about how they tried to control us, and how we'd never let that happen again? You can't get all freaked out just because we're in the woods."

"I'm not getting out of the wagon," she repeated, and folded her arms in front of her.

"Whoa!" Jason pulled on the reins and the horses snorted to a stop. He turned around to grin at them. "Here we are. Everybody out."

"No," Chloe said. "Whatever you're going to do, I'll just wait here." She turned and stared at the small wooden building they had pulled up behind. "What's that?"

Thomas sighed. This was not going well, and he was afraid that all his hopes for this special surprise were going down the drain. "It's a sugar shack. It's where maple syrup and maple sugar is made."

Chloe's eyes appraised the shack, then shifted to the open fire, built on a pile of gray stones. A man in a thick denim jacket stirred something in a huge metal tub. He looked up and waved. "Hi, Jason. Just about ready."

Chloe squinted her eyes at him. "And what's he doing?"

"Cooking the syrup to a stage where it can be made into sugar or candy."

Jason jumped down from his perch at the front of the wagon, and lifted a green cooler from the space behind the seat. "Okay, I'll just get this all set up for you."

Thomas hoped his actions would reassure Chloe. The farmer tramped through the knee-high snow to a weathered wooden table twenty feet away. He set the cooler on one of the benches, opened it and took out a small whiskbroom. He swept the snow from the top of the table, and took a red and white checked oilcloth from the chest, which he spread over the table.

Chloe looked on, and Thomas watched her tension dissolve as Jake set the table with white plates, red napkins, plastic tableware and set a green bottle of wine in the center. She giggled and clapped her hands in glee. "We're having a picnic in the snow?"

"We are. Will you get out of the wagon now, and come with me for lunch?"

She looked over at the table and back, and at Thomas and nodded.

Jason placed a couple of covered dishes on the table. He swept snow from the benches and gestured to them. "Alrighty—soup's on."

Thomas unfastened the back of the wagon from the inside, slid down and held his hands out for Chloe. He helped her wade through the snow, and by the time they reached the table, she was laughing and her face glowed with pleasure.

Jason stomped away through the snow and disappeared into the shack.

Thomas uncorked the wine and poured it into the plastic glasses. He lifted his toward her, and she raised hers to meet it. "Here's to us, and a beautiful future."

She smiled, making his desire for her rise, as she responded. "To us."

The covered dishes revealed typical picnic fare: hamburgers and buns, wrapped in foil and still hot, potato salad, hot spiced apples, pickles, olives and potato chips.

"The farmer arranges all this, the hayride, the lunch, and everything?"

He nodded, basking in her enjoyment. He answered all her questions about the production of maple syrup, pointing out trees that had buckets attached to them.

When they finished eating, Chloe wiped her mouth with a paper napkin. "What's for dessert?"

"Just you wait and see."

Right on cue, Jason came out of the sugar shack. He carried a saucepan which was steaming, and had a wooden spoon sticking out of it. He placed it on the table, along with two clean plastic forks. A light, sweet fragrance filled the air. "There it is. Help yourself. More if you want it."

Chloe, looking puzzled, peered into the pan. "Oh, it smells wonderful—but what do we do with it?"

Thomas stood and put one of his gloves on. He picked up the pan, and motioned to her with his other hand. "C'mon. Bring the forks. This is where the good stuff happens."

He didn't need to go far to find a spot where the snow lay pristine as a cloud. Chloe watched, her eyes wide, as he used the wooden spoon to drip circles of maple syrup onto the snow. Before their eyes, it hardened into soft golden puddles.

Thomas speared one of the syrup candies with a fork and held it out to her. "This is what we natives call 'sugar on snow.' Try it."

He watched as she raised it to her lips and took a tentative nibble. An expression of delight crossed her face, and she ate the rest of it. "Oh, Thomas, this is divine. How come I never knew about this?"

"Probably because you have oranges, cotton and sugar, and an ocean in Florida, and not much snow," he replied, grinning at her. He speared a golden morsel for himself. It was just right—cooled off just enough so that it was still warm and soft.

Chloe helped herself to another piece, and ate it. "Oh, Thomas, I think I've died and gone to heaven. I've never had such a perfect day." She leaned over and kissed him, and he tasted the sweetness on her lips. "Thank you," she whispered. "This is an experience I'll never forget."

As they climbed back into the wagon, a light, fluffy snow began to fall. Thomas showed her how to dig herself a nest in the hay, and they snuggled next to each other, holding hands and exchanging kisses as they rode back to the farm on one of New Hampshire's most perfect late winter days.

"Back to school tomorrow," Chloe whispered. "Will we be okay, Thomas?"

He put his arms around her and drew her close. "Whatever happens, we'll face it together, and I promise, Chloe, I promise I'll protect you this time."

His words echoed in his head almost before he'd finished speaking them.

This time? What did he mean, this time?

Twenty-two

"It's perfect, just perfect." Chloe took off her jacket, threw it on a chair and hugged herself, as she looked around the tiny third-floor apartment.

"It is small." Thomas dropped the suitcases on the floor. "Do you have everything from the dorm room, or do you have to go back there?"

"It's cozy, and yes, I have everything from the dorm. They assigned Hannah a new roomie already."

"I'll go back to the car and get the laptops and whatever else is in the trunk."

She raised herself up on her toes and planted a soft kiss on his chin. He grinned as she rubbed a smear of lipstick off with a finger. "Okay, but hurry back. I want to make sure we christen our new apartment in our own special way."

"And that would—oh." He caught her meaning. "In that case, I'll run all the way to the car, and all the way back upstairs."

She laughed, and called after him, "Don't forget Ivy's brownies."

When the door closed behind him, she went into the kitchen. She'd carried up a couple six-packs of beer, along with the picnic basket containing dinner which Sharon had packed for them. She put the drinks and supper things into the empty refrigerator. Two cabinets over a short counter held an assortment of dishes and glasses, and a door next to the dishwasher revealed a few ill-matching pots and pans.

"It'll do," she murmured to herself. "It's not like I'm a gourmet cook, or that we'll be entertaining the garden club."

She took a few steps to look out the dormer window over the sink. It was framed with white eyelet curtains, and she guessed the third floor of the pale green Victorian house had once held bedrooms. Outside, the street lay quiet in the snow, a few cars parked along the sides. The taller buildings of the Midstate campus showed gray and tan through the bare branches of trees lining the street. She turned and went back into the tiny living room, which consisted of a worn green sofa, two plaid chairs, and a TV stand with a small, old TV. A desk sat against one wall, with built-in bookshelves over it. A painted white radiator hissed in a corner. Her eyes roved the room, as she wondered where she could hang her Mystery Hill painting.

The bedroom turned out to be the largest of the three rooms, with blue flowered wallpaper, and an ornate, old-fashioned brass bed. She went on to inspect the bathroom, which had a claw tub with an attached shower. She looked around and laughed out loud. There was actually a second desk against the opposite wall, with a dangling cable cord and outlets. One of them would have to set up their computer in the bathroom and work from there.

Still giggling, she retrieved the sheets Thomas' mother had sent with them, and began to make the bed. Sharon had also contributed several blankets and a quilt Ivy had made in the one quilting class she had taken. The stitching was haphazard, and the fabric patterns didn't meet in quite the right places. Ivy said that quilting and knitting just 'weren't her thing.' They took too much time and patience, and she didn't have a lot of either.

Chloe had just patted the quilt into place when she heard the front door open. She turned and hurried into the living room to help Thomas.

"Hi," Gaia said. "Hannah told me you were back, and where you were." In her arms she carried a good-sized box of groceries from Thomas' car. "I ran into Thomas downstairs."

She didn't wait to be invited in. She brushed past Chloe, took the box into the kitchen and set it on the counter. Returning to the living room, she took off her jacket and planted herself on the edge of one of the plaid chairs.

Before Chloe could answer, Thomas burst through the door, loaded with bags and suitcases. He shot her a look that plainly said he wasn't thrilled Gaia was there.

He set everything on the floor and turned to Gaia. "Thanks for your help. "We'll probably run into you around campus."

Gaia ignored his obvious hint to leave. "Hey, I haven't seen my best friend since the start of the new semester. I need to catch up on everything."

Thomas tried again. "We're a little busy right now. Both of us missed a couple weeks of school, and we have a lot of catching up to do ourselves, getting this place organized and all. We'll have to socialize some other time."

Gaia assumed her old, playful manner. "What—you don't have time for a glass of wine with an old friend? When did things get to be more important than people, Thomas?"

Chloe gave in. Gaia had been her best friend since the start of her freshman year. Maybe they could start over, be friends again without all the complications that the Druids brought to their relationship.

"She's right, Thomas. We can take a little time off. Wine or beer, Gaia?"

"Beer's fine. Less trouble."

Chloe nodded and went into the kitchen. She took three beer cans from the six-pack, and grabbed a bag of corn chips from the bag on the counter. As she dumped them into a blue bowl from the cupboard, she felt Thomas come up behind her.

"I'll take the beer," he said, loud enough to be heard in the next room. Leaning down, he whispered in Chloe's ear, "Remember what Ivy taught us. If she talks about what we're going to do, or how we feel, don't make eye contact with her. If I think she's trying to get to you, I'll interrupt her."

Chloe nodded. Together they went back to join Gaia.

Gaia acted her old disarming, charming self, and Chloe began to feel nostalgic for their old closeness. Maybe Gaia didn't intend to try to mess with their minds again. Maybe a lot of what happened before was just her own imagination. After all, anyone could break a cord by mistake and get lost in the snowy New Hampshire woods, especially if you weren't used to snow and cold. Lulled by the beer and the warmth of the apartment, she began to relax.

Gaia had her laughing about her adventures with her family at Christmas and semester break. "And my mother!" She rolled her eyes. "She heard someplace that shepherd's pie was delicious, so she ordered one made at the local supermarket. She put it in the fridge, never took it out of the box until we were ready for dessert..."

Even Thomas managed a slight smile at that.

"But we did have the ice cream she was going to serve with it."

Thomas' cell phone rang and he glanced at the window. "It's Coach Walsh. I'll go in the bedroom and talk to him." He threw Chloe a look. "I'll be right back."

The tone of Gaia's voice changed. "I was so sad to hear about your mother, Chloe. How are you feeling about all that now?"

"It's hard," Chloe admitted, feeling her eyes grow teary. "We were never really close, but nobody wants to lose one's mother."

Gaia's big blue eyes fixed on hers with warmth and sympathy. "Well, that's where friends come in. And I am your friend, Chloe. You do believe that, don't you?"

If she tries to get to your emotions, don't look directly at her. That's how they plant their suggestions. That's how they try to control you.

Ivy's warning flashed through her mind, but she already found she couldn't look away. She heard Gaia repeat the question. "You do know I'm your friend, don't you. Chloe?"

Thomas intervened, as he walked between Chloe and Gaia, breaking Gaia's lock on her eyes. He perched on the arm of Chloe's chair and put his arm around her. "Gaia, we really have a lot to do before we start classes again tomorrow."

Chloe caught the fire in both pairs of eyes as they exchanged glances. Gaia slowly rose. "Okay. May I ask, are you coming to the next Druid meeting? It'll be Friday night." She laughed and attempted to end on a lighter note. "Same place, same time."

Thomas was abrupt. "Don't count on us."

Gaia gave him a long, cold stare before she turned back to Chloe. "Well, honey, I'll see you on campus. Maybe we can hang out in the caf for lunch, if your jailer here will let you."

Chloe gasped. "He's not my jailer, Gaia. He just doesn't trust Dyfan, and after what happened last time..."

"What happened last time was a test of trust." Gaia's voice dropped ten degrees. "You're both part of the group now. It's a sacred honor, and you can't just back out."

Thomas matched the chill in her voice as he said "We have no obligation to the Druids. We won't be there."

Gaia threw her jacket over her arm, squared her shoulders and strode to the door. Before she left, she turned back and faced them. "You don't own her, Thomas. We need Chloe in the group, and we're going to have her."

~ * ~

"Are you okay, Chloe?"

She lifted her chin and looked into his eyes. "Oh, I'm more than all right. I'm absolutely furious that she tried that on me. At first, I thought she was the old Gaia I used to know, that we could be friends again, but it's not going to be like that, is it?"

His expression was grim. "No, it isn't. We're going to have to avoid them like the plague.

She nodded. "She almost did it again, didn't she? I let my guard down and she messed with my mind again. Thank God you came back into the room when you did."

Thomas rubbed the back of her neck. "Let's call that a rehearsal. Now you know. You can't get emotional around them, 'cause that's when they see an opening."

"I think I've learned that tonight." She stood up. "C'mon. Let's get everything put away and find what we need for class tomorrow.

"Do you have all the art supplies you need?"

"I have my paints from last semester. If I need new materials, Professor Walsh will tell me, and I'll get them at the campus store."

Later on, with all their gear unpacked and put away, Chloe brought Sharon's prepared meal into the living room. She found a blue flowered plastic cloth in a kitchen drawer and spread it on the floor.

"Not as fancy as the sugar-on-snow picnic," she giggled, "but our first meal in our own place."

Thomas raised his glass of wine. "Thanks to Ivy for the wine and the glasses."

Chloe nodded. "She's something else. I love her. But— tonight, this is for us and to us. She clinked her glass with his.

Thomas helped himself to a piece of fried chicken. He gestured at the wall over the desk. "Do you like where I put your painting?"

"It's perfect. Do you want to use that desk, or the one in the bathroom?" She giggled again at the thought.

He laughed. "Which one do you want?"

She took a sip of her wine. "Call me crazy, but there's more space in the bathroom. I can actually set my easel up in there, and there's a cabinet for my supplies."

"It's yours then."

Later on, as she and Thomas lay in the old brass bed with Ivy's crazily-stitched quilt spread over them, Chloe felt safer and more loved than she could ever remember feeling in her life. The old radiator hissed as it breathed warmth into the night.

"Thomas..." she whispered, but there was no answer. She turned toward him and saw he'd already fallen asleep. She raised herself on one elbow to gaze at his face. She traced his cheek with a finger, but he didn't stir. She leaned over him and kissed the bruise on his forehead. "Thomas," she said again, but more just to say his name, not to wake him. She touched his lips with hers, then drew back, gazing at him. *Thomas, you sleep harder than anyone I ever knew. I wonder where you go when you're not with me.*

Twenty-three

Professor Walsh welcomed her back with a big, Irish grin. "Got your easel all set up for you." He patted the sturdy wooden structure. "Did you get your painting I sent with Thomas?"

"I did, thank you. It's already hanging on the wall." Chloe felt a little embarrassed as the eyes of the class searched her with curiosity. She slipped off her parka and dropped it on a chair until she could get set up. She looked around at the paintings her classmates had either carried over from the last semester, or new ones they had started. There were a few newcomers in the class, but most of last semester's students had returned for the second half of the year.

Several greeted her with waves and smiles, and Ingrid ran over to give her a swift hug, but didn't linger to talk, as Walsh showed no sign of leaving.

"So what's next on your agenda?"

Chloe, feeling flustered, wished he'd go tend to the other students, but she pulled out the photos she'd taken on the sugar-on-snow trip, and spread them out on the table for him to see.

He sorted through them, muttering "hhhmm, mmmmmmm," and "huh!" as he took his time looking at each one. He laid them back on the table. "So which one do you want to work from?"

She held up one of the pictures she'd taken of the skaters on the pond. "This one?" she asked, looking for his approval.

His brown eyes crinkled as he looked at her. "So you want to be Grandma Moses now?"

She didn't know whether he was joking or not. "Is that too corny, is that what you mean?"

He laughed and clapped her on the shoulder. "Do what you want, Chloe. I'll be back later to see how you handle the subject." He strolled off in the direction of Ingrid and Jeb, who had set their easels up near each other by the bank of windows on the far side of the room. They broke off their whispering as Walsh approached them.

Chloe stared at the back of Jeb's canvas, and she wondered what he was working on. Mr. Walsh stood with his weight on one leg and his chin in his hand, as he gazed at Jeb's endeavor without any expression of either approval or disapproval.

Chloe lost herself in her work, and when she finally checked her watch, saw that an hour and a half had gone by. She glanced over at Ingrid, and decided to ask her to take a break and get a Coke or coffee from the machine down the hall.

"Hey," she said, as she invaded her and Jeb's territory. "Need a break? I do."

"Sure." Ingrid stuck her brush in the water jar and gave it a swish.

"Not me," Jeb said. Chloe winced at the squeaky voice, which suddenly brought back a lot of unpleasant memories. She turned slightly to get a better look at what he was painting, and saw, with a jolt shooting all through her, that his new painting was of the Druids' Stonehenge site. The flat, stone altar, complete with pan with glowing coals, took center stage on the canvas, ringed with smaller stones, and trees in the background. At one side, a white-robed figure stood like a ghost between two dark, twisted trees. Chloe shivered and turned away. That was the last thing she wanted to see.

Ingrid's canvas seemed to be a blur of soft colors: blue, gray, purple. She couldn't see any picture forming there.

Around the corner from the refreshment machines, there was an alcove with worn leather furniture where students often lounged between classes. Her Coke in hand, Chloe wandered over to look out into the sculpture garden. Ingrid, with her paper cup of steaming coffee, followed, and carefully took a seat on one of the couches.

Chloe sighed. "It's snowing again. "Does spring ever come around here?"

"Not for another month or two. This is spring compared to Norway."

Chloe laughed, turned and joined Ingrid on the sofa. She paused, then flipped the tab on her soda can and took a sip. She wanted to comment about Jeb's painting, but she didn't know how buddy-buddy Ingrid and Jeb might have become in her absence.

It seemed Ingrid had read her mind. "Isn't Jeb's painting wonderful? I think it's the best thing he's ever done. It really brings out all the mystical feeling you get at a Druid meeting, don't you think?"

Chloe could hardly believe her ears. However, she didn't want to alienate Ingrid, who was the only friend she had in the class. She thought before she spoke, carefully choosing her words. "It certainly does capture the essence of the place."

"Yes, it does, and I'm trying to paint an abstract, which will represent the *feelings* of being there."

Chloe felt at a loss for words. She wondered if Ingrid had completely gone over the edge. "What feelings are those?" she asked.

Ingrid's voice rose with animation. "Peace, unity, oneness with nature. Didn't you feel those things, Chloe?"

Chloe couldn't stand it any longer. Obviously the group had brainwashed this beautiful girl. "Ingrid, don't you remember the last time? Dyfan cut all our cords, and I got lost in the snow, and would have died if Thomas hadn't found me in time."

To her amazement, Ingrid laughed. "Oh, I don't think so, Chloe. It was a test of faith, and Dyfan knew where you were every second. He never would have let anything happen to you."

Chloe's throat tightened. "Don't you realize what they're doing to you, to everyone in that group? They're taking your free will away..."

Ingrid sounded incredulous. "Now, Chloe, how could they possibly do that? Just because you had a bad experience last time doesn't mean..."

Chloe jumped to her feet and faced the other girl. "Ingrid, I mean it. Dyfan, and some of the others, Jett and Gaia, have some sort of psychic power. They're somehow able to take over your mind, and make you think things that just aren't so. You're crazy if you ever go back there. They'll ruin your life."

A shadow flicked over Ingrid's face, and she shook her head. "Now, why would they do that? That doesn't make any sense at all."

"For their own purposes, whatever they are. Listen to me, Ingrid. Thomas and I have experienced it."

Ingrid's voice turned cold. "Maybe Thomas is the one who's taken over your mind. Did you ever think of it that way?"

"Thomas is the one who saved my life."

Ingrid reached out and laid a hand on Chloe's arm. In a softer tone, she continued. "I heard about your mother, and I'm so sorry. But being with the Druids could ease your pain, bring you peace. You'll find that out Friday night at the meeting. Let Dyfan bring you comfort."

"No way!" Chloe turned away, knowing Ingrid was lost to her words. "I'm not going Friday, and I'm never going again. Neither is Thomas. And you shouldn't either. Ingrid, I'm begging you, listen to me."

A slight sound behind her made her turn.

Jeb stood behind her, a grin spread over his weasel-like face.

"What do you want?"

"Just happened to overhear what you and Ingrid were talking about." His narrow green eyes flicked over her, head to toe. "Don't you know you can't leave the group now? You belong to us, and you always will."

Chloe tossed her Coke into the trash container. The dark liquid splashed up over the side. "Don't count on it." She wheeled around and fled back to the classroom.

~ * ~

Too upset to continue painting, Chloe put away her supplies and stored her barely-begun painting in the slatted cupboard where the students left their unfinished work. Mr.

Walsh, his back toward her as he talked with another student, didn't notice as she left.

Her next class didn't begin until after lunch. She wondered whether to run back to the apartment and wait there, or to bide her time in the dining hall. She opted for that, as it was close to Hopper Hall, where her archeology elective was scheduled. Ancient cultures, famous buildings, history, she knew she'd enjoy learning about all that.

As she entered the caf, shivering not only from the cold, but from her conversations with Ingrid and Jeb, she spied Marcy Hughes, captain of the cheerleaders, sitting alone at a table in a corner. Chloe wondered where her usual entourage was, but glad to see her, made her way across the floor to where Marcy sat.

"Hi," she said, dropping her backpack on the floor. "Mind if I join you?"

Marcy looked up with a look of surprise, but flashed Chloe a smile. "Oh, I'm so glad to see you back. Yes, sit down. You are coming back to cheerleading, right? We really need you to hold up your end of the pyramid."

Chloe laughed, feeling her heart lighten. "Yes, I plan on coming to practice tonight. I'm glad you'll take me back, after I ran off like that."

"Desperate times call for desperate measures," Marcy cracked, and Chloe couldn't help but laugh.

Chloe sat down. "One thing I noticed from the email I got. You changed the time of practice to mesh with basketball practice. That's really good for me, because Thomas..."

"Yes, I know," Marcy interrupted. "You and Thomas, joined at the hip."

Chloe raised one shoulder. "Well, Marcy, it works for us." She stood and looked over at the serving line. "What's good today?"

Marcy gestured to her own empty plate. "Pizza, what else?"

As the eleven o'clock class ended, several other members of the squad joined them. "Hi, Traci, Sonya, Jackie."

They returned her greetings, and she wondered briefly why she had never tried to get to know any of them better. All her time last year had been spent with Gaia, who was not on the squad, and this year, with Thomas. These girls would certainly be better friends than the Druids, and she made a silent resolution to cultivate their friendship.

A few minutes before one, the group broke up and scattered toward their afternoon classes. Chloe shrugged into her parka, picked up her backpack and started toward the door.

"Hey, Chloe." A familiar voice stopped her.

She turned and smiled at the sight of her former roommate. "Hey, Hannah. How's everything?"

Hannah grinned. "Okay, I guess. I miss you, though. They assigned me a new roomie, and she talks all the time, never shuts up. It's hard to get anything done with her around."

Chloe laughed. "I'm sorry, Hannah, but I really couldn't stay in the dorm."

"Well, Gaia misses you...that I know for sure. I told her where you'd gone, but I thought it was weird that she didn't know. Aren't you two best buds?"

Chloe hesitated, not knowing how to answer. After a moment, she decided to be honest. "Look, Hannah, things happened between Gaia and me, and I don't feel that comfortable with her anymore. Please don't tell her anything about me from now on, okay?"

"Oh, I didn't know that. Sure, I'll keep things to myself from now on, if I know anything, that is. What's your next class?"

"Intro to Archeology, Hopper Hall. I'm sort of late already, and I hear Miss Myers is a stickler for punctuality."

Hannah's face lit up. "Hey, that's my class, too. Come on, we'll sit together."

They hurried toward the red brick building, chatting and laughing, ran up the stairs to the second floor, and arrived at the room, out of breath.

The class, already seated, talked quietly among themselves. Some had their eyes fastened on their new instructor, no doubt assessing their chances for an easy A. A tall, woman with auburn hair, probably in her mid-forties, wearing a tailored gray suit, she shuffled papers at the desk in the front of the room. She didn't look like the easy-A type.

"Sorry," Chloe apologized, as they approached the desk.

Professor Myers glanced up at them and gave them what might have passed for a tight-lipped smile. "Chloe McAllister, I assume? And Hannah Stuart?" She motioned toward her green gradebook. "I have everyone else checked off. Full class this semester."

A few students looked up.

"Girls, find a seat so we can begin. You're late."

Chloe's eyes scanned the classroom, but she didn't see two seats together. Hannah, with an apologetic smile, slid into a chair in the first row, leaving Chloe on her own.

"We're just about to start a power point presentation," Miss Myers said, with an edge to her voice. "Please find a seat."

Chloe, embarrassed, nodded and looked around the room, looking for a vacant seat, and not focusing on the faces of her classmates.

She saw an empty chair near the back of the room and started toward it. As she edged down the aisle, she stumbled over a book that had fallen on the floor. She lost her balance and fell against a short, stocky dark-haired boy sitting there.

"Whoa!" He exclaimed, putting out an arm to steady her. "I guess you're not a ballet dancer, are you."

Several girls giggled, and she felt the boys' eyes on her, appraising her.

Miss Myers was not amused. "Miss McAllister, would you *please* find a seat. You're holding up the class." She flicked off the lights, and the first picture filled the screen at the front of the room.

Flustered and embarrassed, Chloe's hair fell over her eyes, obscuring most of the rest of her vision. She stumbled her way down the aisle, not looking at anyone, and sank into a chair, wishing herself invisible. She fumbled to set up her laptop in order to take notes.

Miss Myers began to speak, extolling the wonders of the Parthenon, but all Chloe heard was the softer, and very familiar voice from the seat behind her.

Gaia sounded amused.

"Hi, Chloe. I guess we have a class together."

Twenty-four

Thomas couldn't help but admire Chloe's show of strength and resolve. He'd suggested that she see her advisor, and get out of the archeology class, substitute another elective or switch to another section, but she refused.

"I'm really interested in this, Thomas, and Professor Myers is a bit testy, but I've heard she's the best. After I got into it, the first class was fascinating. She really knows her stuff."

"What about Gaia? She's never going to give you a moment's peace."

She straightened her shoulders. "I have to sit near her, but I won't talk to her. That class is only an hour long. I'll just be in and out." She looked up from her textbook and he read the determination on her face. "And besides, I'm not going to let her, or the rest of them push me around or make my decisions for me."

Thomas found it hard to fend off his feelings of misgiving, but as the week went on, Chloe seemed to be handling things just fine. They went to practice together, as the team and the squad met at the same time, in adjoining gyms. He felt considerable relief knowing she was right next door, and safe. After practice they walked back to the apartment together, sharing stories about their day.

At home, they were comfortable with each other. His parents called often, wanting to know how everything was. Mike called to complain about his parents, school, and girls in general. Ivy phoned to check in and she always asked to speak to Chloe. It got to be a joke, as Thomas told her, "Just a sec. She's in the bathroom."

"Ivy's going to think I have a problem," Chloe said, swatting at Thomas playfully. "Every time she calls I'm in the bathroom. Who's going to believe my desk and all my art supplies are in there because there's no room anywhere else?'

Jett called several times, leaving messages about the Druids' meeting on Friday, but Thomas refused to take his calls, and deleted the messages and texts as soon as they appeared.

By Thursday night, everything seemed to be under control. He and Chloe had established a routine that worked for both of them. But the nights were the best, he thought contentedly, as they lay in bed, his arm around her, her head on his chest. He loved the feel of her skin, the soft texture of her hair as it brushed against him. He treasured the delicate, lilac scent of her.

Friday morning, as he shaved and Chloe showered, Gaia's angry last words—hurled at him as she'd left their apartment, made their way into his mind. 'We need her in the group, and we're going to have her.' And, what did she mean, *need*?

Thomas tried to shrug it off. There was a home basketball game that night, and Chloe would be cheerleading. With hundreds of people watching, there was no way they could get at her. As soon as the game concluded, he would meet her and they would go out with friends to celebrate the outcome of the game, whatever it was.

They stopped to say goodbye for the day outside the art complex. "Our schedules don't mesh at all today, so I won't see you until game time." He folded her into his arms. "You take care, okay?"

She pulled back and laughed up at him. "What, you think evil spirits are going to whisk me away or something?"

He wished she hadn't phrased it that way, but again he pushed back his negative thoughts. "Don't talk to Gaia, don't talk to Jett, stay with other people at all times."

She shook her head. "Thomas, I'm a big girl. I can take care of myself." She raised herself on tiptoe and planted a kiss on his mouth. "I'll see you tonight." She shifted her books and the wooden case that held her paints, flashed him a grin, and walked up the path toward the building.

Thomas watched her go in, watched the door swing shut behind her; sighing, he headed for his nine o'clock class.

~ * ~

Strange nervous little feelings needled him all day long. He found it hard to concentrate on the lectures. His notes, when he reviewed them, didn't make sense. He found it impossible to sit around and chat with other students between classes, and paced the halls like an expectant father.

As he passed half a dozen students lounging outside one of the classrooms, a girl's voice called out to him. "Hey, Thomas. Big game tonight. Are we gonna win it?"

He stopped and looked at her without seeing her. "Oh, some team from Connecticut. They could give us a tough time. They're pretty good."

Some guy jabbed him in the elbow. "Is that why you're so uptight? They're not Uconn, so I wouldn't worry about it."

Everyone laughed, and someone added, "Good thing it isn't, that's for sure."

"Good advice," Thomas muttered, but still seemed unable to relax. He knew it wasn't the outcome of the game that bothered him.

After his last class of the day, he grabbed a sandwich and a soda at the caf, then headed for the gym.

A few of the players were already there, running around the gym, working off their excess energy. Thomas joined them, and for a while his concentration on making shots and eluding guards seemed to lessen some of his anxiety.

Excited students from both schools began to arrive, and Thomas joined the rest of his team in the dressing room. He got into his uniform, green and white with the Midstate logo, and settled back on the bench to listen to their pep talk from Coach Walsh.

When they filed out onto the court, he saw Chloe immediately. She looked great, as usual, in her skimpy skirt and halter top, her hair tied up in a ponytail. His anxiety melted away. He was here, she was here, and he was ready for the game.

At the half, the Midstate Elk led 32 to 28. It wasn't a huge lead, but they had played a fast, close game, and Coach Walsh seemed pleased with their performance. Thomas had made several successful foul shots and two three-point baskets.

Walsh clapped him on the shoulder. "Good job, Thorn. Keep it up and we'll walk away with this one."

Thomas wiped the sweat from his brow and grinned at the coach. "Thanks. It feels good to be back."

"And good to have you," Walsh replied, and went off to talk with someone else.

They went on to win the game, 72 to 51. It was a satisfying victory. Thomas showered, bantering with the other guys, feeling good all over. He had done well. He couldn't wait to be with Chloe, see her, hold her, share his feelings of elation.

"We'll meet you at the Elk Horn," he promised his teammates.

He bounded across the court to the cheerleaders' dressing room on the other side of the gym. He met Marcy, coming out. "Hi. Great game," she said, flashing him a big smile, which then turned an expression of surprise. "Hey, are you okay? That girl from Chloe's art class, Ingrid, said…"

He froze. " Ingrid? Why was she here? Is Chloe dressed yet?"

"Chloe? She went with Ingrid. She told Chloe you got into a fight, and…"

The reality of what he had feared all day hit him hard. He could hardly get the words out. "Where did she take her? Where did she say I was?"

"Out in the parking lot. Ingrid said you got into it with…"

Thomas never heard the rest. He raced outside. The student parking lot was mass disorder, with the yellow away-buses attempting to load and everyone else trying to beat the other cars out of the lot. In vain, the parking attendants tried to keep order, and Thomas didn't care that he added to the confusion. Horns blared, brakes squealed, and vehicles, refusing to slow down as he dashed in and out among the cars, splashed him with slush.

He shouted her name, over and over, "Chloe! Chloe!" but with all that was going on, who could hear him? As the lot began to empty, he stopped, out of breath, and leaned against a big black SUV, whose owners had not yet shown up. He let his head clear, and then he knew, as sure as he knew his own name, where she had gone.

The Druids had made good on their threat. Gaia had said they needed her, and for whatever reason that was, they had taken her.

He needed the car. He raced for home, but as he ran into the driveway, he saw with a sinking heart that they had outwitted him again. Both his back tires were flat, and the car sagged on its haunches like a tired gray mule.

Thomas fought for calm. He knew where they'd taken her, the Stonehenge site, of course. It was clear across town and a quarter mile into the woods. How was he going to get there without a car? Any friends he had on the team would have scattered by now, gone out to celebrate their victory, and the Elk Horn was several miles in the opposite direction. Where could he borrow a car?

Donna, the waitress from IHOP. The apartment she'd rented from Rogozzi was no more than a couple blocks away, around the corner. He had no guarantee she'd be there, and he didn't have her phone number, didn't even remember her last name. But, he had no other options he could think of. He started off, sprinting, running as fast as he could.

Out of breath, he arrived at the three story house, another old Victorian like the one he and Chloe lived in. Two cars occupied the driveway. He didn't know which apartment Donna rented, but he raced to the front door anyway and pounded on it. To his relief, she answered.

"Oh, hello...Thomas, isn't it? What's the matter? Come in." She backed up against the door and held it open, as she wiped her hands on a red-checked dish towel.

He bent over, gasping for breath and shook his head. "Donna, please, your car...? Mine has two flats, no time to get them fixed, my girlfriend's in trouble..."

"You want to borrow my car?"

"Yes. Please, Donna, it's an emergency."

He had no idea why she should trust him, except that he had shown an interest in her, had stopped to talk to her kids when he ran into her in his hometown, and he usually presented a calm façade, and now he was a mess. He struggled to control his breathing, as she threw him a concerned look and disappeared back into the house. In a few seconds she came back, and thrust a ring of keys at him.

He grabbed them. "Thanks, you don't know how much. Which car?"

"The blue one. I'm sorry it's so..."

"I don't know how to thank you," he called back to her, already running toward the vehicle.

He found the battered Carolla unlocked, and he jumped in. Much to his relief, it started right up. "Good girl," he muttered, and backed out of the driveway. He had one last glimpse of Donna, standing in her doorway, her hands clapped over her mouth as she watched him leave.

Twenty-five

After her initial struggles, Chloe, wedged in the back seat between Ingrid and Jett, forced herself to calm down and think about her situation. She wasn't scared as much as angry. Ingrid had told her Thomas was out in the parking lot, and hurt from a fight with another student. She thought her fellow art student was her friend. She hadn't asked any questions, just grabbed her jacket and left with Ingrid in a tearing hurry.

The minute she saw Gaia sitting behind the wheel with the motor running, she knew she'd been set up. Jett jumped out of the back seat, and he and Ingrid, who turned out to be surprisingly strong for a girl, forced her into the back seat. She fought and screamed, to no avail.

"Let me go! You have no right to do this. Leave me alone."

Ingrid leaned against her, pinning her against the seat. Jett laid a heavy hand on her knee.

"Thomas will come after me. You'll never get away with this. What kinds of friends do you call yourselves, anyway?"

"The best ones you've got," Gaia said from the front seat. She had parked close to the entrance of the lot, and they were one of the first cars out.

Chloe knew where they were going, of course—the Druids' meeting.

She took a deep breath, and tried to sound rational. "I really don't want to attend this meeting. Doesn't it mean anything to you that I don't want to go anymore?"

Gaia threw her a glance in the rear view mirror. "You're part of the group. We need you."

Her heartbeat picked up again. "You need me? What for?"

Ingrid circled her arm around Chloe's shoulders and gave her a hug. "Don't worry about anything, honey. We just want you to be part of our group. You complete the circle."

Chloe turned to her, forcing herself to stay calm. "Ingrid, they've brainwashed you. I thought you were my friend. How can you do this to me?"

"No, Chloe," Gaia said. "Thomas has brainwashed you. He has a bad spirit. But you are pure, Vala, and Dyfan wants you with us.

Vala—the sacrifice. But—they wouldn't, they couldn't. She shook herself mentally. That was a ridiculous thought in this day and age. Even Dyfan wasn't capable of that. She shot a glance out the car window. A few more minutes and they would be there. Maybe she should just give in for the evening, play the game, pretend to be part of the group, try to convince Gaia and the others that she they had changed her mind, and yes, she needed to be part of the group. Right now there was nowhere to run.

Thomas. She yearned for him. She concentrated as Ivy had taught her, pictured him in her mind, and sent him a message: *I'm okay, but I need your help. I'm at Stonehenge.* She pictured the rocks, the trees, Dyfan standing between them in his white robe, just like Jeb's painting.

Gaia parked the car in a little cove of trees and cut the engine. Ingrid opened the back seat door with one hand and gripped Chloe's arm hard with the other.

Chloe winced. "It's okay. Do you suppose I want to get lost in the woods again? Where do you think I would go?"

Ingrid let up a little, and Jett went around the back of the car and took Chloe's other hand in his. She wanted to pull away, but she didn't. It felt foreign, not like it belonged there, like Thomas' hand always did.

As they walked through the trees and into the clearing, she saw Dyfan standing in his usual spot. His dark stare held hers, and her fear took over, and she began to struggle against her captors. "No!" she shouted. "No!" She fought them with all her strength, but Ingrid and Jett dragged her forward.

Dyfan himself came forward and handed her a blue robe. His voice caressed her. "Vala. It is good to see you here."

Chloe looked around wildly. The group enclosed her, strange smiles on all their faces, and she realized there was no escape, at least not by force. She willed herself to stop trembling and calm down. She would have to use her brains to escape. Trying to avoid Dyfan's piercing stare, she nodded and kept her eyes down as she slipped the robe over her clothing. She fished the rope belt from a pocket and tied it loosely around her waist. She backed into the space where she usually stood. As she appeared to be more docile, Ingrid and Jett gradually loosened their grip on her arms.

The scene looked just like Jeb's painting. A large oval pan with handles on each side sat on the altar stone, and held a bed of coals which burned brightly against the darkness.

The moon, peeking through the heavy, overhanging branches of the trees, created eerie patterns on the snow.

Ingrid and Jett took positions on either side of her. She sensed their vigilance, ready to stop her if she were to make a break for it.

A sudden rustle in the woods attracted her attention. A young fawn, probably only days old, stood there, tethered to a rope tied around its neck and stretched between two trees. It trembled in terror, trying to break free, then stood, staring at the group with its huge, dark eyes.

"Oh, no!" Chloe couldn't hold back the words. She forgot not to look at Dyfan directly, as her eyes flew to his face. "You wouldn't—oh, you can't!"

The head Druid seemed amused. His gaze pierced hers, as he answered in a soft voice. "He is an acceptable sacrifice, Vala. Pain is part of the sacrifice."

"He's a *baby!*" She shrieked, as tears began to stream down her cheeks.

She heard snickers from others in the group, and Jeb let out his high, whiney laugh. She wiped her eyes with her sleeve.

Dyfan pinned her eyes with his. She felt something shift, just a little as she looked at him, and suddenly remembered what Ivy had told them. Don't look them directly in the eyes. Focus on some other part of the face, if you have to speak to the person. With an effort, she tore her gaze from him and fixed her eyes on his hair and the edge of his white hood.

The fawn gave a little bleat and jerked at the ropes, before giving up again. Chloe felt the bile rise in her throat as she watched him. She wondered if she could keep her dinner down. But it wasn't so much nausea she felt as it was pain, running all through her at the thought of killing this beautiful little animal.

Dyfan clasped his hands in front of him. "We will begin. We come in peace."

Chloe looked from Ingrid to Jett and back again, as they all repeated the greeting after their high priest. Were they really going to just stand there and let this happen?

Dyfan began to intone some sort of incantation. Chloe found she vaguely remembered it from other meetings. She had to press her lips together so as not to mouth the responses with the rest of the group. Again she tried to reach Thomas with her mind, picturing his face, trying to feel the security of his arms around her.

Why hadn't he come to rescue her? Had Jett and Gaia managed to do something to him to prevent him? Her distress grew, and she fought to keep control. Out of the corner of her eye she saw a flicker of something shiny. She moved her head ever so slightly so that she could see it. A huge knife lay on the altar, next to the pan of coals. It looked razor sharp. She also saw a silver chalice on the other side of the pan. For a minute, she thought she might faint. It took all her will power to steady herself against the dizziness that threatened to take over.

She felt Dyfan's eyes on her, so she began to mouth a few of the words here and there, pretending to be caught up in the ceremony. She lowered her head, letting the hood hide her face. Careful not to let on what she was really looking for, she stole glances around the circle. On the ground next to Jeb, she saw a branch which had broken off from a tree, lying on the ground between Dyfan and the fawn. The broken end was ragged and sharp, like a spear. And there was the knife and the pan of coals. If she could catch them off guard, if she could create some kind of diversion, and if she plotted every move in advance...

She noticed that the moon, which was full, sometimes disappeared behind a cloud. At those times, the night darkened around them. She decided to wait for the next time that happened, then make her move. She fixed the positions of the trees between her and the fawn in her mind, so she could get to the animal in the dark, when the moon cut off the light again.

Most of the Druids were not wearing mittens or gloves, as the night turned out to be a mild mid-winter evening. Chloe reached into her pocket and slipped her mittens back on. If she grabbed the handles of the hot pan, that would deflect some of the heat.

"It will be done," Dyfan intoned.

"It will be done," repeated his followers.

Dyfan began to walk toward her, intention in every step. He stopped at the altar, and picked up the knife. He held it up, letting the moonlight run across the sharp blade. He turned, and a cruel smile crossed his face. His voice, when he spoke to her, held an edge. Chloe sensed it was a warning not to defy him.

"You will make the first cut. We will share the blood of the sacrifice." He nodded toward the chalice, and held out the blade to her.

She staggered backward. "No, I can't, I won't."

The smile broadened. "Oh, I think you will."

Ingrid and Jett caught her arms as she attempted to back away. They forced her forward again, until she stood facing Dyfan.

"Take the knife, Vala."

Two things happened at once. She heard the screech of a car's brakes, and the group turned to look in that direction, and the moon obligingly ducked under a cloud, plunging the area into darkness. Chloe sprang forward, grabbed one handle of the pan of coals and swung it in an arc. The coals went flying, and the Druids screamed, not able to see what was happening. Several coals found their mark, and their robes caught fire. Others yelled and buried their faces in their hands as coals burned their flesh. Chloe swung the pan back and hit Dyfan in the head, hard. As he reeled backward, he dropped the blade on the altar. Chloe picked it up and raced toward the fawn. With one swift cut, she severed the rope around its neck. It bucked, tossing the rope into the snow, and disappeared into the darkness. She gripped the knife in her hand. She didn't want to hurt anyone, but she'd use it if she had to.

"It's Chloe! Get her!" she heard Dyfan scream.

Jeb threw himself at her. She lost her footing, and they both fell to the ground. She fought him, but he managed to drag her back into the circle, and wrenched the knife away from her. In the scuffle, she felt a stab of pain as the point scraped across the back of her hand. He yanked her to her feet, but she fumbled for the rock she had noticed earlier, picked it up and hurled it at him. It found its mark and he let go of her with a howl of pain, and fell to his knees in the snow.

Several other hands clawed at her, but with the limberness required of a cheerleader, she bent and picked up the club-like branch. She swung it, hitting anything in its path, and it found several targets. She recognized Jett's voice as he yelled in pain.

A flashlight pierced the darkness. She shielded her eyes, and raised the stick again as the light came toward her. "Chloe, stop—it's me."

Thomas grabbed her arm. She dropped the stick and clutched his hand. They dashed through the snow, and with the aid of the flashlight, he led her through the trees, and around the outside edge of the circle. Judging from the sounds she heard, and the brief glimpses of the Druids, some rolling in the snow to snuff out their burning robes, chaos reigned in the circle. At first, there seemed to be no one pursuing them, but as they emerged from the woods, breathing hard, she did hear shouts behind them, and running footsteps, and the breaking of small branches as their pursuers pounded after them.

Thomas clicked off the light and they raced for the car.

The car waited, its motor running.

"Get me the hell out of here!" Chloe yelled, as she jumped into the passenger seat.

Thomas grinned, but there was no humor in it. "With pleasure, my lady."

He had parked the car so it headed out toward the main drag. He threw it into gear, guided it over uneven ground, and onto the road. As Chloe let out a long sigh of relief, the clouds passed and the moon once again lit up the landscape.

He reached over and grabbed her hand. "You're bleeding." He dug a handkerchief from his pocket. "Wrap this around it 'til we can get help."

"It's nothing," she said, but she held the handkerchief to the back of her hand. "Oh, I was so scared, Thomas!" Only now that it was over and she was safe with him in the car, did she allow herself to feel relief and relax.

He flicked a glance at her, and she read the hint of admiration in his eyes. "You did great, Chloe. Wow!"

"Yeah, some knight in shining armor you are, Thomas. The dragon nearly got the princess this time around."

"Well, I did get here with the white horse," he retorted. "The prince ran into some obstacles."

"More like an old gray mare," Chloe said, patting the dashboard. "But all I want now is my canopy bed in the palace."

Thomas grinned again. "That wish, I can grant, baby."

Twenty-six

Dyfan rarely showed his anger. Gaia thought him the most controlled person she had ever met. Today, however, with one side of his face hosting a large, dark bruise, and a burn mark on his left hand, he seemed literally to seethe. Jett had never been assigned a new roommate, so the three of them met in his dorm room. Dyfan presided from the brown leather swivel chair at Jett's desk, while Jett took the absent roommate's chair, and Gaia sat on the floor up against the door, hugging her knees.

She worshipped Dyfan—there was just no other way to put it. She would die for him, any time, any day. If he asked her to jump off the campus bell tower, she would consider it a privilege. If he told her to walk into a fire, she would, without question. There was nothing she would not do for him, and included handing over her former best friend, for whatever purpose Dyfan required.

Jett seemed a little more reserved than usual, Gaia thought. She wished he'd get with the program. He even seemed to have trouble addressing Dyfan as 'Master,' which she did now, quite automatically. It even gave her a degree of comfort, a feeling of security, which she had never experienced. Dyfan was strong, he was in control, and as far as she was concerned, he was never wrong.

Dyfan glared at each of them in turn. "Needless to say, I am not pleased with the way things turned out Friday night."

Gaia covered her face with her hands. She couldn't bear his displeasure, she just couldn't, not for one minute.

Jett stuttered a protest. "It wasn't our fault, Dyfan. We had no way of knowing Chloe would pull a stunt like that. And we had no idea she and Thomas would go to the police and report us."

"What are you supposed to call me?" Dyfan's voice was almost a whisper.

"M-master."

Gaia peeked out from between her fingers to look at Jett as he spoke. "But she seemed to have adjusted to being at the meeting. I mean, she had calmed down and wasn't fighting us anymore. What could we have done?"

Dyfan stared at her coldly and didn't answer.

Her voice trembled. "And the cops just gave us a warning—they didn't take it seriously at all. Just a bunch of college kids on a lark."

Dyfan ignored her as he glared at Jett. "You could have kept your hands on her, and your senses alert. I've trained both of you to feel when someone is not one with our minds."

"She was saying the responses, Master." Jett attempted to defend himself.

"She was." Gaia gazed up at Dyfan, drinking in the features of his beautiful face. When he looked directly at her, she felt as if she were drowning in the depths of his dark, fathomless eyes.

Dyfan seemed to be weighing his answer. "That she was, but she's savvier than I thought. Or..." He tapped his forefinger against his lips before continuing. "Or someone has given her some resistance training."

Jett took a deep breath, as if gathering his courage. "I need to ask you, Master, you don't mean Chloe any harm, do you? I mean—you just want her to be part of our group, right?"

A small smile played around the edges of Dyfan's mouth. "Of course, Jett. I gave her the name Vala, which means sacrifice, but it's absolutely symbolic. However, we do need her to participate willingly, which she's not doing."

"And what do you have in mind for this 'symbolic sacrifice'?" Jett didn't sound convinced.

Dyfan's face reflected the displeasure he felt at Jett's doubt. He answered in slow, measured words. "A great ceremony at the end of the school year, and we'll do it at what they call America's Stonehenge, at Mystery Hill. Thomas' hometown. We just need to get her to cooperate so it will be perfect."

Gaia spoke up. "Maybe I could..."

Dyfan cut her off. "No, Gaia, you tried. It didn't work. I need to neutralize whoever is working with her against us. It might just be that grandmother of Thomas'—what's her name, Iris, Daisy or something like that?"

"Ivy." Jett turned around in his chair to open a drawer of the desk that had been Thomas'. He pulled out a camera, and held it out. "He never came back to get this. He told us there are pictures of the old bitch on it."

The head priest nodded and took the camera. He pressed the buttons until he found what he wanted. He held it out for Gaia and Jett to see. They nodded, and he turned the camera back and examined Ivy's face, looking as though he were memorizing every feature. "Not bad looking for an old lady," he observed. "She looks intelligent...and her eyes..."

Gaia jumped in. "What? What about her eyes?"

Dyfan pursed his lips and nodded his head. "There's something else there. She's a mystical person. She has knowledge. I think she's the one who taught Chloe how to resist."

Jett rubbed his knuckles across his forehead. "I know Thomas is very close to her, closer than he seems to be to the rest of his family. He even said once he thought they had some sort of spiritual connection, whatever that means."

Dyfan let out a soft chuckle. "It means a lot, believe me. And now she has a connection with Chloe, too. Well, we will just have to do something about that."

"What can we possibly do?" Gaia asked, puzzled, but also thrilled that Dyfan seemed about to exhibit some of his amazing powers.

Dyfan held up the camera again so they could see Ivy's picture. "Memorize that face, and concentrate on it. Picture her in your mind."

He turned the camera back toward himself and began to stare at Ivy's image.

Gaia, breathless with awe as she watched him, thought his black eyes might bore a hole right through the camera.

~ * ~

Ivy clutched her chest and staggered backwards, landing hard in her leather recliner. What in the world was this? She'd just had her annual check-up, and passed with flying colors. "Healthy as a horse," her young physician, Dr.

Prentiss, who must be all of thirty-five years old, had said, grinning at her.

Her breathing came quick, and felt shallow to her. She sat back, and struggled to take slow, deep breaths. Her mind reeled; there was no reason for this.

All at once, she felt him, sensed an evil presence as thick as mud wrapping itself around her.

"Dyfan!" She fought against the sludge that clouded her mind, but he'd had the advantage of surprise. She slumped in her chair and felt her mind come apart, like pieces of a puzzle scattering on the floor, and everything went dark.

~ * ~

"Mom! Mom." Are you awake?"

Ivy blinked her eyes open, squinting against the brightness that assaulted them. Sharon bent over her, her face twisted with worry. "Are you okay? How do you feel?"

"I'm dizzy. What happened? Did I faint?"

"Dr. Prentiss says he doesn't know why this happened, or what's wrong. They want to keep you for observation for a day or two."

"No way." Ivy struggled to sit up, then lay back as exhaustion overcame her. She winked at Mike, who stood back a few feet from the bed, biting his thumb. "Well," she conceded, "maybe I could use a rest. I'm so tired. When did you find me?"

"I sent Mike over after school to borrow a cup of sugar..."

"I ran out," Ivy said, closing her eyes again. "Used it up on pineapple margaritas for Russell and me last night. So...I was unconscious for several hours before they found me?"

"I've heard about those margaritas," Dr. Prentiss said as the door to Ivy's room sung closed behind him. "Seems you're famous around Salem for those."

Ivy blinked and tried to focus on the young doctor's face. Sandy hair, eyes of that shade of blue that always made her want to melt, laugh-lines at the corners. A handsome young man by anyone's standards.

"Oh, if I were only forty years younger," she sighed.

Sharon and Dr. Prentiss laughed, and Mike looked as though he'd like to sink through the floor. The doctor turned to Sharon. "Would you mind waiting outside while I talk to Ivy?"

"Of course." She beckoned to Mike, who followed her out of the room with obvious relief.

She didn't wait for his diagnosis. "Okay, Doc, what happened to me?"

He drew a chair up close to the bed and sat down. "I have to admit I don't know, Ivy. What did you feel before you blanked out? Did you have any pain, dizziness?"

Ivy considered what to answer. She couldn't tell him what she'd really felt. *Well, there was this feeling like a big black blanket of mud wrapping around me, and a presence of evil...oh sure. They'd take me from the hospital right to the psycho ward.* "I just felt heaviness in my chest," she said, "and a fuzziness in my head. I got dizzy, couldn't stand up and passed out."

Dr, Prentiss shook his head. "I didn't find anything that might have caused that. But, as your daughter said, I'd like to keep you overnight. Is that all right with you?"

"Sure," she said. "I feel exhausted. I could use the rest."

"Very well, then." He stood up, and moved the chair back to its accustomed place. "You just take a nap, and I'll be in to check on you later."

"Wait." She caught at his sleeve. "I want to ask you something."

He turned back to face her again. "Sure, anything, Ivy."

She hesitated a minute, then took a breath and forged ahead. "Do you believe in 'evil'—I mean, as an entity, as a real power in the world?"

Obviously, by the look on his face, this wasn't the kind of question he expected. He narrowed his eyes. "As in—its ability to attack people, make them sick, or even kill them?"

"Yes. Voodoo, for example. They make symbolic figures of other people and stick pins in them..."

He nodded. "And the chosen victims get sick, sometimes even die. But I think that has more to do with what the people on both sides believe. We all know there is more power in the mind than we have even begun to understand."

She nodded. "Yes, that I do know."

"Is that what you think happened to you, someone actually targeted you?

She hesitated before she answered. "Maybe. Oh, that's silly, Doc. I'm probably just tired, and need a good rest."

He didn't look convinced. "Look, Ivy, if you need to talk..."

She attempted a smile. "No, no, thanks, just wondering, that's all. You don't think I'm crazy, do you?"

He grinned at her. "I've always thought you were crazy. I'll be back to check on you later, okay?"

She nodded, already grateful for the opportunity to lie in a comfortable bed, and not have to do anything.

The doctor paused at the door, grinned and shook his finger at her. "No margaritas, though, Ivy, no matter what flavor."

She managed to return a weak grin. "Better not let Russell visit me then."

~ * ~

Later in the afternoon, Ivy awoke, feeling much more like herself. With her mind clear again, she immediately realized what had happened. She raised herself to a sitting position—no dizziness, which was a good sign. It meant her mind was strong enough to recover from Dyfan's psychic attack. She reached for the phone which sat on the bedside table.

Thomas sounded worried, and his voice echoed his concern. "Mom called as soon as it happened. Chloe and I will be home, as soon as I get my car fixed. The garage is busy today, so they haven't been able to get to my tires." He told her what had happened.

She laughed when he told her how Chloe had swung the pan of hot coals at them and escaped from the circle. "One girl, all by herself, got the best of the entire group?" She shook her head in admiration, even though Thomas couldn't see her. "That's some girl you've got there, Thomas."

"And don't you think I know it. But..." he hesitated. "I'm really concerned about how to keep her safe. She seems to be surrounded by people who are determined to get her into that group, even against her will." He lowered his voice. "And, Ivy, I don't know what Dyfan has in mind, but it's nothing good. I even suggested she leave school for the rest of the year, but she says 'no,' she can take care of herself."

"She could come here and stay with me. I could use a little tender, loving care, and she does that so well." She caught herself as something echoed in her mind. *Chloe at the tiger pen. I came back to marry Thomas and take care of you when you're old and tired.* "Or at the house. Sharon would be glad to have her. She could find a job here until fall, maybe transfer somewhere else."

"I know. I told her that, but she's stubborn, doesn't want to leave." Ivy considered, then made up her mind. "Okay, Thomas, come home for the weekend. I'll be back home by tomorrow afternoon. I have an idea how we can strengthen Chloe's armor against these thugs."

She heard the smile in his reply. "You make it sound like a war, Ivy."

She let a few significant seconds go by before she replied in a soft voice. "It is, my darling grandson, it is. It's a battle for Chloe's soul."

~ * ~

Thomas and Chloe arrived in Salem by early evening, just in time for dinner. Sharon was obviously puzzled about their impromptu visit, and Thomas did his best to reassure her it was just a spur of the moment decision to come home and check up on Ivy. He didn't want to repeat what Ivy had told him, and thought his grandmother would be the best person to tell Chloe of her fears.

"Well, I'm sure she'll be glad to see you both." Sharon shook her head, and sent him a fond smile. "You've always had such a close relationship with Ivy. Sometimes I think you're closer to her than you are to the rest of us."

Mike let out a snicker. "Yeah, I wish he could marry her, then I could have Chloe."

Before Thomas could respond, his father cut in, his usual mellow tone much more severe. "Mike, that is totally inappropriate, and you will apologize to your brother and Chloe—right now."

Mike, for once, had the grace to look embarrassed as he stammered out an apology. "Sorry. Don't know why I said that." He stared at his plate.

Chloe attempted to smooth things over. She smiled at Mike. "It's nice to be wanted by two such wonderful guys."

Charlie's face still looked like a storm cloud. "I don't like some of the things that come out of your mouth, young man. I suggest you go to your room for the rest of the evening. Now."

Mike looked up at this mother. "No dessert?"

Charlie banged his fist on the table and glared at his youngest son. "No dessert, no TV, no computer. Go work on that science project you've been procrastinating on, or read a book. Do you remember what a book is? You're out of here for the rest of the night."

Mike stared at his father, his mouth open, but without another word he got up and shuffled off toward the stairs that led to the second floor.

Thomas, on the spur of the moment, called after him. "Mike, have you been back to Mystery Hill lately?"

Mike turned enough to shoot Thomas a hard look. "If I have, what's it to you?"

Charlie jumped to his feet. "Mike, go upstairs."

The kid disappeared around the corner. Sharon sighed. "You were awfully hard on him. It's just his age. He'll grow out of it."

"He'd better, and soon," Charlie growled. "I'm going to go talk to him."

Thomas leaned over to Chloe. "Oh, oh, the dreaded *talk*. I used to hate that more than anything. Chloe, maybe we should go over to Ivy's and get settled." He looked at his mother. "We both have homework, too."

Sharon shook her head at him. "Not before dessert, you don't." She vanished into the kitchen, where Thomas heard the refrigerator door open and close, plates and silverware being set out.

Chloe kept her voice low. "Why did you ask him if he'd been back to Mystery Hill?"

"I'm beginning to think Mystery Hill might be the source of most of the strange things that have been going on, including Mike's bad behavior. And did you notice, he didn't give me an answer?"

Twenty-seven

Ivy gave Thomas and Chloe her complete attention as they related what had happened Friday night. Even though Thomas had given her a brief account over the phone, she wanted details, everything Chloe could recall.

"And you remembered not to look him directly in the eyes?" she asked.

"Only for a second—when I saw the fawn. I was so shocked, I couldn't believe what he intended to do to that sweet little animal."

"Did you feel anything when you looked at him?"

Chloe nodded. "There was a—sort of shift I felt take place. I fixed my eyes on the rim of his hood instead, and it never got any stronger. I pretended to cooperate, and even mouthed some of the responses, until I got a chance to act."

Thomas put his arm around her. "She did great. I'm proud of her."

Ivy nodded. "So am I. But I'm worried that you're surrounded by all these people who do not have your best interests at heart. Ingrid and Jeb are right there in class

215

with you, and you can't completely avoid Jett and Gaia, can you?"

Chloe shrugged. "No, I can't. They always have access to the dining hall and campus events, and Gaia's in my archeology class."

Ivy nodded. "It's obvious Dyfan has some sort of strong psychic power, and it might be augmented by some other outside force. I don't know how he aimed it at me, but he did, and because I wasn't expecting it, it did a job on me."

"This outside force, as you call it," Thomas put in, "do you think it could be centered in Mystery Hill? Even Mike's behavior is worse, and my folks don't know why. They're at the end of their rope with him."

"Mystery Hill is not an evil place in itself," Ivy said. She attempted to lean forward to make a point, but winced, and sat back. She seemed to ache all over, and didn't know whether that was Dyfan's doing, or just her own body's protests at growing older. She continued. "Evil things happened at Mystery Hill. There are lots of stories— although they can't be verified—but my theory is that some of the power of an evil force lingers on throughout the years. When a person who is open to such influences goes to the site, that force is able to enter that person's mind, so to speak, and strengthen his own evil powers."

Chloe shivered. "So the same thing could happen at the Stonehenge we built outside the town at Midstate? If Dyfan himself is under the influence of evil, he could make the site itself have negative vibes or something?"

Ivy smiled and nodded. "Or something, yes."

Thomas wrinkled his brow. "Still don't know if I believe that, Ivy. I would need more proof that one person's evil can actually influence places and events..."

"Hitler," she said quietly.

Thomas nodded. She was right. That needed no explanation.

Ivy reached for his hand. "Something else to look into, Thomas. Can you find out if anything horrible ever happened at the site Dyfan chose for the Druids' group? That might be why Dyfan picked it."

Chloe jumped in. "I'll ask Professor Walsh. He was born in Middleton, and should know if there's any local lore about that."

"Ivy nodded. "Good idea. That's actually about all you can do. Avoid all those people, and never make eye contact with them. And, Thomas, you stay with her as much as you can. Don't leave her in the apartment alone. Chloe, when you don't have class, study in the library, or someplace else where there are a lot of people."

She nodded. "I will. Please don't worry. I'll be careful."

Thomas put his arm around her and drew her close. "You'd better. You're sort of important to me, y'know."

~ * ~

Ivy brought out her Scrabble set and proposed a game. There was no way Thomas wanted to play Scrabble with Ivy, who was nearly legendary in their family for rarely losing a game, and went over to the house in search of Mike.

His brother wasn't there. He found his mother in the kitchen, baking—no surprise there.

"I don't know where he's gone," Sharon admitted. "I asked him to help Charlie clean out the garage, and next thing I knew, he'd vanished."

Thomas bit his lip. "Why do I have a feeling he went to Mystery Hill? I'm going to take a walk up there and look around for him."

Sharon placed her pie in the oven and set the timer. She wiped her hands on her apron, and turned to face her son. "I know Annie Fisher, who works in the gift shop. I asked her to call me if shows up there."

Thomas grinned. "You don't think he and his buddies go through the gift shop and buy tickets, do you? There are plenty of ways to skirt through the woods and avoid buying tickets, especially if you're a thirteen-year-old kid."

Sharon gave a sigh of exasperation. "I just don't know what to do about him. You and Charlie Jr. never gave us this much trouble."

"We probably did. You've just forgotten what little devils we were." He leaned over and gave her a peck on the cheek. "I'm going to go look for him."

The snow had melted except in places where the trees prevented the sun from shining through. Thomas jogged the mile or so from the house to the site, feeling new energy course through him as he breathed in fresh spring air. Winter was long and hard in New Hampshire, and could drag down one's energy and spirits when it went on too long. Spring was more welcome than one of Sharon's freshly baked pies. It lifted the spirit, renewed one's zest for life.

Annie Fisher had obviously-dyed bright red hair, and wore a kelly green sweater and gray slacks. She looked like a Christmas elf out of place. She smiled at him and extended a hand. "Thomas Thorn, isn't it? I thought I recognized you last time when you came in with that pretty girl, but left in a hurry."

Thomas returned her smile. "I was away for a couple of years, and didn't think you remembered me. You haven't seen my kid brother, Mike, have you?"

Her welcoming smile turned to an expression of frustration. "He might be up there, we never know. The kids go up through the woods, and if we send someone up to check and they're there, we chase them out. But they come right back. We have a limited staff here, and we can't be on them twenty-four-seven."

"I think I'll go up and check." Thomas pulled a ten dollar bill out of his pocket, but Annie waved him on. "No, no—you'll be doing us a favor. Go on through."

Thomas stopped to gaze at the black and white photo that contained the so-called ghost. It was an amazing photograph, and who could deny that the floating white shape among the rocks was actually a ghost? It certainly was something out of the ordinary.

The climb up the hill proved to be slippery, with the melting snow clinging to the rocks on the path. The woods were quiet; the spring birds had not yet come back from the south. Thomas made his way as silently as possible around the edge of the compound, and followed the stone-walled trail to the higher level.

Mike lay sprawled on a large, flat rock, facing upward, his head resting on his hands clasped behind his neck. His mind was obviously somewhere else, as he didn't stir as his brother approached.

"Hi, kid."

Mike startled and sat up. "Jeez! What are you doing here?"

"Looking for you. What are you doing here?"

"Just being here. What's it to you?" He looked away, refusing to meet his brother's eyes.

Thomas lowered himself to sit on the rock. Mike scrunched over closer to the opposite side. Thomas laid a hand on his leg. "I'll tell you what you're not doing, kid. You're not helping Dad clean out the garage, like Mom asked you to."

"'Cause I don't want to. I want to do what I want to do, not clean some stupid garage. You do it, if you want it cleaned."

"Mike, you can't just go through life only doing what you want to do, and ignoring everything else. You have obligations as part of the family."

Mike turned his head slightly to give him a dark look. "Cripes, Thomas. You're what, twenty years old, and you sound ninety. Weren't you ever a kid?"

"Yes, I was, and that's why I'm concerned about you." When Mike looked away again and refused to respond, he went on. "Do you come up here a lot?"

"Yeah, I like it here."

"What do you like about it?"

"Nobody bugging me—do this, do that."

"Well, that's part of growing up, Mike, taking responsibility."

Mike ignored him. "A lot of neat things have happened here," he said, looking off into space. "People have heard voices, actually seen things..."

Thomas felt a chill creep up his spine. "What kind of things?"

Like a church appearing and disappearing..."

"A church would never have been built on this site. Whatever this was meant to be is at least two to four thousand years old."

"Some guy a couple hundred years ago saw a whole line of weird people led by some sort of silver light..."

"He had a dream and thought it was real, or he had a vivid imagination, or he just wanted the attention..."

"Wolf howls and screams, like someone being tortured in the middle of the night."

"And you think that's *neat?* Mike, you need to..."

His kid brother bolted so fast Thomas was taken by surprise. By the time he jumped to his feet to go after him, the kid had vanished among the trees.

Twenty-eight

"Mike! Mike!" Thomas' shouts echoed through the trees and seemed to bounce off the stones back at him in ridicule. He started after his brother, running as fast as he could in the direction he'd seen his kid brother go. There was no sign of him anywhere.

There were no footprints to follow. The snow was almost gone, and damp, matted leaves from last season and faded brown pine needles covered the forest floor. How could he have disappeared so quickly? Maybe, Thomas decided, Mike had ducked into one of the stone huts, storage bins or tunnels. He took his time, searching each one methodically, but the kid was just not there. He'd vanished as completely as the visions some people claimed they'd seen at Mystery Hill.

Thomas retraced his steps and sat back on the flat stone he'd recently shared with Mike. He ran his finger up and down the groove carved around the edge of the rock. If it had been used for human sacrifice, this allowed the blood to run down into some sort of vessel placed under the stone. Other scholars debated that theory, however, claiming that the indentation was used for the collection of wine, which was then used for sacred ceremonies.

Hard to say which was the truth. Mike obviously had become enamored of the site, but was that the cause of his recent bad behavior? Mystics, and Ivy was one of them, theorized that the stones held the essence or spirit of evil, and its lingering influence could infect other people, especially those with psychic sensitivity. Could a tinge of whatever it was have gotten to Mike?

He dug his cell phone out of his pocket and called home. Sharon didn't sound too alarmed. Mike went there by himself often, and Thomas was there waiting for him. He'd come back, but call her again in an hour.

He called Chloe. Ivy answered and told him she'd beaten her in two games of Scrabble and Chloe had decided to take a shower and a short nap before dinner.

"You keep that up and no one will play Scrabble with you, Ivy," he joked. "You have to let someone else win once in a while."

"That's not ethical," she retorted, and her voice was serious. She meant it.

He laughed, and told her he'd be back with Mike in time for dinner.

Mike would come back of his own accord. Of course, he would.

The late afternoon sun was hot and forced its way through the laced, upper branches of the trees to warm his arms and face. It felt so good, so comforting after all the tension of the past months. He removed his light jacket and lay back on the rock. The heat from the rock felt like a hot massage on his back. He sighed, and closed his eyes. He just wanted to bask in the sun's warmth and not think about everything that had happened. Just for a little while, he didn't want to have to worry about Chloe, either. Just for a minute or two. Then he'd get up and go into the woods and look for Mike.

~ * ~

He must have been tired, as he slept for a long time. When he woke, he rubbed his eyes, unable to focus on where he was. *What a strange dream. Running in the forest, dressed in Indian deerskins, pursued by a bigger, stronger brave. Feelings of fear, desperation and guilt. Then—unbearable pain as an arrow pierced him in the center of his back. He fell, and the other brave stood over him, grinning.*

"Now, Achak, I will be the chief's favorite. I will lead the tribe."

He knew he was dying. He felt his life force ebbing away. He could only manage one word as his spirit left his body... "Kanti..."

Thomas sat up. He felt tired to the bone, discouraged and thirsty, as if he'd been wandering in the woods for a long time. He rubbed his eyes. He could go down to the entry shack and buy a soda or bottled water—but suddenly he remembered Mike. He had to find him first.

He stood and looked around.

"I'm here, Dude." Mike leaned against a large tree, his eyes round and curious as he regarded his older brother.

Thomas glanced at his watch. "Good. We'd better jog on home. I'll help you with that garage tomorrow, okay, kid?"

Mike nodded. "Uhm, Thomas?"

"Yeah?"

"You must have had some dream. Who's Kanti?"

Twenty-nine

Something was wrong. Jim Walsh felt it, could almost smell it as he prowled his classroom. Chloe McAllister seemed to have painters' block, if there were such a thing, as she sat staring at her canvas and not making a mark on it. He didn't think the assignment he'd given them was that difficult: choose a painting and use elements of it, the technique, the colors, the style—whatever, and paint something of your own using something borrowed from that painting or artist.

Three students had zeroed in on Vincent Van Gogh, a rather obvious choice, and were starting works using his famous Sunflowers, Starry Night or the café at night as their inspiration. He smiled to himself as he recognized the Elk Horn taking shape, using Van Gogh's colors and composition. The Elk Horn had been there, looking much the same, since he had been a student.

Walsh glanced over to the windows, where that odd couple, small nerdy Jeb and tall, beautiful Ingrid huddled together over their paintings, talking in low tones. Jeb seemed to have a bad burn all down one side of his face, and he had spotted a dark bruise on the back of Ingrid's hand, which stretched all the way up under the sleeve of her sweatshirt. He wondered what had happened there.

He selected two books of assorted paintings and dropped them off on the table near Chloe. He gazed down at her. "No ideas?"

She shook her head, but picked up a blue pastel crayon and made several meaningless marks on the canvas. She looked up and shrugged.

"Well, take a look through these. Maybe something will hit." He wandered away, bent to speak to another student, but kept his eyes on Chloe, wondering. This just wasn't like her. He kept his ears open as Ingrid said something to Jeb, got up and walked over to Chloe.

"Hi," she said. "Want to go out and get a Coke?"

"No." Chloe looked away, refusing to meet Ingrid's eyes.

"Why not?" he heard Ingrid ask, but there was something in her voice he'd never heard—almost a mocking tone.

Chloe turned a page in the book he'd given her and didn't answer. Ingrid waited a moment, then moved away and went out into the hall alone.

Walsh's profiling training kicked in automatically. He'd seen Chloe and Ingrid go off on break together, but now Chloe wouldn't even look at her. He knew it wasn't over a boy, because he still saw Chloe and Thomas together all over campus, and they were definitely a couple. What then?

It got 'curiouser and curiouser', as Alice had said.

"Professor," a girl called to him. "Can you take a look at this?"

He bent to help her. A few minutes later, out of the corner of his eye, he watched Jeb get up, cram all his dirty brushes into his water jar, ostensibly with the intention of getting clean water and washing off his brushes.

A sudden noise distracted him, and he wheeled around in time to see Chloe's easel crash to the floor, and her canvas skitter across the floor. Had Jeb done that on purpose?

"Oh, sorry," Jeb said, in the same mocking tone as Ingrid had used, but he didn't stop to help her. He glanced at the instructor, and clapped a hand over the burned side of his face. "I can't see out of this eye." He continued his trek to the sink and made a big show of dumping his water into the basin.

A boy seated near Chloe threw a look of disbelief after Jeb, and got up to help Chloe set up her station again. Another student returned her canvas.

Walsh watched as a flush crawled up over Chloe's cheeks, and she buried her face in her hands. After a minute, she dropped her hands and a look of determination replaced her embarrassment.

Good girl. Don't let those jerks get the best of you, whatever the problem is.

But what was it? From the burn on Jeb's face and the bruise on Ingrid's arm, and their treatment of Chloe, it was almost like retribution, as if Chloe had beaten both of them up. But that was ludicrous...wasn't it?

Trying not to be obvious, Walsh drew up a chair and sat down beside Chloe. He brushed a finger over her canvas, as if pointing something out to her. He kept his voice too low for anyone else to hear. "What's up, Chloe?"

"No ideas," she said. "My mind is a blank slate today." She said it loud enough to be heard, as if she thought he was asking about her project.

"Is something the matter? I thought you were friends with Ingrid. I've noticed you going on break."

"Not anymore." Chloe picked up the blue pastel and drew a few more lines on the canvas.

His concern grew. "Is it just a little spat—or something more serious?"

"More serious." She kept her eyes on her canvas and her voice almost a whisper.

"Want to talk about it?"

She turned her head and met his eyes. "Yes."

"Can you stay after class?"

"Yes."

Noticing that several students had taken an interest in their quiet conversation, Walsh stood up, pointed to the blank canvas and nodded his head. "Just go with that idea," he said, and moved away.

Just before the end of class, Chloe seemed to come alive. She squeezed her paint out onto her palette, and began to paint in earnest. Walsh circled behind her, wanting to see what idea had finally hit her, but not wanting to disturb her.

"Aaah, I know the painting—can't think of the artist at the moment. Oh, yes, Magritte's *Carte Blanche*." He was pleased she had chosen something different, something unusual, but he'd expect nothing less of her.

A sparse woodland, the trees gray and light brown, filled Chloe's previously empty space. Woven over and between the slim tree trunks she'd sketched the delicate figure of a fawn. Everything was very tentative still, but she'd captured the eyes of the young deer, huge, staring, terrified.

Where did this come from—why was this meaningful to her?

The classroom began to empty out, but Chloe seemed lost in her work. Walsh busied himself at his desk, preparing for his after-lunch class. He had several hours, and he could wait until Chloe felt satisfied with her effort. At last she put her brush down, sighed, and flashed him a smile.

After she cleaned up, he pulled the chair up beside her again.

"Okay, shoot. What the hell's going on here?"

Her voice trembled as she began to speak. Whatever had happened still had the power to frighten her.

He listened as she related an almost unbelievable story. If it hadn't been coming from Chloe, a girl he perceived as unusually mature and grounded, he wouldn't have been able to believe it.

"Ingrid and this other guy, Jett, kidnapped you and made you go there against your will?"

She nodded.

"And—this Dyfan, whoever he is, was actually going to sacrifice a fawn?"

"Yes. It was so little and so beautiful, and so scared. I couldn't stand it."

"And that's how Jeb got that burn, and Ingrid her bruised arm?"

She nodded again.

If it hadn't been such a serious situation, he would have laughed. Imagine this pretty, feminine girl getting the best of a whole circle of people! He took a deep breath, sat back and folded his arms. "You're a brave girl, Chloe. I should think you'd want nothing more to do with them or this school. He paused and tapped a finger on the table. "And if I didn't know you and Thomas, I'd think this was one big, made-up story."

"It isn't," she said.

"I can see that. Now, what are we going to do about it?""

She lifted her chin. "I'm not going to let them scare me. I have a right to be here, and I'm going to stay."

He admired that streak of stubbornness, her determination to face whatever came her way, in spite of her terrifying experience.

He rubbed a hand over his eyes. "I wonder if Dyfan picked that site for a reason."

"Oh," she cut in. "I was supposed to ask you that. Did anything—something violent or unusual ever happen there?"

He didn't need to think about that. Everyone who'd lived in Middleton knew the answer to that, and he'd been born here and lived all his life in this town. "Oh, yeah. Several hundred years ago there was a massacre there—Indians against the settlers. Horrible story, killings and torture. There's supposed to be a marker there that tells the story, but over the years it's been neglected, and it got buried in the overgrowth."

"The cops told us about the marker, too..."

"So you have gone to the police about what's happening there?"

"Uh huh, but they said they couldn't do much about it, except send a patrol car up every now and then."

Walsh stood up. "Well, I'm going to make sure that they do more than that. I'm going to see that they remove the stones and the altar and put up a barricade around the site."

"How can you do that?" she asked. "When Thomas and I told them what they were up to, they acted like it was a bunch of college kids on a lark, and nothing more."

He smiled at her. "The cops are used to college kids pulling pranks and doing stupid things, but this has gone 'way beyond amusing."

"But…"

"When you live in a small town all your life, you know everyone and have a bit more pull than the person just passing through our little piece of heaven. I'll take care of it, Chloe. The chief of police is my brother, Joe.

~ * ~

Jim Walsh had very few occasions to visit the police station. A small red, brick building sat on a worn-out patch of grass, and housed a single barred cell for the occasional resident who'd had a bit too much to drink, or once in a while, a pair of barroom brawlers.

One of Middleton's three policemen sat behind the solitary desk, drumming his fingers on the glass top and watching the small TV in the corner. He looked up as Walsh entered and the door swung closed behind him.

Walsh greeted his brother, Joe.

"Hi, guy," Joe said, with a grin at his brother. "What brings the esteemed professor down here? And what have you got there? A present for me? It's not my birthday yet."

Walsh forced a smile, and laid Jeb's painting on the desk. "It's not a present, but I want you to look at this."

Joe picked up the painting and gave it a good once-over. "Whooo—this is weird. One of your students did this?"

"Yeah, Joe, a couple of kids came to see you a few weeks ago about things going on out at that old Indian massacre site?"

Joe shrugged and lay the painting flat on the desk. "Yeah, sounded like a bunch of college jerks fooling around, like usual. Not much we can do about that if they want to play Druids, or whatever they're doing out there."

Walsh pulled up a chair and straddled it backwards. "Listen, Joe, it's a lot more than that." He tapped the painting. "This is what's going on out there, and I believe one of my students is in real danger."

Joe narrowed his eyes and regarded his brother. "Go on, Jim. I'm listening."

Walsh related Chloe's tale, referring to the painting as he told about the arrangement of stones, the central altar, the student Druids in robes, and the chief priest, Dyfan. "It's gone beyond simple goofing around, Joe," he finished up. "They were going to kill that fawn, and..." He couldn't finish the sentence. He swallowed, bile rising in his throat.

Joe completed his brother's thought. "You think they might actually try to sacrifice a human being next time? You can't believe that, Jim. Nobody's that nuts."

"My intuition tells me this weirdo Dyfan does intend to do that. And, yes, he is nuts."

Joe got out the ever-present note pad and began to scribble. "Is this guy a student at Midstate? And what's his real name? I assume his parents didn't lay 'Dyfan' on their baby boy."

Walsh shrugged. "Jack Wayland. I wasn't able to find anything on him. That's why I'm here, Joe. We have to stop this guy."

Joe nodded, his face tight. "You betcha."

Walsh leaned forward and placed a tight fist over the painting. "I want this site dismantled. Can you do that?"

Joe nodded. "Piece 'a cake, big brother, though not one I'd choose to eat. Give me a couple of days, and this Dyfan character will be history."

Walsh nodded. "I think we'd better take care of this nasty piece of business before we have a real tragedy out there."

~ * ~

Jim Walsh lived in a modest gray Cape a few streets over from the college. He had a car, but rarely used it, choosing to walk to school, and nearly everywhere else he needed to go in the small town. This and several sessions per week at the college gym kept him in acceptable ex-Marine shape. He left the police station at a jog with Jeb's painting under his arm. He'd return it to the wooden storage file before class tomorrow, and Jeb would never miss it.

His mind was on the big game the next evening, the last of the season. Although everyone else in the country would be watching the NCAA, and rooting for Florida, Duke or Uconn, all Middleton would be rooting for their own community college, Midstate. It would be televised locally, and the college stadium would be filled to capacity. He thought of Thomas Thorn, and hoped he would have a good game. The guy had real talent, and next year he would be even better. *If* she stayed at Midstate. Chloe was a year ahead of him, and Walsh suspected that where Chloe went, Thomas would go also.

He heard footsteps pounding on the sidewalk behind him. He turned and moved aside to let the three runners pass, but the next thing he knew he had been knocked to the sidewalk. He never had time to look at their faces. Taken by surprise, he let out a yell and grabbed for their ankles, but they were younger and faster, and eluded him easily. One hit him with a club of some kind, and the others kicked him. Ignoring the pain, he fought back until a kick in the head was the last thing he knew. He came to sometime later. He had been dragged into a yard and hidden behind some bushes, so he couldn't be seen from the street. It was dinner hour, and evidently no one had observed or heard the attack.

He sat up, his aching body protesting every move, and rubbed his aching head. "Some Marine you are, Walsh," he muttered.

His head reeled as he tried to figure things out. What had they wanted? This kind of thing hardly ever happened in Middleton, and certainly not in a neighborhood like this. He felt in his jacket, and found his wallet still there. He dragged himself to a sitting position. Everything hurt, although as he examined his clothing, he didn't see any blood.

He got to one knee and, with an effort, forced himself to stand. He was sore all over, but it wasn't any worse than some of the street fights he'd been in as a tough Irish kid growing up. The problem was, he wasn't sixteen anymore.

He suddenly remembered Jeb's painting. He searched the bushes, looked around the section of yard where he'd been deposited, scanned the sidewalk and street. It became clear to him that the painting was what they'd been after—but why? Jeb was a member of that group, and they could have gotten it from him. He began to limp toward home, and then the light dawned. He had taken the side of the opposition. He had gone to the college authorities and the police.

They didn't need to steal the painting. They wanted to send Jim Walsh a message.

Thirty

"Guess what? Miss Myers said today that our archeology class is going to take a field trip to Mystery Hill." Curious, Chloe waited for Thomas' reaction.

Thomas swung around in his desk chair, alarm on his face. "Oh, no, you're not. Not without me, and obviously I can't go on your field trip."

Chloe took another bite of the pizza that served for dinner. "I knew that would upset you, but honestly, Thomas, I'll be okay. Hannah will be there with me."

"Gaia will be going, right?"

"Yeah, but she absolutely ignores me now. To my face, that is." She wiped her mouth with a paper napkin and took a swig of Coke from the can, but she couldn't prevent a small shiver. "Except that I can feel her eyes boring right through my back in class.

"I don't like it," Thomas said. "People like her and the Druids never give up."

"The police disbanded them," Chloe protested. "The Druids are no more. Gaia's no threat, and Ingrid and Jeb look right through me in art class. I'm not even a person to them anymore."

Thomas shook his head, his expression adamant. "Even though the police dismantled the site, moved all the stones back into the woods and sledge-hammered the altar to pieces, I can't believe Dyfan has vanished from our lives. I have a very strong feeling he'll be back."

Chloe lifted a shoulder. "The cops never found him on campus, did they?"

"Nope." Thomas pushed his paper plate with the uneaten pizza crusts away. "Mr. Walsh told me there's no record of him at the college, and everyone they asked denied knowing him—including, Jett, Jeb, and Ingrid."

"Well, that's not so strange. Nobody wants to get into trouble, or admit they knew about what went on out there in the woods."

"Mr. Walsh told me he was going to take Jeb's painting down to show his brother, but even with that, it's just our word against his."

"Then it's over," Chloe said, feeling a wave of relief wash over her.

Thomas looked grim. "I wouldn't bet on it."

She decided to change the subject. "Getting back to the field trip. I'd like another really good look at Mystery Hill. The time we went and I took those photos, it had just rained, and everything was sort of gray. I'd like to see what it looks like in better weather, explore some of those caverns. And Miss Myers knows the place so well. I want to hear about the history of it."

Thomas groaned. "Chloe, please wait 'til we go home again, and I can go with you."

"Thomas, I have to go with the class. It's a required trip,

and our final project is based on a comparison of that site, and another of our own choice."

"Chloe, I really…"

Her stubborn streak rose, and she cut him off. "Thomas, I love you and I know you have my best interests at heart, but you can't control everything I do, and you can't tell me what to do and what not to do. I want to go with the class, and I'm going to do that. You're just too protective sometimes."

He heaved a sigh. "I know I can't prevent you. Just stay away from Gaia, okay?"

"I will, I promise. I'll hang with Hannah, like we do in class anyway. I have no desire ever to speak to Gaia again."

"I just bet Gaia loves your palling around with Hannah."

Chloe threw him an impatient look. "She has her own buds. Why should she care?"

Thomas sounded as if he weren't giving up. "And when is this going to take place?"

"Next Friday." She held up a hand as she read his expression. "I know, I know—it's also the last game of the season that night. I'll be back in plenty of time for cheerleading."

"You'll be tired after being out all day walking around."

"Thomas! I'm nineteen years old, not ninety. I'll be fine."

He put his hands up as if defending himself. "Okay, I know you will. I just hope you'll be back in time, because the game is early, at five, and my whole family's coming over to see the game and watch you cheerlead. Mike will be impossible if you're not out there in your next-to-nothing skirt."

She laughed. "Miss Myers promised we'd be back. I wouldn't want to disappoint Mike. And we're all going out to dinner afterwards, right?"

"We are, and you have to be there. You're part of the family now."

She picked up her paper plate, and walked over to his desk to pile his leftovers on top of hers to throw away. She bent down and kissed him on the bridge of his nose. "I know I am, and there's nowhere else I'd rather be."

He put his arms around her before she could move away. "I love you, Chloe, and I just can't bear to think of losing you to something or someone as evil as Dyfan. There's something deep inside me that tells me I *know* this bastard all too well. I can't shake this weird feeling that he's not finished with us yet."

~ * ~

Late March and early April in New England can bring the heaviest snow storm of the season, or the gift of a perfect spring day, with blue skies, a warm sun, the promise of new green grass and budding new leaves on the trees. The morning of the archeology field trip warmed up early and it looked to be one of those fresh and beautiful days.

Chloe waited until the last minute to board the bus, waiting for Hannah, but Hannah didn't show. Her feelings of apprehension grew. Miss Myers had the bus wait as long as possible. She called Hannah's cell herself, and Chloe called and texted her. Everything went to messages, and Hannah never called back.

Where the hell was she? This was a required trip, unless you were sick enough to have a doctor's note...or you were dead. *Ridiculous, Chloe!* She pushed the thought from her mind.

Chloe got off the bus at Mystery Hill, her camera strung around her neck. There had been an empty seat next to Gaia, and Miss Myers had waved her toward it, but Chloe had shaken her head and moved to the rear of the bus. She was the last one to get off, and she hurried to catch up, as the other students had already began moving toward the gift shop.

Miss Myers spoke to the red-haired woman at the desk, whose nametag said 'Annie.' Annie looked at her credentials, checked them against a notebook on the counter, and waved them through. "Have a wonderful time. Take a few minutes to look around the gift shop." She waved to her left. "We have some books, one a fascinating research book about the history of Mystery Hill, and a new novel based on this site."

Chloe's eyes lit on an orange cover with *America's Stonehenge* in bright yellow letters, and she started toward the display.

Chloe wondered if Annie remembered her coming there with Thomas. Probably not. A lot of people went through there every day. Annie did notice her interest in the book, however. She started toward her. "Yes, that one..."

Miss Myers interrupted with a curt, "Not now, students," and beckoned to everyone to keep up with her as she went out through the back door. "Later, if we have time," she called back over her shoulder in Chloe's direction.

Chloe trailed along behind the group. She breathed in deeply, wanting to feel the cool, crisp air go all through her. It was amazing, she reflected, on how different the scent of the air was in New Hampshire—and all the northern states, compared to Florida. Here it was lighter, laced with the fragrance from the pines and other evergreens. In the Sunshine State, the air was heavier, moister, but tinged with the wonderful salty smell of the ocean. It was something you never realized unless you experienced both places.

The trail led upwards, the same as it had when she'd been there with Thomas, and Chloe listened intently to what their professor told the class as they walked.

Miss Myers pointed out the stone walls lining the path up the hill. When they reached a small, stone structure, she stopped and gestured the class to gather around. Chloe moved closer, taking care to be on the opposite side of the group from Gaia. She caught a glance that Gaia threw her, and felt a sudden stab of regret for the lost friendship. She averted her eyes, tossed her hair back and fixed her attention on what Miss Myers was saying.

"This is called 'The Watch House' and is thought to have been a structure built as a shelter for a sentry, whoever was standing guard at the time. Obviously it's too small for storage, or any other use."

Everyone nodded. Miss Myers pointed upward along the path. "Perhaps the sentry, or an acolyte, led a procession up the hill to the site for religious ceremonies."

A voice called out a question. Gaia.:"What kind of religious ceremonies did they have?"

Miss Myers looked thoughtful. "It's hard to say, because we don't know who really built this site. It might have been a native tribe that lived here, or it might have been the Indians who came down from Canada, and they would have followed their own religious traditions." She paused. "The problem with that is that the Native Americans did not build in stone."

"So who did build this?" a boy named Josh asked. He had the build of an athlete, boy-next-door good looks, and soft, curly brown hair, and Chloe had noticed how the girls flocked around him at break time. She couldn't blame them. If she were not so involved with Thomas, she might have tried to attract his attention too.

Their instructor shook her head. "Nobody knows for sure. Archeologists have noted similarities to sites in Ireland, and some even speculate that the Norsemen could have sailed up the Spicket River and built here." She paused. "And there's an even wilder speculation that it might have been the Phoenicians. Nobody knows for sure."

She continued up the path and the class followed her. "Unfortunately," she continued, "a lot of damage has been done to the original site, so we're left with more questions than answers." She stopped and waved her hand around. "Other people think Christian monks were here, and they would have built some sort of church, and of course an altar."

And had visions. Ivy had told her and Thomas the stories that had grown into local folklore over the years.

The group arrived at the highest point of the site, which was open and empty except for the large altar stone. Chloe looked at it, shuddered and looked away. It was too much like the one Dyfan and the others had rigged up at the Midstate site, although that one was not as large, of course.

"Four and a half tons," Miss Myers noted, with a trace of satisfaction. "Was it dragged here on purpose, or did one of the glaciers, during the ice age leave it here? We'll never know."

Gaia spoke up again. "Did any of the group who were here over the years use this as an altar for human sacrifice?"

Miss Myers looked at the stone, and nodded slowly. "Nobody can say for sure, of course, but if you notice the groove carved around the edge, most experts think that's a dead giveaway." She winced, as several students giggled at her unintentional pun.

"And the groove is for what?" Gaia persisted.

Feeling more and more uncomfortable, Chloe looked away from the group, up through the branches of the huge trees, stretching their branches regally toward the sky.

"To collect the blood." The professor pointed to the base of the stone. "There would have been a vessel here to collect the blood—which would then be used in some sort of ceremony. Maybe thanks for good crops, or a sacrifice asking for good hunting."

Chloe took a few steps away from the group. She wanted to revisit the small chamber where she and Thomas had first made love.

Miss Meyers had gone over most of the material about Mystery Hill in class, using a Power Point presentation she'd put together for them. Once she'd pointed out the major constructions, and the sacrificial table, she encouraged them to look around on their own, and to take pictures if they were so inclined. A number of them had brought their cameras, and they scattered about, taking pictures of things that interested them, and of each other.

Chloe picked her way among the rocks with care, trying to recall where it was located. Yes, this was it, she decided, as she found the entrance. She stepped inside, and the feelings that had begun there surfaced within her again. A thrill went through her as she remembered that first time, how they had come together with gentleness and passion, and even though that first time had been special, whatever had been born between them that day had only deepened and become more beautiful through the year.

~ * ~

As Chloe stood there, she suddenly felt another presence in the chamber with her. No, not one presence—two. She couldn't see them with her eyes, but a new kind of awareness told her they were there, one on each side of her, an Indian brave and a young Indian girl. She knew what they looked like, what they were wearing, and she sensed their deep love for each other. And, more than that, she felt a part of both of them, as if somehow they all overlapped and were one entity.

The young brave was slight of build, and thin, and Chloe felt his despair and pain. The girl was younger and somehow Chloe knew she was pregnant, although it was not something she saw with her eyes. They both wore deerskin garments, fringed and decorated with beaded designs. The girl, strikingly beautiful, had long hair, raven-black, loose against her slim back.

The boy said something in his native language, but Chloe didn't need a translator to understand him. "I failed to protect you, Kanti. But someday we will meet again, and I will not fail you then."

The young woman said nothing, but Chloe felt her anguish. In a flash of insight, she knew they had been here, once long ago, and they had come back to tell her their story. But why? What did it have to do with her? Was this the reason Thomas was always so protective?

"Chloe."

Gaia stood in the narrow doorway.

The awareness of the other presences vanished as if they had never been. Chloe's anger flashed hot against her former best friend. She'd been granted a special moment in time, and who had come along to ruin it—Gaia, of course.

"What do you want? Why can't you leave me alone?"

Gaia looked terrible. She seemed to be trembling, and she stared at the ground, biting her lip. Tears ran down her cheeks, and her face was pale. She looked up at Chloe and reached out her hands, palms up. Her lips quivered. "I didn't come to annoy you—I just wanted to tell you something."

"I'm not interested in anything you have to say. Just go away, and stop bothering me."

Gaia didn't move. "Oh, Chloe, Jett just called me. Dyfan is dead."

Chloe rolled her eyes. "Sorry, Gaia. I don't believe that for one freakin' second." She pushed past her and hurried back to the safety of the group.

Thirty-one

Chloe stared out of the bus window and pretended not to notice, as Gaia, with Josh in tow, slid into the seat behind her on the bus. She spoke in quiet tones to Josh, telling him about her 'friend' Jack's terrible death—but Chloe knew she was meant to hear. It seemed Jett had gone looking for Dyfan, or Jack, and found him in the small apartment he rented, dead. He had hanged himself.

Poor innocent Josh swallowed every morsel of what Chloe still believed to be lies. He tried to comfort Gaia, putting his arm around her and letting her cry into his shoulder. Even Miss Myers left her seat and asked Gaia what the problem was, and how could she help?

Gaia, playing the martyr, sobbed that it 'was personal,' and to please just let her handle it in her own way.

Something rang false about it. Chloe had no feelings for the supposedly-dead Dyfan, except relief he would be out of her life, but she didn't completely believe it either. Gaia had proven herself a capable fibber, as well as an actress, often enough. She couldn't wait to tell Thomas. She dug out her cell phone. In fact, she'd text him right now. He'd have Jim Walsh's brother, the cop, check it out.

The bus back to Midstate was delayed for nearly an hour by an accident on the Interstate. Chloe raced toward the stadium. She shoved her way through the crowd piling inside the gym. Inside, students and their families packed the bleachers for the last game of the season.

The cheerleaders were already dressed and warming up the audience. Marcy threw her a scowl and Chloe mouthed, "I'm sorry!" at her as she flew into the dressing room and yanked open her locker. She threw on the green satin briefs, the short skirt that barely covered anything, and wriggled into the green and white halter top that boasted the Midstate logo. Her second pair of sneakers, the immaculate white ones she kept sacred for cheerleading, were there, too, and she plunked down on the wooden bench to change her shoes. No time to talk to Thomas.

Out on the floor, the Midstate team ran about the boards, passing the ball and making long shots. The crowd roared its approval. Chloe took her place in the cheerleading line, and scanned the bleachers, looking for his family, and finally spotted them, as Mike waved frantically at her.

She caught a glimpse of Thomas, and at that very moment he turned, caught her eye and gave her a quick grin and a thumbs-up. She wished she'd had a chance to tell him Gaia's supposed news, but she hadn't had a moment of privacy to do that. On the bus there'd been no opportunity to call him either. She had sent a brief text, but maybe Thomas hadn't checked his phone for that. Who knew for sure? Maybe Dyfan was dead, but if Gaia had loved him as much as she claimed, why wasn't she absolutely devastated?

If I lost Thomas that way, I'd be a basket case. I wouldn't be sitting on a bus relating details of the worst thing that ever happened to me to a casual classmate. Her heart hardened toward Gaia again. The girl was quite an actress.

Telling Thomas Gaia's 'news' would have to wait until after the game; and even then they had a date to have dinner out with the family. Ivy, of course, knew everything that had happened concerning Dyfan and the Druids, but Sharon, Charlie and Mike had no idea, and Thomas had told her in adamant tones that he didn't want them to know, and she agreed. Why drag anyone else into this tangled web?

The game began in earnest, and Chloe missed a few cues and earned more frowns from Marcy. When she made a wrong turn during one of the routines, the girl next to her hissed, "Pay attention! What's the matter with you tonight?"

Jim Walsh didn't look great, either. He actually had a black eye, and moved with a limp, as though everything hurt. She wondered what had happened to him.

The first twenty minutes of the game galloped by. At half-time, the Midstate Wildcats were five points behind. Jim Walsh looked as upset as Chloe had ever seen him. He herded his team into the dressing room.

Marcy had a few things to say to her squad, too. She put her hands on her hips and glared at Chloe. "This is the last game of the season. It's a big deal, and the way you're cheering tonight, it's like you've never been on the floor."

Chloe spread her hands in apology. "I'm sorry." She knew that no excuse was valid, either that she'd had upsetting news or that she was tired from the field trip.

Second half, the Wildcats came back with a vengeance. The other team fell behind and never seemed able to regain its confidence, as Midstate surged ahead. Chloe cheered as Thomas played like a demon, making several three-pointers, and never missing his foul shots. As the buzzer rang, the crowd jumped to its feet, shouting, their arms waving in the air. Sixty-seven to fifty-two. It was a great victory.

~ * ~

Thomas shifted from one foot to the other as he waited outside the girls' dressing room for Chloe.

"Great game, Thorn!"

"Way to go, guy."

Teammates and classmates, and even students he didn't know stopped to clap him on the shoulder and congratulate him. It felt great, but not as wonderful as the pleasure he'd felt knowing how well he'd played with his family watching him from the stands, and not nearly as satisfying as knowing Chloe was back safe and sound from her trip to Mystery Hill. Her bus had been late—but his relief was tangible when he saw her rush into the stadium at last.

He'd taken the quickest shower of his life, just wanting to get back to her. He heard the hair dryers buzzing, and settled against the wall to wait. It wasn't as long as he'd expected.

She flew through the door into his arms. He buried his face in her hair. She smelled like soap and hot water, shampoo and the faint lilac scent she always wore.

As she pulled away, she had that look in her eyes, a look he recognized by now that said to him: "I have something to tell you." He could tell it wasn't anything good, but before she could share her news, however, his family surrounded them.

"Later," he mouthed at her, but looked at her with concern. He knew her well enough by now to know something was eating at her, and besides he had seen her make several mistakes in the cheering routines, and he had noticed Marcy snapping at her. That wasn't like Chloe at all. He had questions of his own; Jim Walsh looked as if he'd been in one hell of a fist fight, but the coach hadn't said anything, and when one player asked, he brushed it off. "Irish street fight, shades of my childhood. Nothing serious. Keep your attention on the game."

"Why didn't you leave your cheerleading outfit on?" Mike demanded, grinning at Chloe. "You got great legs."

Two college guys passing the group laughed out loud. "That she does, kid!" one of them called back.

Charlie herded his family through the crowd toward the doors, everyone talking and laughing at once. Thomas walked with Ivy, holding her arm, and made sure she didn't get lost in the crush, although he was fairly sure she could take care of herself if that did happen. Chloe went ahead of him, and Mike hopped along at her side, trying to keep her attention all for himself.

As they neared the exit, he heard Chloe gasp, and she turned enough to throw him a look of alarm. He tensed as he put his other hand on her shoulder. "What is it?"

He hadn't needed to ask. His family paused as another group approached the exit, blocking their way.

Charlie, oblivious, stepped back to let them go first. "After you," he said, with a courtly wave of his arm.

Thomas, Chloe and Ivy stood face to face with Gaia, Jett, Jeb and Ingrid. Thomas avoided Gaia's eyes, which were fixed on him. He felt Chloe freeze.

"Great game, Thomas," she said in a sweet voice, tossing her blond curls in a flirty way. "You were awesome tonight."

"Thanks," he said briefly.

"Is this your family? I'm so glad to meet them at last." She made it sound as if she'd heard all about them. She extended her hand to Sharon. "Hi, I'm Gaia."

There was nothing he could do. He and Chloe introduced everyone all around. Charlie and Sharon greeted them all warmly, country-friendly, and evidently not sensing the tension that swirled around Thomas and Chloe. Ivy, however, was a different breed of cat. She took everything in with one glance at their faces, as she looked from one to the other, fixing her gaze long and hard on Gaia, and Gaia was the first to look away.

"What a sweet girl," Sharon said, looking after Gaia. "Good thing you saw Thomas first, Chloe."

Chloe choked on her answer. "Yes, isn't it?"

"We'll meet you at the restaurant," Thomas said to his dad as they headed for the parking lot. "I have my car. We can't all fit in yours."

He turned the key in the ignition and flicked on the heater, as it was a chilly evening. He turned to Chloe. "Okay, what gives?"

She threw him a look of gratitude. "You always know, don't you? Well, get a load of what Gaia told me back at Mystery Hill, and I don't believe a word of it, by the way."

"I thought you weren't going to talk to Gaia..."

She waved her hand at him. "I didn't. She sort of way-laid me where I couldn't get away from her, and just blurted out that Dyfan is dead..."

"What?"

"That's what she said, and she looked awful, red-eyed, and sort of freaked-out. I said I didn't believe her, but then she sat behind me on the bus and told this other kid, Josh, all about how he hanged himself."

"She didn't look so freaked-out a few minutes ago."

"No. You'd think if that were true, they wouldn't be at the game, acting more or less normal—for them, that is. Are they trying to throw us off-guard? Why else would they want us to believe that?"

Thomas backed out from the parking space and edged his way into a line moving out of the lot. "I don't believe it either. They're toying with us. We'll call Mr. Walsh when we get back to the apartment and see what he's heard from his brother."

"What's with him, anyway?" Chloe asked. "He looked awful."

"He didn't tell us any details, just said it was an "Irish street fight'."

"Weird," Chloe said. "I never thought he was the type for brawling."

Thomas shrugged. "Maybe he got jumped, and didn't have a choice."

Charlie had made reservations at a well-known steak house on the edge of town. It was situated on a picturesque lake, although this late in the evening there wasn't much to see in the way of scenery.

Everyone had a variation of the restaurant's famous steak. When their meals arrived, everyone's meat was cooked to their individual tastes, and the accompanying vegetables were colorful and crisp.

"Your mashed potatoes are better, Mom," Mike said, as he pushed the creamy white mound around his plate. "These taste like they've got Elmer's glue in them."

"Wow, a compliment from Mike!" Sharon smiled at her son. "Will miracles never cease?"

Everyone laughed, and Thomas made an effort to participate in the family outing and enjoy it. But when his eyes met Ivy's, even for the flick of a second or two, he saw the concern reflected in them, and knew she wasn't fooled at all.

~ * ~

The wind blew off the lake, ruffling Chloe's hair as the Thorn family said their goodbyes. Thomas watched her as she hugged his mom and dad, and Mike, and thought of how much he loved her. Her news about what Gaia had said disturbed him more than he wanted to admit. There were the same old feelings, surfacing again, that Evil with a capital E was in the air, and its eyes were fastened on Chloe.

Ivy was the last to hug him. "Call me," she whispered in his ear.

He returned her embrace. "I will."

As soon as they returned to the apartment, Thomas flicked on the TV, trying several local stations in search of possible news of a local suicide. There was nothing, but the usual, which included a shoplifting incident, but no serious crimes in Middleton or vicinity.

"Is it too late to call Mr. Walsh?" Chloe asked, casting a concerned look at the clock on the wall.

"Maybe, but I'm calling anyway." He pressed in the numbers.

"Coach, it's Thomas. I heard something tonight that..."

Walsh interrupted him. "I was just about to call you. What did you hear?"

"Gaia told Chloe that Jack Wayland, otherwise known as Dyfan, committed suicide by hanging himself at his apartment. Is that true?"

Coach drew in a long breath. "I haven't heard anything about that. But I'm afraid Joe called and told me something even worse. Is Chloe with you?"

"Yeah. We didn't hear anything on the TV. You want me to put her on?"

"Yes. I guess I should tell her myself." He sounded distraught.

Thomas raised his eyebrows and handed the phone to Chloe. "He wants to talk to you."

"Me?" She took the phone. "Mr. Walsh?"

"Chloe, I have something to tell you, and it's very bad. My brother Joe just called me with this—I wanted you to be the first to know, before all the media gets it in the morning."

She drew in a breath. This sounded bad, but if it wasn't Dyfan, what could it be? "What is it?"

"Chloe, I hardly know how to tell you this, so I'll just say it. A body was found out at that student pretend-Stonehenge site today, but it wasn't Dyfan's."

She could hardly breathe. She managed a weak, "Whose was it, then?"

He blurted it out. "Your former roommate—Hannah's."

Thirty-two

By Monday, a thoroughly shaken Chloe gathered up her books and mini-computer and prepared to go back to class.

Thomas urged her to wait a few more days, and do her work at the apartment, as she had cried all weekend, alternately in sorrow and in rage. Her eyes were red and puffy, but her stubborn streak asserted itself. Thomas had also filled her in on Jim Walsh's beating, which accounted for his condition at the game, and the disappearance of Jeb's painting. Everything he told her seemed to make her more determined.

She had watched the first TV account of Hannah's death. The breathless young blond anchor, who looked more like a high school beauty queen than a newscaster, delivered the grisly account. "Hannah Stuart, a sophomore at Midstate Community College, was found dead Friday in the woods on the east edge of town. A mini-Stonehenge site had been built there recently by some Midstate college students, but due to recent complaints, had been dismantled. Hannah had been tied to a tree, and an arrow shot into her heart." The girl swallowed and paused for a moment, as if reading the account was just too distasteful for her. After a few seconds she continued. "The crossbow was left on the ground near her. Police are interviewing her friends at the college, but they have no suspects at present. The family…"

Chloe ran from the room, and slammed the bedroom door.

Thomas rapped on the door. "Chloe?"

"Leave me alone, Thomas," she answered, her voice choked with tears. She didn't come out the rest of the day.

A girl he hardly knew emerged from the room that evening. The lightheartedness, the humor, the breeziness was gone. Thomas saw and felt the difference in her. This girl was hard and determined.

"I'm not hiding out from them, Thomas, no matter what they do."

"Chloe, be reasonable. Gaia tells you Dyfan committed suicide by hanging himself. The police couldn't find any trace of a dead Jack Wayland, alias Dyfan, but Hannah is found dead out on the Druid site. Isn't it obvious they've sent you a message? They want you confused and terrified, for their own purposes."

"What can they do?" Chloe asked. "The police are all on alert now. Jack wouldn't dare show his face around town, or the campus, and if Gaia so much as looks at me, I'm going to rip her eyes out."

Thomas sighed. He had known that beneath her light-hearted manner Chloe had a toughness she rarely showed, but he wasn't sure she would be able to handle an all-out attack if the others all ganged up on her. He slung his backpack over his shoulder, trying to push back his misgivings. "Okay if I walk you to class, then?"

"Sure," she said with a shrug.

She went down the stairs ahead of him, and walked toward the college, barely replying to his attempts at conversation. When they reached the art building, he attempted to put his arms around her, but she shook him off. "Not now, Thomas. I have things to work out first."

"Why can't we do it together?"

She met his eyes, and it seemed to him that there was no sign of recognition in them. "I'll be back, Thomas, emotionally, that is, but it's going to take a while, just like it did after my mother died. Just please, don't push me."

He struggled with his need to stay with her and protect her, and her need to process her sorrow in her own way, but finally gave in. A sense of unease washed over him, but he tried to push it back. "I'll see you back at the apartment then," he said. "I'll get a pizza for dinner, okay?"

"Sure." Toneless, as if she didn't care. She turned toward the door.

He had to try just once more. "Be careful, honey...please."

She almost smiled at him. "Sure, Thomas, you know me."

As he watched her walk away, so straight-backed and sure of herself, he wondered if he did know her, after all.

~ * ~

Chloe retrieved her painting from the storage rack, set it on her easel, and sat staring at it for a long time. The eyes of the fawn, so desperate and pleading, pierced her heart, but also hardened her determination. The painting was coming along well. It was everything she intended, but she just couldn't go on with it. She felt Jim Walsh's concerned looks as he walked around the room, helping his students with their projects. He started toward her once, but she glanced up at him and shook her head. He changed direction and bent to confer with a pretty, dark-haired girl on the other side of the studio.

Chloe didn't go out for break, but nearly everyone else seemed to need to get out of the classroom and take a breather from the obvious tension. Jeb went over to the storage rack on his way out and rustled through the paintings stacked there, making more noise than he needed to.

He turned to smirk at her, then said in a loud voice to the professor. "Mr. Walsh, my painting isn't here. Do you know where it is?"

Chloe couldn't believe his nerve. Oh, he sounded so innocent!

Walsh gave him a cold stare. "I think you know where it is."

Jeb shrugged and left the room with Ingrid.

He did that to provide himself an alibi by pretending he doesn't know what happened to the painting. But he knows. She looked after him with loathing.

But—who had seen Jim Walsh leaving the building with Jeb's painting? It wouldn't even have been unusual to see him carrying a canvas or two. Everyone knew he walked everywhere he went, and the campus wasn't that large. Probably someone going to or leaving the dining hall, or on their way somewhere, had seen him. Maybe Jeb himself had seen Walsh leaving the Redfern complex.

All at once Chloe made up her mind. She got out the Gesso, chose a wide brush and, with determination, wiped out the painting of the fawn in the woods, and laid a fresh, new white surface on the canvas. She glanced up to see Walsh watching her. He gave her a brief nod. He understood.

By the end of class, her portrait of Hannah had taken on a mission of its own. Was it related in style or color or pose to another painting? She didn't know and didn't care as Hannah's pretty, serene face came to life on the canvas. What she did know was that it was the best thing she'd ever done, and it was this that would express her love for Hannah, and let the healing begin.

Gaia didn't show up for archeology class in the afternoon. The mood was definitely somber as the students filed in. Chloe ignored her usual seat in the back of the room and sat where Hannah had sat, near the front. Miss Myers raised her eyebrows, but didn't comment.

Professor Myers waited until everyone was seated and quiet. Usually so articulate and sure of herself, she seemed at a loss how to begin. Finally, she cleared her throat, and stumbling over her words, plunged ahead. "Students, we've had a tragedy on campus, of which you're all well aware by now. We missed Hannah on the field trip, and now we know why. It is beyond my comprehension how anyone could do that to anyone, much less a beautiful young woman like Hannah. In honor of her, I am going to dismiss class today, and as you have heard, the campus will shut down on Friday as a tribute to her. Her family arrived in town yesterday, and invites anyone who wishes to go to attend her memorial service."

Chloe had a brief stab of memory, as she thought of meeting Hannah's parents and younger sister, Becca, when they had moved into the dorm the first year. They had seemed like lovely people, and Becca was as lively and talkative as Hannah was serious and quiet.

Nobody said anything. Silently, the students filed out of the classroom, leaving Miss Myers standing in her usual position, staring at the floor.

~ * ~

"Chloe."

She stopped short and raised her eyes. She recognized Joe Walsh, Professor Walsh's brother, whom she had met when she and Thomas had first gone to the police station to report on the Druids. Taller and slimmer with darker hair, he still resembled his brother. He had been waiting for her.

"Do you have a few minutes?"

She nodded. "Sure."

He motioned down the hall to where a bench sat in front of a window. Chloe wasn't surprised that nobody was there as usual, drinking coffee or a soda, chatting with another student, or just staring out the window. The whole campus seemed in a depressed mood, with a heaviness hanging over everything. Things like this just didn't happen in Middleton.

Joe got out his pad and unhooked a pen from his jacket pocket. "Mind if I ask you a few questions?"

She shook her head. "No, but Jack Wayland killed Hannah. I have no doubts about that."

"Well, let's work up to that. She was formerly your roommate in the dorm, right?

"Yes."

"How well did you know her? Ever go home with her on break or hang out with her on campus?"

"No. I met her family when we moved into the dorm last year. She had her group, and I had mine. We weren't close friends, but we suited each other well as roommates."

"Why did you move out of the dorm?"

She hesitated. The whole thing sounded so crazy. She began again. "My former best friend..."

"That would be Gaia Butler, right?"

"Yes. Well, she and I started to not get along very well, and I had started seeing Thomas Thorn and we decided to move in together."

"And do you mind if I ask? What was the source of contention between you and Gaia? Was it Thomas?"

Chloe took a deep breath. She knew she appeared strong and composed, but they didn't know how terrified she felt inside. She hurt for Hannah and her family; she was scared for Thomas and herself. It looked as though she would have to get into the whole Gaia-Jett-Dyfan thing, and she hated talking about them. Nevertheless, if it would help in catching Hannah's killer, she'd do it. She'd do anything.

"In the beginning, it was. Then Gaia wanted to get involved in this Druid group. I didn't want to, but she talked me into it, and Thomas, who was rooming with Jett Mason, agreed to go, too."

"And did you like it once you got involved?"

"No!" she said with emphasis. "But—well, it was strange. We kept going anyway."

"Why, if you didn't like it?

She took a deep breath, crossed her arms to keep herself from shaking, then plunged into the mind-control knowledge that Jack, as Dyfan, seemed to have, and how somehow he'd taught Jett and Gaia to use it, too.

She gave out a nervous laugh. "This all sounds crazy, right?"

"Strange things happen, Chloe. Just keep talking. I'm not making any judgments."

Joe nodded soberly, making notes as he listened. "And after one of the basketball games, you say Jett and Gaia and a couple other kids actually kidnapped you and took you out to that Stonehenge site?"

She nodded.

He wrote down their names, then closed the pad with a snap.

"I didn't take this all too seriously until my brother was assaulted, and of course this grisly murder. We're going to get whoever did this, you better believe me."

She set her mouth. "Jack Wayland did it, I told you."

"I'm inclined to think so, but we have to look at other possibilities."

"You don't need to look any farther. He owned a crossbow, and he left it right there. He wants you to know he did it."

Thirty-three

After Thomas filled her in on Hannah's murder, Ivy called Thomas and Chloe every day and spoke to both of them. Some of the news they had to tell her was good, some not so good. The police couldn't find any trace of Jack Wayland, alias Dyfan, and everyone they spoke to denied knowing him. Although the police grilled Ingrid and Jeb for several hours, they had nothing to say, and even denied knowing him at all. Gaia never came back to the archeology class, and no one seemed to know where she was.

One day Thomas told her no one had seen Jett lately, either.

"I don't like it," Ivy said. "All three of them missing. I don't get good vibes about this. Has anyone contacted their parents?"

Ivy could almost feel Thomas' shrug over the phone line. "Jim Walsh went to Administration, and they said Jett's parents and Gaia's aunt all said they had heard from them, and there was nothing to worry about. They said they'd be back in time for exams. Professor Walsh's brother, the cop, said as long as the families had heard from the kids and didn't seem concerned, there was nothing they could do."

She could tell that Thomas didn't want her to worry. He tried to reassure her. "Well, as far as we're concerned, we have less to worry about with them gone."

"I know," she said. "But I have a bad feeling they're not really gone. Just be really careful, around town and the campus, too. Don't leave Chloe alone."

"I won't, and the school year is nearly over."

"I can't wait until you're both back here to stay. Then, next year when you transfer to Keene, you'll be out of their clutches forever."

She heard Thomas blow out a long breath. "Yeah. I can't wait 'til this is all over."

Ivy hung up, and stood gazing out her kitchen window. The magnolia tree on the edge of the lawn had started to come to life. Leaves sprouted on the other trees, and the lawn was coming in fresh and green.

Ivy shook her head. "I don't know what's going to happen, but I know this isn't over. And I don't know how to help them."

Nevertheless, the days passed without incident, although Ivy's nerves jangled like shattered glass, and she felt as though she were walking on nails. She counted down the weeks until the end of the school year...six, five, and finally, only a month to go.

"Mom, what's the matter with you?" Sharon asked one night at dinner. "I've just never seen you so antsy."

Mike smirked. "Antsy? She's a wreck. Every time I say anything, she yells at me."

Ivy felt instant remorse. She'd been so focused on Thomas and Chloe, so anxious to have them safely home, that she had snapped at Mike repeatedly. She simply had no patience for his antics and outrageous remarks.

"What can I do to make it up to you?" she asked.

He didn't even think about an answer. "Drive me over to spend a weekend with Thomas and Choe," he demanded.

"That's a great idea," Charlie commented dryly.

Ivy threw Mike a grin. "We could do that. We have to wait a few weeks for the end of school, though, as they have exams soon and they have to study for them. And Chloe has a big art project to complete. They'll have a few days free after exams. We'll go then, okay?"

"Could we do something else sooner?"

"What do you have in mind?"

"Go up to Mystery Hill with me, and tell me everything you know about the place."

"No!" Ivy surprised herself at how loudly her voice came out. She clapped her hand over her mouth. "Sorry, I didn't mean to yell."

Sharon and Charlie looked at her in amazement. "Mom," Sharon said, "what in the world is the matter with you?"

"Told'ja," Mike said. He stood up and leered at Ivy. "Maybe you should go spend a night with Russell and work off whatever's bugging you..."

"Mike!" Charlie yelled. He jumped up so fast his chair fell over.

Mike took one look at his father's face and ran. Charlie went after him.

"Well," Sharon said, looking around the table as if everyone were still sitting in their places. "Who wants pie? I made apple and cherry."

Ivy rose from her chair. "I'm going back to my place. I need something stronger, like a margarita—or three."

~ * ~

All evening long Ivy stewed, trying to figure out what was bothering her. It had to do with Thomas and Chloe, yes, but what was she so concerned about that kept her so on edge? A couple of unflavored margaritas later, she got out her journal, the one in which she had chronicled all the strange things she'd experienced, sat in her rocker and read it from start to finish. The only entries that hit her as being meaningful were the two about Chloe at Disney World. She'd had no premonitions about future events involving Thomas or Chloe.

She closed the journal, sat back and shut her eyes. It was about Chloe, then. Maybe meditation would give her a clue. Perhaps she could connect with Chloe's mind and get a better handle on whatever was digging at her.

She closed all the curtains until the inside of the trailer was as dim as she could get it. She lit a candle, set it in front of her and tried to lose herself in its flame. She forced her mind to go blank, to picture Chloe's face and nothing else. Nothing happened, and no image came.

Forty-five minutes later, nothing had pierced the gray haze, and she gave up in frustration. She had never mediated and had nothing happen. Sometimes it wasn't much—just a feeling or a shape passing before her eyes, or a memory that became more vivid as she dwelled on it. Sometimes she had a premonition, but she'd never sat and experienced nothing at all. She sighed and opened her eyes. Then it hit her, and a cold chill swept over her. It was a knowing, that's the only way she could describe it. She'd been right all along. Chloe was in mortal danger.

She had connected with Chloe, but it was like a one-way phone call. Right now there was no one on the other end of the line.

She paced up and down the length of her mobile home. The full moon, as it rose, flooded the yard with light, and she began circling around the pool, trying to work off her restless energy. It didn't help.

She went back into the trailer, and sat in her favorite recliner. She had already checked in with Thomas that morning, but now the fear that filled her concerned Chloe. She decided to call her, just to make sure.

There was no answer on Chloe's cell, and that didn't surprise Ivy, but it did increase her worry.

She called Thomas. His voice message said that he was at the Sports Banquet, and wouldn't be taking calls until later that night. Leave a message.

Ivy choked the words out. "Thomas, I called Chloe and there's no answer there. Call me crazy—but you know these feelings I get, and they are seldom mistaken. Something's wrong—she's in danger, Thomas, I know it. Call me as soon as you can."

When she rang off, she sat back in despair, knowing there was nothing she could do. Then a very strange thing happened. She heard a phone ringing, but the sound was all in her head. She knew it was Chloe, but how did you answer a phone that isn't real?

Thirty-four

Chloe's feet felt cold, and she awoke. Instinctively, she moved, trying to stretch out her arms and legs, but they were met by the hard edges of whatever confined her. The sudden knowledge that she lay captive, wrapped in a blanket, in an enclosed, dark space brought her to full and sudden consciousness. Her feet were cold because whoever put her there had removed her shoes. The sound of a motor and the uneven motion told her that she was in the trunk of a car.

Panic set in. Her stomach knotted, and a small scream escaped her, but she forced it back as she realized that whomever was responsible for her abduction might hear her, and come to do something worse to her. Her mind felt foggy, and she needed time to figure things out. As her eyes grew used to the dimness, she shifted her position, and frantically explored the spaces around her with her hands, trying to discover what else was in the trunk with her.

She choked back a sob. Nothing. Not a jack or a wrench, or anything else that could be used as a weapon, or to make noise, or to poke out the taillights to attract attention.

Her heart beat like a tom-tom, and her head whirled in confusion. She closed her eyes and concentrated, willing herself to keep calm, as her mind cleared. Who had taken her, put her in the trunk of a car, and where were they going?

And where was Thomas?

She gasped as all of a sudden everything came back.

Marcy had called her while she waited for Thomas to come home from the basketball team banquet. All the sports teams came together with one big bash at the end of the year. "Just a couple of beers at the Elk Horn to celebrate with the squad," Marcy had said.

Chloe considered. Thomas had made her promise not to go out. But if she left him a text message that she was going to the Elk Horn with Marcy and the rest of the girls, just a final time together before they all went their separate ways for the summer...well, he couldn't object to that, could he? After all, it had been weeks, the school year was nearly over, and no one had seen any trace of Dyfan, or Gaia or Jett, so how dangerous could hanging out at the Elk Horn be?

The police had searched the town for the trio, and found nothing. Jack Wayland had apparently fled his apartment, leaving a month's rent unpaid. The cops, as well as the college authorities, contacted Jett's parents and Gaia's aunt, and all reported they'd heard from the kids, and they were okay. Of course, they continued their search for Jack, but other than what Chloe had told Joe Walsh about the crossbow, they had no evidence against him.

She made up her mind. She was tired of sorting, cleaning and packing, and didn't see why she should sit around doing nothing while Thomas celebrated with his team. "Okay, Marcy, I'll go, just for a while. Can you pick me up? My car died months ago."

"Sure," Marcy said, and gave a little cough. "Be there in ten minutes."

"Your voice sounds funny," Chloe said. "Do you have a cold?"

"My allergies acting up, that's all. See you in ten."

She sent a brief text to Thomas. She would be at the Elk Horn with Marcy and the rest of the squad.

Chloe ran into the bedroom and fished through her closet for something a little special to wear on her last night out in Middleton. She chose a white, lacy-knit pullover dress that stopped just short of her knees. As she held it up to her in front of the dresser mirror, Marcy's words came back to her: 'my allergies are acting up'. Allergies? She'd known Marcy for two years and never heard her complain about allergies. Oh, well. She shook herself mentally. She didn't know everything about everyone, did she?

She barely had time to dash on makeup and pull a brush through her hair before she heard the knock at the door.

She grabbed her purse and raced to the door. As she unlocked it, the door pushed forward against her, forcing her back and knocking her off balance. She gasped and blinked her eyes in disbelief. "What are you two doing here?"

"Surprise!" Jett said, grinning.

"Hey now," Gaia said. "Is that any way to greet old friends?"

They closed the door behind them and stood blocking it.

Fear beat at her. What did they want? "You stopped being my friends a long time ago. Get out of here!" Her voice rose. "I don't want anything more to do with you."

"Oh, come now." Gaia pinned her sharp blue eyes on her, then brushed over her dress. "Well, don't you look nice? Very appropriate."

Chloe looked away, remembering how Gaia's gaze had been able to affect her before. "Do you have any beer in the fridge? No need to go to the Elk Horn. Let's just have a drink here, and renew our previous friendship."

"No." Chloe yelled. Her nails bit into her palms "I want you both out of here—now."

Gaia looked at Jett. "I'll get something from the fridge, juice if they don't have anything else. Keep an eye on her."

As soon as Gaia headed for the kitchen, Chloe seized the only opportunity she knew she would have. She grabbed a ceramic lamp from a side table, pulling the cord out of the socket, sprang forward and swung it at Jett's head. He ducked just in time to avoid the blow, and it crashed against the door. She dashed past him and got her hand on the doorknob, but he grabbed her, pulled her back and pushed her roughly into one of the armchairs.

"Stay right there!"

"I will not. Let me go!" She jumped up. Jett slapped her hard across the face, knocking her back. She stared at him, incredulous. Her face stung with pain.

Gaia returned with three bottles of beer.

"I do hope you're going to cooperate. It will make things so much easier." She raised the bottle in a pretend toast. "C'mon, kiddo. Let's have a last drink together."

A last drink? What the hell did she mean by that?

Chloe took the beer, but before she could hurl it at Gaia's face, which was what she intended to do, both Jett and Gaia pinned her to the chair.

"Chloe, you're going to drink this," Gaia said. Chloe kicked and twisted, fighting as hard as she could, but Jett was much stronger than she'd have thought, and held her down with his own body. Gaia forced the bottle between her lips. She tried not to swallow, but she had to—or choke. She managed to spit some of it out, but most of it went down her throat.

Jett glanced at Gaia. "Think she needs another?"

"Let's wait and see." Gaia sat back, and put her own brew to her mouth.

Chloe looked at the door. She should make another attempt to escape. But the door seemed to waver, like one of the carnival mirrors. When she shifted her gaze back to Jett and Gaia, she had trouble focusing on their features. Their faces seemed to be changing shape, melting.

She fought to stay conscious, but she felt her resistance melting away. She heard Gaia's voice asking something, and Jett's reply, "date rape drug."

Chloe made one more great effort, as she threw herself out of her chair and tried to crawl toward the door. She heard their laughter as they picked her up and set her back in the chair.

"Just relax, Chloe," Gaia said. "You're going to like to way you feel in a few minutes."

"Yeah, she'll mellow out. Hey, Gaia, was there more beer in the fridge?"

Chloe's head felt as though it was stuffed with wool, but the thought went through her that she was drinking beer with two of her best friends and she should try to be a good hostess. Thomas would be home soon, and he would want to join them...

"...I'll get more." She tried to get up, but she felt so heavy. She hadn't realized how tired she was, but she made a try.

"I'll get them for us." Her words sounded as if they came from a great distance.

Gaia put a hand on her shoulder. "I'll get them, Chloe. You just stay here and rest. You must be so tired from all the packing you've been doing." Her voice sounded so soothing.

Chloe heard the refrigerator door open and close, and the sound of beers being popped open. Gaia came back into the room and handed her one of the cans.

Jett raised his drink. "Here's to the three of us, together again."

The beer tasted good, cold and smooth in her mouth.

Gaia said something to her, but she couldn't make it out. "What, what are you saying?" Was that her own voice, sounding so hesitant, her words slurring?

She heard Dyfan's voice—what was Dyfan doing in her apartment? Wasn't he dead? Gaia had told her he was dead.

Then everything had gone gray, and now here she was, trapped in the trunk of someone's car and being taken somewhere against her will, and scared to death. What did they intend to do with her?

She fumbled around for her cell phone, but she knew they wouldn't have left it with her. She had to get a message to Thomas, but how was she going to do that? What would Thomas have done when he got home and found her gone? Did he figure she'd gone out and would be home later? Had he decided just to go to bed and wait for her?

When would he realize something had happened to her, and how would he go about finding her?

The car bumped along. Chloe fought to keep herself calm, thanking God she wasn't claustrophobic. Actually, she found small, confined spaces comforting. There were plenty of times as a child when she had curled up in a corner, shielded by furniture or boxes, and remained there for hours, feeling secure.

She tried to reason it out. Okay, Gaia had masqueraded as Marcy—thus the voice that didn't quite ring true, and Gaia and Jett had obviously drugged her. Dyfan had been waiting in the wings, so to speak, and the three of them had kidnapped her from the apartment, wrapped her in a blanket and imprisoned her in the trunk of a car. She wondered how they had carried her down three flights of stairs without anyone seeing or hearing them. It was already evening, dark out, so probably no one saw them put her in the trunk.

She wriggled around as much as she could, trying to ease her cramped legs. Why had they removed her shoes? So that she couldn't kick out the taillights? Somewhere she had heard that was what you were supposed to do if you got locked in the trunk of a car.

She wondered how long she had been confined there, and how far they had driven. There was no way to tell. But her mind was clearing, and whenever and wherever they stopped, she had better be ready. And she couldn't afford to give in to fear and risk making any mistakes, if she had any chance of escape.

Suddenly she thought of Ivy. What had Ivy told them? That minds could link with each other, and knowledge and power could be transmitted that way.

She closed her eyes and pictured Ivy's face. Slowly the old woman's face came into focus, and her gray eyes, so like Thomas' and Mike's fastened on hers.

She put all the mental energy she had into two words as she gazed into Ivy's eyes: *Help me.*

~ * ~

Help me. It was Chloe's voice, and the words rocked Ivy to the core and went through her body like an infusion of icy water. She'd been right. Something had happened to Chloe and she needed help. But unlike the time when she'd been lost in the snow, there didn't seem to be anything around her but darkness. Where was Thomas?

She glanced at the clock. It was quarter past eleven. She grabbed the phone and pressed the numbers for Thomas' cell phone. He answered, sounding sleepy.

"Hi, Ivy. Got your message and just about to call you. I'm on my way home from the sports banquet. What are you so worried about? Chloe's okay."

"Thomas, where is she?"

"Either home or at the Elk Horn with the other cheerleaders. She sent me a text she was going out with Marcy…"

"Thomas, she's in danger. She needs help."

"What are you talking about? I told you, she's either home…"

"No, she isn't! Thomas, call her, and check out both places."

He hesitated, but only for a few seconds. "Okay, Ivy. You're usually right. And-—I'm almost to the Elk Horn now. I'll stop in and check, and call you right back."

"No! I'll hold. Hurry, Thomas!"

Ivy could hardly sit still. She drummed her fingers on the table, ran her fingers through her hair, tapped her feet on the floor, as she heard Thomas slow the car, pull into the parking lot and turn off the ignition.

"Thomas, hurry up!" She felt close to tears. She couldn't help Chloe if she didn't have a clue where she was, or how to help her.

He tried to humor her, reporting in a sing-song voice. "I'm getting out of the car now, Ivy, closing the car door. I'm walking to the door of the Elk Horn...opening the door, lots of kids here."

"Thomas!" She fumed at him, wishing she could yell through the phone loud enough to alarm him.

"I'm looking around now, Ivy, don't see Chloe. Oh, there's Marcy and a few of the other girls. I'm walking toward them now—Hi, Jesse, hi, Mark, 'lo there Haley..."

"Thomas! I beg you!"

"Checkin' in with Marcy now. Hi, Marcy. How long ago did Chloe leave?"

Ivy tried to hear Marcy's reply, but the noise in the Elk Horn blocked her words.

Thomas said something else. Ivy caught, "she told me you called her and..."

Another muffled reply, and she heard Thomas say, "You never called her?"

The noise from the bar faded. Thomas came back on the line. He sounded much more awake, and she detected an undercurrent of worry in his voice. "She was never here, but I'm sure she's at home, Ivy. She must have changed her mind."

"Did you say Marcy said she never called Chloe?"

"Yeah." Thomas didn't sound so jolly now. "I'm going to have to hang up, Ivy, so I can call her cell. I'm going right home. I'll call back as soon as I get there and find her."

Ivy let him click off. *She's not there, Thomas. She needs us both to help her, but I don't know where she is.*

Thirty-five

Thomas ran up the three flights of stairs, calling her name as soon as he entered the building. The door to their apartment wasn't locked. His heart in his throat, he raced from room to room, calling her, looking in every possible place someone could have stashed a body. Nothing and nobody, and no note. Her cell phone lay on the floor. His desperation built. Chloe just wasn't there. He called 911.

"Yes, what's your concern?"

"My girlfriend! She's supposed to be here, but she isn't. Someone's taken her."

The operator sounded amused. "Well, sir, I'm sure she'll come back. Why don't you just relax…"

"You don't understand! These people have been after her for months! She never would have left without telling me." His voice rose until he was shouting.

"Sir, if you will just calm down, I'll send a policeman around to talk to you."

Thomas rarely cursed, but he let out a stream of profanity that surprised even himself. "If I don't find her, they'll kill her!"

"Who are *they*...?" the woman began, but Thomas hung up in frustration and dialed Coach Walsh's number.

Coach listened for a bare ten seconds, and grasped the situation at once. "I'll call Joe to get people out here, and I'll be right over." Several minutes later, Thomas heard him pounding up the stairs, and rushed to the door to let him in.

Red-faced and breathless, Walsh put a hand on Thomas' shoulder. "When did you last see her?"

Thomas began to pace the room, unable to stand still. "Earlier tonight, before I set off for the banquet. She texted me about an hour later that she was going to the Elk Horn with Marcy and the girls. But I just checked there, and Marcy said Chloe'd never been there."

Walsh rubbed his chin in agitation. "Okay, okay, let's try to figure this out."

"And look at this, Coach. She left her cell phone. Who goes anywhere without their cell?"

Walsh nodded. "Bad sign. Is there anywhere else she might have gone off by herself?"

"No, I can't think—and she would have let me know. I made her promise!"

"If—just think about it. If someone took her, where would they take her?"

"Oh, God! Out to the Druid site where Hannah was found?" Thomas folded in on himself as the thought hit him. He started for the door, but Walsh restrained him.

"No, I don't think so, and Joe and his crew are on their way out there now, anyway. Where else?"

The answer struck him like a bullet. "Mystery Hill!"

Walsh nodded. "That's what I think, too. Let's go!" He dug out his phone. "I'll have my brother alert the police in East Salem to get out there and see what's going on. We'll stop by my place so I can pick up my gun."

"It'll take us an hour to get there." Thomas had never felt so helpless. It was like *déjà vu*. All those strange and inexplicable things he'd seen in dreams or visions, or imagined—Chloe was in danger and again he couldn't protect her.

~ * ~

Donna Rigozzi didn't have the money for a real vacation, but her sister in North Salem had invited her to spend the week with her family. On this perfect spring-into-summer day, she felt a little restless.

Emily asked, "What would you like most, Donna, that I could actually give you, or do for you? Please be honest."

Donna swallowed hard. Did she dare ask for this? "Time. Just one day for me alone, no kids, nothing I have to do."

"You got it." It was a Friday, a teachers' in-service day, so the kids were all out of school. Emily and her husband had decided to take their two and Donna's three to the Children's Museum in Boston, and to stay overnight at a motel to give the kids more time to experience the city, and Donna another patch of time for herself.

"Just take a day off," Emily insisted. "We can handle all of them, and you're always so tied down. Brett and Hilary are older and can help with your three. Just do what you want to, all day long."

It was a welcome change. It felt luxurious, as if she were at a four-star hotel, on a vacation she couldn't afford. She slept late in the morning, made herself a late breakfast of French toast and bacon, and read the newspaper while she ate.

She spent the day pampering herself, taking a walk, having her nails done. About eight in the evening she decided to treat herself to a movie. No, she wouldn't get home 'til after eleven, but so what—she could sleep in, the next morning.

The movie theatre, just a two-screen complex, and not much of one at that, was in the next town over. Donna threw her purse in the car and headed out.

The movie hadn't been that great, in spite of the raves she'd heard from other people. Donna guessed that maybe she just couldn't appreciate those other-worldly sagas with paranormal elements. Her life had been grounded in reality, and she was one of those gotta-see-it-to-believe-it people.

She passed the sign for Mystery Hill on the east side of route 28. Like that, for example. She'd heard all the stories—what New Hampshire native hadn't? But she'd been there, walked the paths, looked into the rooms and tunnels, and it was just a pile of rocks to her. She didn't care who'd built them, or who'd lived there, or what they did there. It just didn't pertain to her life.

Thump! Thump! Thump! Oh no! She recognized that sound, and remembered that the guy at the garage had told her the back right tire was worn and needed replacing. She'd intended to do that, but Jackie had needed braces, and well, the money only stretched so far.

The Mystery Hill entrance lay fifty feet ahead. She slowed the car and guided it into the parking lot. Her sister and brother-in-law were in Boston for the night, so there was no use calling them for help, and she was sure all the garages would be closed. She looked around, and saw to her surprise a car, partially hidden, parked under a large tree at the side of the lot. It looked as though whoever left it there didn't want it to be seen. Could be some teenagers making out—

she'd heard it was a favorite spot. Who else would be there at this time of night? Maybe they'd put the spare tire on for her. She didn't have much of a choice, did she?

She dug a flashlight out of the glove compartment and got out of the car. Yep, the tire was flat as an IHOP pancake, so to speak. She shone the flashlight up the path she knew led to the site, and sighed wearily. This was a great ending to her day off, but she didn't have any choice. She turned back toward the road as she heard the squeal of tires.

~ * ~

Ivy sat in her kitchen, staring out at the night, waiting to hear back from Thomas. He'd told her his coach, Jim Walsh, was with him, and that they had alerted the East Berlin police to check any suspicious activity at Mystery Hill. He and Walsh were on their way there, too, and he would call her as soon as he knew anything. She glanced at the clock—ten-thirty. Something inside nagged at her. She felt a strong need to get out to Mystery Hill, but still she hesitated.

Thomas had told her he would call if there was any news.

On edge, she waited. *Why?* she asked herself, but there was no answer, just a nagging feeling that she had to go there, that she was needed there. She shook her head. Sometimes her feelings overwhelmed her, convinced her to do something that didn't seem necessary at all.

After her third cup of coffee, the feeling was even stronger. She sighed. There was absolutely no point in going to bed and trying to sleep. Sleep would never come. Evidently she would have to go there and see for herself that it was a useless trip before the nagging would stop.

Her phone rang. Thomas. She knew it before she looked at the screen. She snatched it up. "What is it?"

She listened, and it all came clear in her mind, and she gasped as the realization hit her. "It's full moon tonight, the last of the school year. They'll take her to Mystery Hill. Have you heard from the cops yet?"

"No. We're waiting." Ivy heard the desperation in his voice, and her heart bled for the pain she knew he felt.

When Thomas clicked off, she sat at the kitchen table, leaning her chin into her hand, thinking. What should she do—stay there and wait, if by some miraculous chance Chloe should show up there? Was there any point in waking Sharon and Charlie and enlisting their help? What could they do that the police couldn't? Then it came, faint but clear, and as real as if she'd been standing next to her. She trembled as she heard Chloe's voice again.

Help me!

There was no more time to think. Ivy had an extra key to Charlie's car, just in case she had an emergency, and this certainly was one. Trying to fight down the panic in her stomach, she grabbed the key from the hook over the calendar, let the door slam behind her, and ran for the car.

~ * ~

The lone policeman sent to investigate saw the green car, sighed wearily, and climbed the path to the top of the hill. He found two teenagers sitting on the altar rock at Mystery Hill.

"What are you two doing here? The site closes at six p.m., you know. You shouldn't be here after hours."

The boy grinned. "It's not like we're sight-seeing. Just a little making out with my girl here. Don't you remember doing that?"

The cop didn't smile. "What are your names?"

"Ingrid Felseth," the girl said. "Do I need to be a certain age to be here?"

He wanted to snap at her not to give him smart-ass answers, but he restrained himself. He looked at the boy. "And yours?"

"Jeb Rubbel." The kid actually produced a driver's license.

The cop rubbed his eyes. The call from Headquarters had interrupted a promising evening with his pretty, young wife, and sent him on a wild-goose chase out here to Mystery Hill. Still, he'd better make sure.

"Are you here of your own free will?" he asked Ingrid.

She tossed her long braid back over her shoulder. "I'm here because I want to be here."

He had to give her that. She was tall and muscular, and the boy was short and wiry. Guys built like that were often strong, though, but he didn't think he could dominate Ingrid physically, and she certainly didn't sound intimidated.

"Guess not," he muttered. He looked around. The site looked eerie in the light of the full moon, filled with shadows and dark spots where the openings to tunnels and storage rooms were. He shuddered. He'd always felt uncomfortable here, even as a kid.

"There was a report of some sort of disturbance here. Have you kids seen or heard anything out of the ordinary?"

They both shook their heads.

"Okay." The cop took a last look around. "Well, I'm going to have to insist that you leave, and find somewhere else to continue your romance. Is your car here?"

"Down in the lot," the boy said with no trace of animosity. He gave his hand to the girl. "C'mon, Ingrid. We'll go to my place."

The cop followed them down the path and into the parking lot. He saw them into the dark green car that sat there, sitting right out in the open, and waited until it pulled out onto the main road and started off toward the next town.

What a dumb waste of time. Well, he'd call in his report, and hurry home and see if Lauren was still awake and willing.

~ * ~

Ivy saw a blue car in the lot, and a woman with a flashlight standing by it, looking to see who else had driven in. She drove up beside it, then noticed the other car nearly hidden by the bulk of a huge tree. She cut the engine and got out.

The other woman, hard to see in the moonlight, looked middle-aged, chunky and relatively harmless. "Hi," Ivy said as she approached her. "Ivy Harris. Why are you here?"

"Got a flat." The woman gestured at the car, hesitated and added, "Donna Rigozzi. I was on my way back from the movies. I don't suppose you can change a flat? Or that you could call someone to come and help me?"

Ivy nodded. "Yes, I can do that, but it'll have to wait. I'm here for another reason. Have you heard or seen anything going on around here tonight?" Her voice cracked with anxiety, and the woman called Donna took a few tentative steps backward.

"No. Is something supposed to be going on?"

Ivy caught her breath and looked toward the hill. "I hope not, but..."

Her words were cut off by the arrival of still another car in the lot, which swerved crazily as it roared into the parking lot, and screeched to an abrupt stop.

"Thomas!" Ivy ran toward the car.

Her grandson and a man she recognized as the basketball coach, Jim Walsh, jumped out of the car.

"Ivy! What are you doing here?" Thomas gave her a fierce hug. "This is Coach Walsh..."

"I remember," she replied, as she gave him a brief handshake, then realized how she must sound. "Sorry, I don't mean to be so curt, but..."

Donna joined them, giving them both curious looks. "Thomas—and the professor from Midstate. What are you two doing here?"

"You all know each other?" Ivy asked, looking from one to the other.

Thomas ignored the question, except for a cursory "yeah." Ivy saw him tense as he looked around the parking lot. "The cops are supposed to be here. Have you seen them?"

Both women shook their heads.

"So much for law-enforcement," Walsh said in a sarcastic tone. "Somebody probably came, didn't see anything, and left, thinking everything was okay."

"Someone else is here," Ivy said, and pointed to the car behind the tree.

"Whose is that?" Walsh asked, with a concerned look at Thomas.

He shook his head. "I don't know, but I don't like it. I think we'd better go up the hill, *pronto*."

Walsh whipped out his phone. "I'll call my brother again. He's probably had a report if anyone came and checked. Meantime, we'd better go up there and have a look-see for ourselves." He started toward the trail, and Thomas and Ivy followed.

Donna looked from one to the other, bewildered. "What's wrong?"

Ivy grabbed her arm. "Come on. We'll take care of your tire later, but right now, somebody might need all the help we have to give."

Thirty-six

Chloe concentrated so hard on trying to send Ivy a mental message that her head began to ache in protest. *Help me! Help me!* she breathed over and over again, hoping with all her heart that Ivy's supposedly highly-developed psychic powers were alive and working. Again she searched the crevices of the trunk for some kind of tool that could be used as a weapon. They had been thorough; there was nothing.

All right, she had nails and teeth. And she could pretend to be still knocked out when they opened the trunk. Then, if she could catch them off-guard, if she could inflict a little damage and run—she might get away.

The car went on for what seemed like a long time. It was dark in the trunk, and she couldn't read the numbers on her watch. But, finally she felt the vehicle slowing. Her ride became bumpier, and she guessed they had turned off the main road and were on some sort of side road or access road. She felt as though her heart was in her mouth, and her stomach ached with fear. Whatever was happening to her was not good, and she had never been so scared in her life.

She swallowed hard, guessing that the end of the trip was near. Then the ride became even rougher, as if they had left any kind of actual road, and were driving over rocks and gullies and fallen tree limbs. She was jounced up and down, hitting both the top and bottom of the enclosed space. It hurt, but she bit her lips, not wanting to make any noise they could hear.

The car stopped. With a supreme effort, she relaxed her body, closed her eyes and feigned sleep. She heard Jett and Gaia's voices as the doors opened and closed again. Her throat tightened again as she heard their footsteps approaching the rear of the car.

"Lucky we sent Ingrid and Jeb on ahead," Gaia said. "They were able to throw the cops off the trail."

Jett laughed. "Yeah, just a couple of college kids making out. They won't come back tonight."

Dyfan's voice: "Can you two get her up to the site by yourselves? If you don't need me, I'll go and prepare for the ceremony."

Chloe used all her will power to control her shaking.

"We'll be fine, Master." Gaia sounded confident. "I haven't heard anything from back there. I think she's still out."

"Okay. See you up there."

The car door opened again. "Got the rope?"

"Yeah, but I don't think we'll need it—not yet anyway."

"Okay, let's get her out."

The trunk creaked open. Chloe felt the welcome rush of fresh air, but remained still.

Gaia slipped an arm under her shoulders. "Jett, get her legs, will you?"

She let them lift her from the trunk. As they struggled to balance her weight between then, she made her move.

She had planned her attack. She jabbed her fingers into Gaia's eyes, and raked her nails down her cheek, digging into the flesh.

Gaia screamed in surprise and pain. "Arrrghhh! You bitch!"

At the same time, she doubled up her knees and kicked out at Jett with all the force she could summon, hoping she would hurt him where it really counted. Jett made a sound like a wounded animal. Both staggered back, dropping her on the ground. She ignored the pain that surged through her as she hit the dirt, scrambled to her feet and ran. As she had guessed, they had driven the car into the woods, and she headed in the direction she thought the road might be. Then it occurred to her they could catch her much more easily on the open road. They would alert Dyfan, and she would stand no chance against the three of them—and there might be more of the Druids here. The full moon lit patches of the uneven, pine-needle covered ground, and she changed direction, and circled around behind some large trees, and crouched, hugging the ground.

Gaia yelled, "She'll head for the road! C'mon!"

She heard Jett, already on his cell phone, hollering for Dyfan.

They raced past her, sure she'd try to run out of the woods. When they had gone, she turned and headed the other way. She didn't know where she was, but she knew if she were to survive she'd have to hide from them until they gave up, or she could find help. And where could she find help in an unfamiliar woods in the middle of the night?

Her breath caught, as she realized where they might have brought her—Mystery Hill. But she couldn't be sure of that, and there was no way she could have gauged the duration of the ride. She could be anywhere; she'd have to choose her way carefully.

She picked her way cautiously among the trees, trying to choose those with thick enough trunks to hide herself behind. The ground seemed to slant slightly uphill. It might not be good, she reasoned, to end up on top of a hill, where she might be spotted from below, so she changed direction and began to circle around to the right. Maybe there would be another road on the other side of the hill, and she could walk along the edge of that until she found a house or a gas station—or anything. She kept on, walking with caution, avoiding the shafts of moonlight.

She listened for noises that might mean Jett and Gaia were in pursuit, but the night was quiet, broken only by the mournful calls of an owl. How much time had gone by? She didn't know.

There was a sudden glint of something white ahead. Chloe froze in her tracks. When it didn't move or make a noise, she walked cautiously toward it. It was the beginning of a stone wall, and it stretched out in the direction she was going. She sagged against it in relief. A stone wall meant people, civilization, and maybe a farmhouse. All she needed to do was follow the wall to safety.

She followed the perimeter of the wall, now and then stooping to trail her hand along the top as she walked. She loved the rough feel of the rocks, and felt an unreasoning gratitude to the farmer who had built the wall. She hardly realized that her path had grown steeper and turned sharply to the right. She threaded her way through the trees, until ahead of her she saw the dim outlines of a small stone building. A storage bin, part of a silo, maybe? She hurried her steps. Just a few more minutes, and she would be safe.

A white-robed figure stepped out of the stone building and blocked her path.

"Welcome, Vala. Now we can begin."

~ * ~

She drifted back to consciousness, and discovered she couldn't move. Her wrists and ankles were tied with ropes, binding her tight and flat against a large, cold rock. Her bare legs were cold. She shivered. She blinked her eyes, trying to focus. They had placed something on her head that felt like a tiara, and it prickled against her scalp. She made out the vague forms of four robed figures holding torches, circling around her and chanting. With rhythmic motions, they tossed flower petals into the air, which drifted down and settled on her prone body.

"She's back," a voice she recognized as Gaia's said.

Chloe squinted to make out her face. The dim torchlight distorted the features she had once thought so pretty. Gaia's face looked as if it were made of melting wax. Chloe shifted her eyes to the other faces: Ingrid, whose strong Nordic features had turned hard and fierce; Jett, his dark good looks suddenly sinister, and Jeb, whose never-attractive features now resembled those of a troll.

Frantic, Chloe struggled against her bonds, and attempted a scream. Nothing came out. The ropes binding her bit into her flesh, and hurt. She fought to stay conscious against her fear.

Gaia held up a small bottle and directed her question to someone behind Chloe's head. "Should I give her some more?"

Dyfan! She suddenly felt as though she'd been drenched in ice water.

"No. She's just aware enough. She's perfect."

Through her terror, she saw Dyfan smile down at her. "And she wore such a perfect dress for the sacrifice.

"She'll scream."

Dyfan laughed. "Let her. There's no one around to hear her."

She heard Jeb's voice, sounding excited. "Just like those stories of long ago—when hunters heard screams in the night and were too scared to go see what they were."

"What if someone does hear and calls nine-one-one?" Ingrid asked. "There'll be cops swarming all over the place."

Chloe saw Gaia smile. "By then it will be too late. We'll be done here."

What did she mean by that? All of a sudden all her strength seemed to leave her body, and she nearly fainted from the feelings of terror that raced through her. But still, it was all going to be symbolic, wasn't it?

"It's three minutes 'til midnight," the voice behind her said. "Place the receiving vessel in its sacred place, Jett."

Chloe continued to struggle, panting and pulling against the ropes that tied her, feeling their rough edges cut into her skin. She heard her voice come out in whimpers, like those of a trapped animal. "Let—me—go..." she managed to croak, before her head began to swim again, and she felt herself start to drift. She fought to stay conscious.

Jett picked up the same terra cotta jug that had been used for the bonding ceremony months earlier, and knelt down with it at the base of the rock. She tried to kick at it, but her feet were tied too tightly to give her enough movement. She remembered that there was supposed to be a hole beneath the altar stone where a receptacle would collect the blood that ran down from the grooves cut in the rock.

Her head cleared for a moment, and the realization of what was happening finally hit her. No, they wouldn't! They couldn't!

Vala, the acceptable sacrifice.

Dyfan came around the altar stone and stood at the foot, gazing down at her, with an expression on his that resembled love. The moonlight hit his head and shoulders, lighting him up like the image of a god.

The light from the others' torches played twisted shadows on their faces.

"Vala, an acceptable sacrifice."

"No! No!" Her voice sounded weak, that of a helpless child.

He raised a knife, a wicked looking thing with a fat, sharp, shining blade. He raised his eyes to the moon. "To the gods of nature: we bring you an offering. We ask you to guide our steps, and to show us the way, as we seek to grow in love, creativity and wisdom.

"Vala, the perfect sacrifice. You have been honored above all others." He raised the knife. Chloe screamed.

~ * ~

Thomas, several steps ahead of Jim Walsh, saw the gleam of the knife in the moonlight, and knew exactly what was about to happen. He turned, wrested the pistol from the coach's hand and aimed a shot at the figure in white, outlined in the moonlight. The high priest staggered, dropped the knife and clutched at his arm in shock. Thomas and the professor raced out from behind the trees and into the open, where the other four Druids in their robes stood transfixed. He ran toward Chloe lying on the altar stone, but Jett suddenly sprang to life and tackled him. Furious, Thomas punched him in the face, and with a groan, Jett lay quiet. Walsh whipped off his belt and tied the boy's hands behind him. Jett moaned and writhed on the ground, to no avail. Thomas, casting a frantic look at Chloe, and ascertaining she was all right for the moment, turned the gun on the others.

"Stand over there, and don't move," he ordered.

"Spoken like a cop," Walsh grunted. "Joe couldn't have said it better."

Ivy and Donna arrived on the scene, panting.

"Ivy!" Thomas yelled. "Check on Chloe." His words were unnecessary, as Ivy threw herself on her knees at Chloe' side. Donna had her cell phone out and frantically punched in numbers.

Thomas turned the gun over to Walsh. "Hold them there. Where's that bastard, Dyfan?

Gaia took that moment, as they both glanced around, looking for Dyfan, to launch her own attack. She made a dash for the altar, bent and grabbed the knife Dyfan had dropped. She yanked Ivy to her feet, and held the blade to her throat.

Ivy struggled, her arms flailing in the air, but she was no match for Gaia.

"Let us all go, or this old bitch dies!"

"Gaia," Thomas said, taking a few small steps toward her. "Be sensible. This is over. The police are on their way."

"It'll take them awhile," she said. "Then they have to get up the hill on foot. I have time to bargain." She tried to pin him with a hypnotic stare, but he refused to meet her eyes, knowing that was where her power lay.

Ivy had managed to loosen Chloe's bonds, and she had one hand free. Chloe tugged at the ropes on her other hand, turning her head and using her teeth.

Gaia kicked her in the side. "Lie still, you whore. We're going to finish what we came here to do."

Chloe screamed in pain.

Thomas advanced another step, tensing to throw himself at Gaia. "No, we're not. Mr. Walsh has a gun, and he'll use it if you try to hurt anyone."

"Will he?" Gaia leveled a grin at Thomas. "I doubt it. He hasn't the guts to shoot anyone, especially a girl."

"Don't bet on that," Thomas growled. "He's an ex-Marine."

Gaia yelled at Jeb and Ingrid. "You two! Don't just stand there—you can take him. Don't disgrace Dyfan by being cowards."

Jeb and Ingrid exchanged looks, but didn't move.

"Don't disgrace the Master!"

The sound of distant sirens wailed in the distance. Jim Walsh made the mistake of glancing in the direction of the sound, and both kids jumped him together, knocking the gun from his hand. Thomas went after it, and as the four of them wrestled on the ground, Donna waded into the fray. Using her considerable bulk, she wedged herself between Walsh and Jeb, which allowed Thomas to grab the gun and jump to his feet.

Although Jeb fought like a demon, Donna outweighed the skinny kid by at least seventy pounds, and she seemed to absorb his kicks and fists with ease. He spit in her face. She lifted one hand and leveled a hard blow across his cheek. He moaned and turned his face into the leaves. Finally, she sat on him, and pinned him to the ground with her weight. Jim dragged Ingrid over to where Jett lay and fastened her wrists to his.

"Okay, Gaia, it's over." Thomas held the gun with both hands, FBI style, and pointed it at her from six feet away. "I'll kill you to save Chloe and Ivy, and you know it—so let her go."

Cars screeched to a halt in the parking lot below them. Car doors opened and slammed shut.

Gaia smiled at him, and for a moment he had a glimpse of the pretty, bubbly girl he had met on campus earlier in the year. Slowly she began to draw the blade across Ivy's throat, and a thin line of red appeared. "Are you man enough, Thomas? Show me."

Thomas fired. Gaia dropped in her tracks, and as she fell, threw Ivy across Chloe on the altar stone, where she lay, moaning. Ingrid screamed. Jett and Jeb thrashed on the ground, trying to free themselves as Walsh ran to help Thomas. Thomas dropped the gun, picked Ivy up and held her in his arms. Her throat was bleeding, but he could see the wound was superficial, and would not be fatal. Jim Walsh already had his shirt off and had ripped strips off to wrap around her throat.

Thomas let Walsh take charge of Ivy, and turned all his attention to Chloe. Gently he removed the wreath of white flowers from her head. He knelt beside her and wrapped his arms around her, holding her close, feeling their spirits merge, and inhaling every inch of her with his soul, as if he would never let her go.

Again, the voice from another time, another place. You're all right now, Kanti. We have forever to celebrate our love.

Thirty-seven

There was no sign of Dyfan or Gaia or the gun. Although Thomas was sure he had hit her, there was no blood on the ground, and she had disappeared as completely as if she had never been there. The police called an ambulance for Ivy, and took the rest of them to the police station. The police didn't know whom to believe, but the officer who had questioned Jeb and Ingrid earlier identified them, and they, along with Jett, were removed to a separate rooms to be interrogated again.

Two other officers, Scott Holden and Rob Pierce, sat down with Thomas, Chloe, Donna and Jim Walsh. They sat around a rectangular table, which was pitted and scarred with cigarette burns on its worn surface. The story the two young people told was so bizarre—Thomas could tell from the skeptical looks on their faces that the cops couldn't tell fact from fiction.

Jim Walsh called his brother, Joe, and both policemen spoke with him. After that conversation, they seemed more willing to hear all the details of what had happened.

The younger one, Rob, well-muscled with sandy hair, squinted at Thomas. "And you say you shot the other girl—Gaia? Where did she go?"

"I don't know. It's possible, I guess, that I missed her, or didn't hurt her badly, and she ran off into the woods."

"Uhm hum." Scott, who had blond hair and straight-from-Hollywood cop good looks, made notes on his pad. "And this other character, the one who thought this all up, where did he go?"

"Dyfan, or Jack Wayland," Walsh replied. "As my brother told you, he's probably responsible for the murder of Chloe's former roommate, Hannah Stuart, in Middleton. Thomas fired at him, but I think just hit his arm. He disappeared into the woods before Gaia did."

A couple of hours later, the police seemed no less bewildered, and still at a loss to charge whom with what. Since there were no victims who claimed to be shot, and no gun, they couldn't charge Thomas with anything. Ivy had obviously been injured by someone, but that someone was nowhere to be found.

"We'll send out search teams tomorrow and comb the woods," Scott said, closing his pad with a weary gesture. "And of course, we'll put out an APB on them. We'll keep the other three here overnight, and call their parents. I don't know what we can charge them with except trespassing."

Rod nodded and waggled a finger at Thomas and Chloe. "And you two can go home. I don't know if I'll ever believe this story, but it sure will go down as one of the weirdest ones we've ever heard." He stood and extended a hand to Donna and Jim Walsh in turn. "Would you two like some place to spend the rest of the night? I can give the guy who owns the Wayfarer Inn down the street a call."

Walsh shook his head. "I don't think I could sleep. I don't mind driving at this time of night, and I'll drop Donna off at her sister's."

"They'll never believe the night I'd had," Donna sighed. She looked at Thomas and forced a weak smile. "And to think something like this all began at IHOP. And I thought that job was boring."

~ * ~

Jack Wayland and Gaia Butler disappeared as if they had never existed. In vain the police from three towns combed the hill and the woods. There was no sign of them. After several days, law enforcement backed off, but put out a nation-wide alert for the pair. The police managed to keep the whole situation quiet, as any media hype would be bad publicity for the town, which depended on tourists coming to Mystery Hill.

"It's not an evil place in itself," Ivy noted, as she, Thomas and Chloe sat over cherry-pineapple margaritas at her kitchen table. "It's just that when someone with evil intentions is able to focus his energies in a place with a history like that, their power is increased, and I think, reinforces the evil."

Chloe shivered.

Thomas put his arm around her. "Are you okay? Anyone else who went through what you did would be in a recoup facility for a while."

She smiled. "I'm stronger than you think."

He gave her a squeeze. "You are, babe. You're awesome."

"Absolutely," Ivy agreed. "But I'd stay away from that place for a while, if I were you. Gaia and Jack may still be lurking around, waiting for another chance."

Thomas winced, but shook his head. "Oh, I don't think they'll be showing their faces around here anytime soon. But

I'm not going back there either, 'til I hear they've both been caught."

Chloe looked at him over the rim of her glass. "Your folks want to have a picnic up there when Charlie and January come home, in a month or so. Somehow we have to not let that happen."

"Oh, I don't think there's any danger to anyone else," Ivy said. "Tourists go through there every day. It's Chloe they want. But—we'll make up excuses not to go on the picnic."

Chloe giggled. "Yeah! I'll have a toothache."

"And I'll have to drive you to the dentist in Portsmouth," Thomas agreed, rocking back in his chair.

Ivy nodded. "And I'll make an appointment with a vendor to show them my jewelry at the same time, so I'll be going with you."

"Well, that's settled." Thomas drained the rest of his drink. "I think I'm ready to turn in now. Coming, Chloe?"

She stood up and leaned over to give Ivy a big hug. "Thank you for everything. Believe me, if I ever have the chance to take care of you when you're old and tired, I'll feel privileged to do that."

Thomas raised his eyebrows at her. "And how about the rest of that promise—will you marry Thomas, too?"

"I think I'll keep you guessing for a bit," she said.

They started across the lawn, leaving Ivy standing at the door looking after them.

As they passed the pool, Chloe's phone rang. She dug it out of her pocket.

"Who is it?" Thomas cast a look at the window.

"I don't know. I don't recognize the number." She put the phone to her ear. "Hello?"

There was no answer. "Hello?" She repeated, then held it out so Thomas could hear, too. "Doesn't seem to be anyone there."

"Oh, we're here, Vala," Jack's voice said over the line. They heard Gaia giggling in the background. "And don't ever think we've gone away, or forgotten you, because…"

Chloe dropped the phone on the ground.

She melted into Thomas' arms, holding on to him as if she might fall. He held her tightly against him. He saw the moonlight play across her hair, and he stared at their reflections shimmering in the water of the pool. The image seemed to be one person standing there, and that thought gave him the strength he needed. He had vanquished her enemy once, and if needed, he could do it again.

He took Chloe's face in his hands and their eyes met. "I love you, Chloe, and our love is stronger than anything *they* can do. End of story."

"I know," she said softly. She turned her head and stood very still, as though something had caught her attention.

He followed her glance, and saw that she was staring at the merged image in the pool. "Do you see that?" she asked. "We're one person."

He caught at her hand. "We are," he said. "And we always will be."

Hand in hand they walked toward the house, knowing that whatever fate threw at them, they would never be separated again.

The End

Meet
Joan Conning Afman

Joan Conning Afman graduated from the University of Hartford Art School with a BFA in fine art. She taught art in the Hartford school system, then retired to sunny Florida. She keeps up her love for art by painting and exhibiting in local art shows, but also pursues her new found love of writing. "Sacrifice at Mystery Hill" is her fifth published novel.

Addicted to and fascinated by all aspects of the paranormal, Joan's novels often echo these ideas, which she hopes will encourage readers to be more aware of the invisible, spiritual worlds all around us.

Joan has four grown children and six beautiful grandchildren. Retirement is a wonderful time of life, especially when surrounded by blue skies, an ocean, and palm trees. Life is good.

VISIT OUR WEBSITE
FOR THE FULL INVENTORY
OF QUALITY BOOKS:

http://www.wings-press.com

Quality trade paperbacks and downloads
in multiple formats,
in genres ranging from light romantic
comedy to general fiction and horror.
Wings has something
for every reader's taste.
Visit the website, then bookmark it.
We add new titles each month!